RENOWN OF THE RAITHLIN

BOOK ONE OF THE RAITHLINDRATH SERIES

Robert Ryan

Cover Design by www.ebooklaunch.com

ISBN-13 978-0-646-91670-5

(print edition)

Trotting Fox Press

Contents

1. Dawn of Change   3
2. Clear Like Water; Cold Like Ice   17
3. Footfalls of Doom   28
4. Death in Every Glance   40
5. Dark as the Tomb   52
6. Chance Meetings   61
7. Dead Man Swamp   74
8. A Choice that is no Choice   90
9. The Blood of Kings   104
10. The Witch in the Wood   115
11. Esgallien   126
12. The Wisdom of the Raithlin   139
13. They Have Many Names   152
14. Even the Earth Remembers   165
15. The Eye of the Storm   177
16. Light of the Half Moon   189
17. All that I Desire   201
18. We who Mastered the World   212
19. All the Days of his Life   223
20. Nightmare   235
21. On the Brink   245
22. Death is Become Life, and Life Death   255
23. Erlissa's Choice   264
Epilogue   277
Appendix A. The Red Cloth of Victory   281
Appendix B. Encyclopedic Glossary   291

1. Dawn of Change

Lanrik endured hunger, and the humiliation of the situation, with patience. He could not allow Mecklar to break him.

First light colored the grasslands, and he sensed change in the air. The world he knew was slipping away. He studied his companion and saw the embodiment of that force at work: a man lacking the desire to strive for anything except self-gratification, yet with the power to destroy the achievements of others.

They sat on the ground, separated by a small and smokeless fire. Mecklar ate with slow relish, his sausage-like fingers slick with grease. His lips and chin were smeared too, but he ignored that and continued to chew methodically. His stubbled jowl rolled with each movement, and his heavy-lidded eyes glazed with pleasure.

He casually wiped his hands on dirty trousers and spared Lanrik a glance. Whenever he spoke, it was only to probe for a reaction like a *nudaluk* bird that relentlessly hammered its beak against a tree in search of insects.

"You'd have something to eat as well – if you were any good at hunting."

Lanrik shrugged and looked away. This was another attempt to provoke him. His hollow stomach tightened in anger, but he resisted pointing out that Mecklar only had food because it had been brought from the city. Lanrik had carried it, along with Mecklar's tent and heavy sleeping rug, though he made do without such comforts himself. He slept under the nighttime sky, his head resting on mounded dirt and his body wrapped in his Raithlin

3

cloak. Yet he liked it that way, and the cloak of the scouts of Esgallien City offered more than warmth: it symbolized all that was good in his life.

The silence did not discourage Mecklar.

"I'd share some food with you, but it would defeat the purpose of the exercise. I'm supposed to see how good the Raithlin are." He sipped watered wine from a silver goblet, his gaze fixed on Lanrik. "And I haven't been impressed so far."

Lanrik tensed but sat perfectly still. *Nothing I do would ever impress you.* The taunting was difficult to ignore, but Lanrik was not going to retaliate and provide an excuse for an unfavorable report to King Murhain.

The king, trying to reduce expenditure, had sent Mecklar to evaluate the Raithlin. He had gained his position in Murhain's retinue by cutting costs in the past, and likely sought advancement by doing it again, placing the Raithlin in jeopardy. *I'm not going to let you goad me.*

He relaxed and answered in an even tone. "It's my part to show the skills of the scouts – yours to judge their usefulness."

There were a hundred Raithlin, but their leader, the Lindrath, had chosen him to demonstrate their capabilities.

Constantly tested by Mecklar, he had represented the Raithlin over the last week. They had set out from Esgallien, crossed the white-watered ford of the Careth Nien, and headed south onto the plains. He had run for miles with a heavy pack, climbed trees, and despite Mecklar's surly watchfulness, crept unseen through grass and shrubbery to within feet of him. He had also found water, built shelters against the weather, concealed his tracks and laid false trails.

These were the basic skills of the Raithlin, but he was proud to be more than just a scout. In times of war, though not part of Esgallien's army, he might have to spy

4

out enemy positions and sow confusion. In times of peace, he and others watched Galenthern, the plains beyond the ford.

Nothing moved over the grasslands within a week's march that the Raithlin did not see: not a hare that cautiously fed or a hawk that wheeled in the sky. That, Lanrik admitted to himself, was the problem. Not a single enemy warrior, much less an army, had been seen for decades and the king felt secure. He might think it safe to disband the Raithlin; but they knew otherwise. Not for nothing did Esgallien's enemies swear an oath during tribal ceremonies to conquer the north. The desire had infused their blood since antiquity, and their leaders often fanned it to life. If they sacked the city it would yield untold wealth.

Mecklar belched and renewed his verbal assault.

"If you hadn't missed your shot you wouldn't be in this predicament."

In an attempt to diffuse the constant taunting Lanrik changed tactics. *He'll find it difficult to fault someone agreeing with him.*

"I've only got myself to blame," he said.

This was more truthful than Mecklar knew. Yesterday afternoon, they stalked a herd of aurochs in one of the wooded swamps scattered across the plains. They closed on a young bull. Its blackish coat was glossy with health and the pale stripe along the length of its spine shimmered in the waning light. It stood man high, though it still had growing to do, and was in range of Lanrik's bow.

The beast sensed danger and lifted its head. The black snout quivered and tested the air. They were downwind though, and their scent had not reached it. Its lyre shaped horns swept from side to side; the long ears flicked with uncertainty. Angrily, it stamped a hoof to chase persistent flies.

5

Mecklar tapped Lanrik on the shoulder and urged him to shoot, but the bull was a magnificent creature and it was not the Raithlin way to kill such an animal when the majority of its meat, tough and strongly flavored anyway, would be wasted. Yet Mecklar was not the kind who understood such things, and Lanrik, knowing he had shown the Raithlin skills to good effect all week, deliberately loosed the arrow wide. It struck a willow trunk with a crack. The bull and his herd crashed away through the thick scrub.

Lanrik's thoughts returned to the present. Eastward, an unbroken column of smoke was rising in the still air.

Mecklar had seen it too. "What's that?"

Lanrik stood and strained his eyes over the grasslands. He did not know what it signified, but a gnawing worry gripped his stomach.

"A finger of smoke pointing to calamity," he said at last, and there was a catch in his voice. "Over there the flat ground rises into a tor covered by rock and overgrown with scrub. The Raithlin use it as an outlook."

"So one of the scouts lit the fire?"

Lanrik nodded. "Yes, but *why?*"

"Then when we return to Esgallien I'll have them punished. Only an incompetent would reveal their location."

Lanrik dragged his gaze from the horizon. His eyes narrowed with suppressed anger.

"You don't understand. None of the Raithlin is incompetent. We light fires such as the one I used to cook your breakfast: small and smokeless. This is a deliberate signal – the sort made by someone in desperate trouble."

"Well, we're due to head back to Esgallien soon. No doubt we'll find out the truth then."

Lanrik shook his head. "We can't go back to Esgallien. We have to find out what's going on."

Mecklar came smoothly to his feet. His bulk and slovenly manner gave the impression of lethargy, but the opposite was true: he was strong, fast and nimble.

"You Raithlin think you run the world, don't you? But you're not in charge of this expedition. You'll go where I say."

Lanrik pointed to the east. "Someone over there needs help, and the next lookout is further away than us. Events have overtaken the demonstration, and the Raithlin skills are needed in earnest. You can come with me and observe what I do, or you can return to the king, but I bet he'd like to see how we perform in a real emergency."

There was a cold silence while Mecklar thought.

Lanrik waited patiently. *Snake-hearted bastard. You're not weighing up what's right and wrong – you're deciding how to make the Raithlin look bad.*

"Very well," Mecklar said. "We'll see why the fire was lit, but my report to Murhain will surely emphasize the arrogance of the Raithlin."

Lanrik did not answer. He kicked in dirt from the rim of the fire-pit to put out the flames without smoke. Shouldering his heavy pack he set off, and Mecklar strode angrily beside him.

He could have wished for things to be different, but wishing was in vain. He must make the most of the situation and knew that none of the other scouts, and certainly not his uncle who had instilled Raithlin values in him since childhood, would ignore someone in trouble. Besides, it was his *job* to find out what had happened, and he could not see a way for Mecklar to twist that into a fault.

The two men moved swiftly across the grasslands. Profuse flowers of purple vetch and lush whorls of red-flowered clover stood out against the green of the plains. The column of smoke bent in the rising morning breeze until it looked like a half-fallen tree. Neither man spoke, but Lanrik sensed Mecklar's irritation.

He thought about his companion as they walked. Mecklar was overweight, sloppy and difficult to get on with, but his mind was rapier sharp. Lanrik did not know anybody else of such contrasts. He sensed a ruthless intellect weigh and judge him every time the heavy-lidded gaze turned in his direction. It was no surprise that he was adept at saving the king money.

His ability as a swordsman was a shock, though. He was too big to move fast yet shifted rapidly between retreat and attack with seamless grace anyway. His size lent strength to his blows, and beneath layers of soft flesh was a framework of iron-hard muscles.

They first met a few weeks ago in the sword tournament of Esgallien's Spring Games. They each won through the early rounds, facing and beating a series of increasingly skilled opponents, before the king judged their clash in the final bout.

The sword was Lanrik's specialty weapon. His uncle, a former Raithlin of renowned sword craft, had trained him. But his uncle could not have prepared him for what happened.

Most bouts lasted about six rounds, but the final had gone twice that without a blow landing. The crack of the oaken practice swords reverberated through Conhain Court, the square in the city named after Esgallien's first king. The crowd, rowdy at first, grew quiet as they watched, and though time did not stand still, it barely shuffled past.

Finally, Mecklar broke through. He thrust forward and Lanrik twisted to avoid what would have been a lethal stroke with a real weapon. Instead, the wooden blade merely skidded across his ribs.

To Lanrik's astonishment, King Murhain did not call an end to the round. Instead, he awarded Mecklar the Red Cloth of Victory. Uproar broke out in the square.

The Lindrath spoke to Murhain but eventually turned away and called for quiet.

"The king has invoked the ancient right of the judge," he said.

There was more shouting, and the Lindrath waited for it to subside.

"There's a rule that if a bout continues an unreasonable time, the judge can award victory to the competitor he thinks is likely to win."

There was renewed mayhem in the crowd, but a single voice rose above the din.

"Maybe for the early rounds. Not the final!"

The Lindrath's gaze shifted to the king, and he spoke with thinly veiled sarcasm. "It's true that in the nine hundred and fifty three years since the first games in Esgallien, the rule has never been invoked in a final. But it still exists."

The crowd eventually dispersed, and the Lindrath came over to Lanrik.

"There'll always be next time, son. You know better than most that the king dislikes the Raithlin – as well as your family. It's no surprise that he's favored someone from his retinue."

Lanrik wondered, as he often had since then, if Mecklar really was better. He had a feeling that they would find out one day. For the moment, his main concern was the column of smoke, and he noticed that it was thinning.

Mecklar glanced at him. "It seems that your incompetent friend has realized their stupidity."

Lanrik clenched his hands into fists, and then breathed out slowly and relaxed.

"Perhaps the person is injured and only had the strength to build a small fire."

"Then they're weak as well as stupid. Characteristics that don't go well with the primary Raithlin trait of arrogance. All these faults must cause your people lots of problems."

Lanrik could sense Mecklar's anticipation for his response. It was like a vast pit before him, and his antagonist was *willing* him to stumble into it. He refused to allow the man to break him though. Instead of saying what he really thought, he just laughed. It was no time for humor, but there were worse reactions to the absurd.

Mecklar went rigid, and Lanrik felt that he had won a kind of victory. Irrespective of what happened, Mecklar's report would be bad; it was what the king wanted, but he would not get it easily.

Lanrik wondered what he would do if the scouts were disbanded. Could he learn other skills? He would have to, but his heart would never be in it. The Raithlin were his life and identity. His uncle had made it so.

Other concerns crowded his mind. Why would one of the Raithlin, for whom stealth and caution were second nature, light a fire to deliberately make smoke but only feed it for a short time? Whatever it signaled, it was not an enemy attack. No army could approach the lookouts without being seen, and at first sight, the outlying scouts would return to Esgallien and give warning. The inner ring of scouts would monitor the enemy and assess its strength, intention and morale.

The tor was in plain view now, and Lanrik studied it as they continued to close the gap from its southwestern side. It was a time to be cautious, for something must have happened, but without knowing its nature, he did not know what to be wary of.

Underneath his boots, the lushness of the plains changed. The fertile earth dried and turned into shallow and rocky soil. The grass was now wiry and yellowish; the vetch ceased to scramble over grass stems and became sickly, while the delicate red clover disappeared altogether.

He veered to the northern side of the tor, and Mecklar looked at him questioningly.

"There's an easy path up the southern side," he explained. "We've been visible since dawn, and whoever's up there knows we're coming. They'll probably be expecting us to take that way, but until I know what's happening, it's best to be unpredictable."

Mecklar only grunted but changed course readily. They moved as quickly as possible up the tor's slope but had to slow frequently to navigate around boulders and find a way through thick stands of stunted ash and birch. The air became still and dead. The light grew dim beneath the trees, and the only thing they could hear was the ceaseless hum of insects.

When they broke through to the top it happened so suddenly that the full light of the sun dazzled Mecklar. Lanrik, expecting it and careful to shield his eyes with his hand, was the first to study the small plateau.

It was bare of trees but strewn with massive boulders. Climbing the last few steps, he reached the top, and mile after mile of the bright green plains came into view. He did not give this any attention. The summit, perhaps only fifty paces across, held his interest. He saw on its southern side the remnant of the fire.

There was no sign of the Raithlin who should be there. Where had they gone? He did not doubt that a scout had lit the fire and saw clear signs of their activity. Low branches along the southern trail had been broken to fuel it, and there were deep scrapes on the ground indicating the Raithlin had been injured and dragged themselves across the earth. That being the case, they could not have gone far.

He studied the plateau more closely. The boulders cast large shadows, and if he were injured it was in just such a place that he would rest. He walked slowly across the summit.

He saw the boots first. They were of the soft doe-hide that the Raithlin preferred for comfort and maneuverability. He noticed the rest of the body immediately afterward. The gray pants and tunic were ordinary, but the forest green cloak and hood were the garb of the scouts. He knew when he got closer that he would see on the cloak the Raithlin motif: a trotting fox looking back over its shoulder. It would be woven with red thread above the heart just like his own. The etching on the blade of his sword showed the same design.

He hesitated before taking the last few steps. Both of the scout's legs were broken, and he saw the gleam of exposed bone. The cloak was tattered and bloodstained. A large rip tore one side, exposing a long wound, blackened at the edges and raw in the center. The scout's face was burnt, almost beyond recognition of being human. The hair that was left was shriveled, and the skin of the face covered in blisters and seeping blood. He knew all the Raithlin but could not tell who this was. He felt sick but forced himself closer.

He knelt down carefully beside the body. Impossibly, one eye flicked open and held him with its gaze. Of the other, only a ruined socket remained. The hair on the back of his neck stood up. How could anybody suffer such injuries and live? Not only had they endured unimaginable pain, they had worsened it by dragging themselves along the trail to collect branches for the fire. How many torturous journeys had they made, alone and uncomforted, to gather enough material? And for what purpose?

He had little time for such thoughts as the scout gripped his shoulder and tried to speak. He pulled off his pack and retrieved a water flask, dribbling a little at a time into the Raithlin's mouth. He sensed Mecklar approach from behind. An idea occurred to him, and he turned quickly and saw that his companion had drawn his sword.

"You won't need that. Whoever's done this has gone. What I need now is a tuber from one of the *elendhrot* bushes that grows on the path to the summit. Do you know the plant I mean?"

"I know it," Mecklar said, his eyes fixed on the wounded Raithlin.

"The tubers are near the surface. I only need one."

Mecklar shifted his attention to Lanrik. "No medicine can heal those injuries."

"Just get me the tuber!"

Lanrik knew the injuries were beyond help, and he guessed the scout had at most half an hour to live. The elendhrot was not for healing though; immediately beneath the purple skin of the tuber was a pithy substance that yielded a pain-easing juice.

He held the scout's hand until Mecklar returned, then put down the water flask and took the tuber offered to him. He worked quickly with a knife to peel away its dark skin and obtain some of its interior. A pinch was all he needed, and he placed it in the Raithlin's mouth. The scout swallowed and mumbled.

Mecklar looked agitated. "Did you understand that?"

Lanrik shook his head but the scout tried again.

"It's bitter."

Mecklar backed away. "It's a woman!"

Lanrik found Mecklar's observation annoying but ignored him. What he wanted to know was who she was.

He leaned closer. "What's your name?"

He flinched at the anguish that showed in her remaining eye.

"You don't . . . recognize me . . . Lanrik?"

He bit his lip, unable to answer.

She closed her eye. "Don't think of me as I am now . . . Promise to remember me as I was when I won the archery tournament in the Spring Games."

Lanrik's memory flew back to those special three days of the year, and he knew her instantly. "I promise, Lathmai," he said. He would try to keep it but knew he would struggle all the days of his life.

The archery tournament was held the day before the sword final, and he was near her when she took the winning shot. Her brown hair was luxurious, and her eyes shone with mischief. She surprised him with a kiss after receiving the Red Cloth of Victory, and then danced away with her friends giving him a backward glance and flashing smile. They had been friends, perhaps something more, ever since.

He looked at her now: shriveled, blackened, broken and robbed of her vitality. He had not understood before this moment how much hurt filled the world.

"There's something . . . you need to know," she said. "Look to the south and you'll see an army. The enemy is coming . . . Esgallien is in peril."

He could barely grasp what she was saying. It was all he could do to hold her hand and not cry.

"Other scouts will have noticed your fire. They'll do whatever needs to be done."

Lathmai shook her head violently. "The other scouts are dead," she said. "All of them. You're the last hope of Esgallien."

"They can't be dead," Lanrik said. He wondered if she was delirious.

Lathmai's grip tightened. "Gwalchmur betrayed us . . . he knew where the scouts were positioned."

Gwalchmur was a Raithlin and Lanrik's mind reeled.

"He's only one man," he said at last. "He couldn't kill them all."

"He's not alone," Lathmai said. "He's with an elùgroth. Gwalchmur led him to the other scouts . . . and the sorcerer killed them. They stalked me at night . . . told me I was the last . . . then left me to die."

She shuddered, and he knew her time was short. He squeezed her hand and felt no response, but she spoke once more.

"I watched you move across the plains. The smoke was to attract your attention, though I didn't know it was you. I've done all that I can . . . my strength is gone. You're the only one who can save Esgallien now. Promise me . . . you'll not let my suffering be for nothing. Promise me you'll save our home." Her grip suddenly tightened. "Promise me . . . you'll kill Gwalchmur!"

Lanrik closed his eyes and bowed his head. He felt a foreshadowing of fear at what such a promise might lead to. He also knew that he would defy an entire army, even an elùgroth, for Lathmai's sake.

"I will," he said.

Her grip relaxed, and her breath became shallow and ragged. He held her hand between both of his for her last few moments.

The presence of an elùgroth explained much. If the other scouts were dead, the way to Esgallien was open. And without being alerted, the city would not respond in time. They *must* be warned.

The sun began to beat down, and the sheen of perspiration on his face turned to heavy beads of sweat. The hum of insects was loud, but there was no sound from the three people on the summit until Lathmai spoke for the last time.

"Remember me," she whispered.

"I'll always remember you. Esgallien will remember you, for you are the Raithlin who saved it."

There was, perhaps, a hint of a smile on her ruined face before her final breath rattled harshly in her throat and she died. One instant he was holding her hand; the hand of a living person, and the next it was a lifeless object. What had happened to her thoughts and memories? Where had the will that animated her body gone? Could such things be present, and then cease to exist in the span of a single moment?

He looked over Lathmai's body toward Mecklar, and his voice was cold.

"Do you understand now that the Raithlin are not careless and do not light fires for nothing? Lathmai suffered in ways you and I cannot imagine for the mere hope she could save her people. Do you still say she was incompetent?"

For once Mecklar made no comment. Lanrik ignored him and stood to look over Galenthern and saw what he had not noticed earlier. There was a vague dust cloud on the horizon and below it, pinprick flashes of light from sword hilts, shields and spear tips. There was a shifting of colors and an impression of movement as well. It was, as Lathmai had warned, an army. It was an army intent on destroying his homeland and would travel fast to do so.

There was a more urgent danger. The enemy scouts would have seen the smoke just as he had. They would come to investigate, if they were not already stalking up the tor. If he and Mecklar were killed, who would warn Esgallien?

2. Clear Like Water; Cold Like Ice

Lanrik dragged his gaze from the approaching army. There were things to do and panicking about its approach, or the proximity of enemy scouts, would not help.

He looked at Lathmai's broken body. "We'll build a cairn," he said. "I won't leave her unburied in the wilderness."

Mecklar was going to object, but something in Lanrik's mood made him hesitate.

"There are rocks everywhere. I guess it won't take long," he conceded.

Lanrik retrieved her rapier; he had an idea on how to use it later. They formed the cairn against the lee of the boulder by using smaller stones first and then rocks of increasing size. When they covered Lathmai's face, grief stabbed at Lanrik's heart like a knife, but he was unwilling to share it with Mecklar and they labored in silence.

All the while a feeling of rage against the shortsightedness of the king, the provocation of his counselor, and most of all, Lathmai's killers began to build. He hardened his heart. *It'll motivate me for what I must do next.*

Everything was still. The only sound came from the hammering of a nudaluk bird seeking insects in a tree trunk on the southern side of the tor. He was glad of the noise, for it meant that no scouts approached from that direction.

They finished the cairn, and he fixed Lathmai's rapier in its crest with the hilt set firmly into the rocks. He did not tell Mecklar why.

17

There was no time for a ceremony, but Lanrik placed his right hand over the trotting fox motif on his cloak and voiced the simple Raithlin creed that he knew meant so much to her:

Our duty is to serve and protect
Our honor is to fight but not hate
Our love is for all that is good in the world

He did not look at Mecklar. The king's counselor represented everything that was going wrong. Why did the good like Lathmai die while the lesser lived?

Mecklar shuffled his feet. "That's all we can do. We'd better get back to Esgallien quickly."

Lanrik lowered his hand and turned toward him. "Quickly won't be soon enough."

"What does that mean?"

"It means the enemy will march rapidly. They killed our scouts to provide an opportunity to take the city by surprise, and they won't squander it. We'd only reach Esgallien a little before them."

"They'll still get a warning – the army will just have to respond quickly."

"It's not that simple," Lanrik said. "The defenses are well organized but it'll take time to mobilize them. Orders must be given, messages relayed and equipment retrieved. Men must gather in their companies and march several miles to the ford. Without sufficient warning they won't be ready in time."

Mecklar chewed at the nail of a grubby thumb.

"There's nothing to be done about it. Why worry about something we can't change?"

"There *is* something to be done about it," Lanrik said. "I'll stay behind and slow the enemy. If I can give Esgallien an extra half day it would make all the difference."

Mecklar dropped his hand and spat. "You can't be serious?"

"There's no other choice."

"*No other choice?*" Mecklar repeated in astonishment. "Surely not even a Raithlin can be so arrogant and deluded. One man can't defy an army!"

Lanrik answered him evenly. "If you're correct, then nothing is lost except another *incompetent* scout. You'll still return to the city and warn them."

He reached down to the pack on the ground and took out one of the water flasks and some packages of food. He passed the rest to Mecklar.

"There's no more time for talk. You'd better go quickly, and I suggest you discard the tent and sleeping rug. You'd find them heavy."

Mecklar grabbed the pack and swung it awkwardly over his back. He tightened the straps and stared hard at Lanrik for a long moment. Then he turned and trudged off without speaking.

Lanrik watched until he disappeared. He had done his best to carry out the mission the Lindrath had given him and avoided being provoked into saying something foolish, despite Mecklar's needling. What report the man gave was out of his control, and he must now concentrate on the task at hand. He climbed the boulder, careful to hug close to its surface so as not to outline himself, and studied the green expanse of Galenthern once more.

The enemy would have sent scouts ahead of the army; it was just a matter of finding them. They would be moving, and that was what would give them away. Unless they had already reached the cover of the tor, in which case he was a dead man.

His eyes carefully scanned the vast grasslands, but he knew it would be easier to find them if he could put himself in their situation. If he were down there, how would he approach the tor?

The plains appeared perfectly flat from this height, but that was illusory. In reality, there were folds and gullies, small patches of trees and areas of long grass. He would travel beneath the trees and along the gullies in order to take advantage of their concealment.

It was in a gully that he spotted a half dozen of them. They were about five miles away, working their way through scattered ferns that grew nearly man high. It would be at least an hour before they reached him, and he had some time to think.

Was Mecklar right? Were the Raithlin arrogant and over sure of their abilities? Perhaps, and yet they had real skill, acquired and honed over many generations. If he could accomplish his aim, it would surely prove to King Murhain the necessity for maintaining them. It would also ensure Lathmai's death was not in vain. And there *were* ways that one man could slow an army.

He cast his mind over the ancient legend of Galathar. Stories had been told for a thousand years about the Halathrin hero. He was a prince among those immortal people and had slowed an army that would otherwise have destroyed their realm. He had done it alone, and though he was a great warrior, he had achieved the feat by other means.

Lanrik shivered. It would be folly to think of himself as anything like the Halathrin. He was no prince in hiding either; not even a minor noble. Nor was he a golden-haired hero with a piercing gaze like they all were in stories. He was just an ordinary man with a liking for peace and quiet. But being ordinary was no reason not to attempt the extraordinary.

Whatever the case, it was time to make a plan. Events were unfolding, and his life and that of his people would be made anew. What had his uncle taught him about a crisis? His voice always carried a bitter edge, unless he was talking about the Raithlin skills, and he could almost hear him speak one of his favorite axioms now. *Clear like water; cold like ice.*

His eyes looked over the plains but saw nothing as his focus turned inward, and he assessed the situation dispassionately. One man could not fight an army. That was a weakness. What then were his strengths? He was independent. He could hide and maneuver. He was able to transform thought into instantaneous action. An army could not do these things, being enslaved to habit, order and the slowness of chain communication.

What else? There was always more. No problem was insoluble, nor was there only one way to solve it. How could he put these strengths to use? Elugs, who would constitute most of the enemy, were deeply superstitious. That would be the key to it all. If he could not physically slow an army, he must use his strengths to trigger a mental state so that the soldiers were hesitant to march and therefore slowed themselves. Plans unfolded in his mind. They all lead to one final gamble at the end though; a gamble about which he was not yet ready to think.

The end would come when it was time. For now, he must make a beginning. He slid off the boulder and retrieved charcoal from Lathmai's fire.

The elugs would probably approach along the southern path. They could also circle the tor's base, split their force, and come up the northern way as well. He would prepare for all contingencies.

Quickly he traced a pattern on both sides of the boulder in broad, black strokes. The pattern was three slanted lines, going from right to left and each one longer than the previous. It was a sign of death in the Graèglin Dennath, the harsh mountain range to the south that was the homeland of the elugs. They called it a drùgluck, and it served as a warning to stay away from a place, usually because of poisonous fumes escaping cracks in the earth, but it also marked sacred areas that served as gateways to the spirit world or locations where the dangerous effects of elùgai, the sorcery of an elùgroth, lingered. Often it signified all three at the one spot.

Working swiftly he laid out rocks in the same pattern in front of the boulder. Next, he broke a leafy branch from a nearby tree and descended the northern path. He went onto the plains and did his best to brush out Mecklar's tracks heading toward Esgallien. Coming back, he made no effort to hide their older prints from this morning and their ascent of the tor. He wanted the elugs to think that they were still up here and hide the fact that the city was being warned.

He glanced at Lathmai's fire. It had gone out, and to light it again would reveal to the elugs that someone was still on the tor. On the other hand, what was most necessary was that Mecklar reached Esgallien, and fire would help concentrate the elugs' attention away from him and toward the tor. He swiftly gathered more fuel, including green leaves that would produce dark smoke, and stooped to relight it.

He looked about him grimly. The scene had been prepared, and when the elugs arrived they would have much to contemplate. He used the branch once more to erase all sign of his movements. Irrespective of the risk, it was vital to his plan that he stayed on the tor, and he positioned himself in the shadow of a boulder toward its eastern edge. From here he had a good view of most of the summit, especially Lathmai's cairn and her rapier.

Time passed slowly; his mind moved between states of anticipation and dread, but none of his inner turmoil showed in his body. After stringing his bow, he sat cross-legged and still, an arrow knocked to the string, and the weapon resting loosely in his hand.

He heard and saw nothing out of the ordinary for a long while yet still knew when the elugs arrived: the nudaluk bird grew silent. There was now only the intermittent hum of insects on the hill.

Many minutes later, he saw the first elug. It had crawled up the southern path and only its head was visible. It watched until it was satisfied that no immediate threat was present, and then stood slowly, taking several steps onto the plateau. There it stayed, its scimitar drawn, and an alert look in its eyes as it scanned the summit. A long while its gaze rested on Lathmai's cairn.

The elug's dark skin, tinged with green and slick with sweat, was visible where its rough tunic did not offer cover. It had been a hasty journey to the tor.

Lanrik surmised this was a test: a bait to see if anybody was still on the plateau and to induce an attack that would reveal their location. The lone elug remained close to the rim and could make a quick retreat while his companions remained safe, awaiting a signal to come up. Sensing no threat, the elug gave an impatient flick with the point of his scimitar.

Another four emerged. They each wore their scimitars on back scabbards in characteristic elug fashion. Their long limbs were ungainly and they moved awkwardly, yet Lanrik knew they had speed and strength equal to any man and perhaps greater endurance. They were deadly fighters in a group, but individually they often lacked courage.

Fear touched him as they stood upon the summit, and their cruel gaze swept over it. One of the elugs stared into the shadows where Lanrik waited, and his breathing slowed. *Clear like water; cold like ice.*

The elug's eyes turned away after a while and focused on Lathmai's cairn. It drew their attention as he hoped it would, and the longer they studied the signs he had left and the sword rising from its top, the more he sensed their uneasiness increase.

The elugs moved forward cautiously. One kicked dirt over the fire to stop the smoke. They continued to scan

23

the summit, faces turning and hard eyes darting to and fro, and yet always their gaze was drawn back to the one place. Hesitantly, they gathered before the cairn.

Lanrik was worried because there were only five. *Where was the sixth?* Regardless, he knew he had no choice but to put his plan into action at the moment of maximum effect on the enemy's superstition. That moment had nearly arrived.

One of the elugs stepped closer to the cairn, and the others watched him intently. This was something beyond their experience or expectation. What were drùgluck signs doing here, in the homeland of the enemy? Was its warning legitimate?

The elug stepped forward, one foot resting on the cairn, and reached with its left hand toward the blade. Pausing, its eyes roved the summit. From where Lanrik watched, he could see fear in its expression, but perceiving no threat it regained a measure of confidence. It tensed, ready to pull out the blade.

This was the moment Lanrik was waiting for, and he acted instantly. In one practiced motion he drew the bow and loosed the arrow. The shaft flew straight and pierced the elug's neck. He stiffened and stood transfixed for a moment, then toppled away from the cairn.

Cries of dismay came from the remaining elugs. Lanrik stood and knocked a second arrow to the string. He pulled and released and another elug reeled and fell. Three remained, and now they knew where their attacker was. They rushed toward him, scimitars flashing wildly as they bridged the gap. Once more Lanrik fired, and another elug screamed and collapsed. The remainder came on.

They were too close now for the bow, and Lanrik dropped it and drew his rapier. Darting to the left in order to ensure he faced only one opponent at a time he deflected a wild swing and stabbed forward. His blade ran deep and his enemy convulsed. He had only moments to withdraw the blade before the remaining elug would be upon him. Just as he found the right angle of release he heard a wild howl and looked up to see the sixth elug, until now unaccounted for, leaping from the top of boulder under which he had himself hidden. A wicked knife, bent as were their swords, slashed at his throat.

Lanrik released his sword and rolled. The knife-blade gashed his shoulder, and he felt warm blood seep over his back, but he paid no heed to it.

Coming to his feet once more in a smooth movement, he stood motionless. Both hands rested easily by his side, and he looked at his attackers coolly. The elugs paused, unsure what to do. They were wary because he had already killed four of their companions, and though now outnumbered and weaponless, he was showing no fear.

They stood before him, and in the hand of one a scimitar cut slow arcs in the air, and the other held high its bent blade, which still ran with blood.

Lanrik reached to the sky with his empty left hand and formed a claw as though calling down powers from above.

"Attend!" he said, his voice resonant with authority. "You have transgressed against a drùgluck and defiled a hallowed place. Death shall march in the shadow of your army. Each soldier will hear doom with their every footfall. The very land will turn against you!"

The elugs paused. All was still. The hum of insects droned through the air. Lanrik's hand dropped, and as they watched it fall, his other hand drew a small knife from a belt sheath. In the same action he flicked it forward, and it struck the throat of the elug who had gashed his shoulder. The creature fell. Thrashing and gasping it reached desperately for the blade and pulled it out. This caused spurts of blood to surge from its neck. In vain the elug clamped both hands to the wound to halt the flow, but nothing could stop that deadly stream, and in moments it tumbled to the ground.

25

The two remaining combatants looked at one another in silence. All the elug's companions had been killed, and though it still carried a sword Lanrik read fear in its eyes. A slow smile spread across his face, and he took a step forward.

That was too much for the elug. It sprang away and fled across the summit and down the southern path of the tor. Lanrik could have retrieved his bow and winged an arrow after it but chose to watch instead.

He *wanted* one elug to survive and take word back to the army. In this way the breaking of the drùgluck taboo, and the consequences, would spread and the elug's superstition be aroused. It would infect them, spread through their ranks and fester. And he would work to deepen their fear. Soon the steps of the army would slow, and though driven on by their commanders, vital time would be won for Esgallien.

"Fly!" he called after the elug. "Fly, but listen for the footfalls of doom that chase you!"

The elug crashed down the slope, and Lanrik worked quickly to bandage his shoulder and stop the flow of blood. The wound, though painful, was superficial. He hoped it would not interfere with his plans.

He climbed the boulder once more and studied the plains. The army was coming closer, and the lone figure of the elug raced toward it. He chuckled. The elug ran as though the fear of death was upon it. His plan had started well, but there was much more to do. He must continue in a like vein until the army marched in dread. Let their masters drive them on! They would go forward, but reluctantly, and each moment they lost was time gained for his people.

He dropped off the boulder and lit the fire once more, piling it high with green branches until smoke rose in billowing clouds. That would give the army something to wonder about.

He was grateful to his uncle, for it was he who had taught him the skills put to use just now. How he wished he could tell him, but his uncle was lost.

Sadness nearly overwhelmed him, and he glanced at Lathmai's cairn. *Does your fate await all Esgallien?*

His determination reasserted itself, and his thoughts turned back to the approaching army. There was more that he must yet dare in order to protect his home.

3. Footfalls of Doom

Lanrik gathered his weapons and started on his plan. What he did now would give him the opportunity to slow the army. But only if he seeded into the enemy's consciousness the illusion of a supernatural agency at work that punished them for breaking the drùgluck taboo.

He dragged the slain elugs to the base of Lathmai's cairn and positioned them on their knees with their heads bowed to the ground. It made them look as though they offered repentance. He felt these actions were macabre, even if they were necessary. He quickly removed a back scabbard and scimitar from one of the elugs. Adjusting the strap, he fitted the weapon on himself. It felt cumbersome but would serve a vital purpose later.

He took the remaining blades and scabbards and heaped them in the fire. Carefully, he kicked live coals over them and the hardened leather smoldered and discolored. The hilts of the scimitars were partly visible, and the next wave of enemy scouts would quickly discover that one was missing if they dug them out. It would give them a clue to his intentions, but he doubted they would be so thorough.

He stepped back and surveyed what he had done. It was a disquieting tableau and would insinuate itself into the enemy's superstitious mind. A final touch occurred to him and he retrieved some charcoal, which he rubbed over each elug's left palm. He placed their blackened hands upwards and retained a handful of charcoal to finish off his idea when he descended the tor. His plan was taking shape.

He looked sadly at the cairn and wished Lathmai a silent farewell. Much had happened on the tor, but there had been too little time for the important things. *I wish I could talk to you one more time. I wish I could tell you how I felt.*

Even as that chance had been lost with his uncle, so it was again. In future, he would try to say these things while he still could.

He turned away and walked down the southern path of the tor toward the approaching enemy. The route twisted around trees and jagged rocks that protruded from the earth like long buried bones exposed by wind and rain. At the bottom of the path was a massive boulder. It was just what he was looking for.

He ground the charcoal on his left hand and mixed it with a little water to form a paste. Reaching up as high as he could, he spread his fingers and marked the face of the boulder with the drùgluck sign. The imprint of his fingers and thumb were clearly visible, and that it was a left hand was obvious. He repeated the process several times until there was a band of five drùglucks. When the enemy saw them, they would wonder what they signified. But when they found the five slain scouts atop the tor, and their marked left hands, it would unsettle them. Why would the scouts have left a warning before discovering what was on the crest? But having reached the crest and being killed, how could they have marked the boulder?

It was now past noon and the day was on the wane. The elug army was only miles away, and other scouts would be in advance of it. He must remain unobserved. Nightfall would allow him to move with less risk, but he could not wait until then. The army would pass close to the tor on its direct march to Esgallien and would establish camp for the night several miles to the north and closer to his home. Soon this whole area would be thick with the enemy.

It was not enough to leave the tor and stay ahead of the advancing army. When the elug he had allowed to escape returned to his leaders, they would send further scouts and perhaps regular troops to find him. It was vital that they failed. Otherwise, the illusion of otherworldly power would be destroyed. He reasoned they would be expecting him ahead of them. After all, they were approaching enemy territory and they would think that anybody trying to hinder them, natural or supernatural, would stand between them and their goal. He must therefore circle behind.

His next task would be to infiltrate the army. This could only be done at night, for even disguised he would certainly be recognized during the day. The scimitar on his back would give him the expected outline in the dark but would be insufficient to fool anyone in daylight.

Once he had penetrated their camp, he would be in a position to cause damage, sow confusion and inflame their superstition. He had to make them fear that the words he had yelled after the fleeing elug were true: that the footfalls of doom followed them.

He moved northeast across the green expanse of Galenthern. It grew lush once more and was again speckled with vetch and red clover. His passage was clear for anyone with the skill to read it from the bruised grass, though. A good tracker would also know how long ago he had passed by the amount the bent blades had sprung back.

He would have stayed where he was and allowed the enemy to sweep by him if there was a suitable place to hide. Staying still was usually safer than moving, but there was nowhere he trusted enough on the plains.

A good way ahead was a large stand of trees, and he decided to skirt its northern side to provide cover between him and the enemy. He walked at a steady pace until he saw tracks and came to an abrupt halt.

The grass was greatly disturbed, and he smiled to himself. It was a stroke of luck, for the tracks were from a herd of aurochs. The beasts spent most of their time in the scrub-choked swamps, which were common on the plains, but they sometimes moved onto the open grasslands to graze at night or move between wetlands. Whatever the aurochs had been doing did not matter: what was important was that he could follow their tracks and use the trampled earth to hide his own.

He increased his pace and glanced at the sun. It had begun its downward arc, but hours of daylight remained. He consciously noticed something then that he had been hearing for some time without realizing – drums.

The elugs always marched to the beat of drums: they were a part of their life and integral to their ceremonies. They also used them to communicate in the mountainous lands of the Graèglin Dennath. These were all things to be mindful of. If he infiltrated the army, he would look to make use of them to inflame its superstition.

Lanrik put this thought aside, for he saw movement among the trees in the timbered area he was nearing. He could not quite make out what it was then realized it was a flock of birds, probably wood pigeons. They were a common sight in the forested patches on Galenthern, but these were not flying in the high and lazy circles that he often observed or in the direct line they used when heading to feeding grounds. They had been scared and taken off in an abrupt and scattered way.

It could mean anything, but Lanrik thought it signified something very specific: elugs had arrived. They were passing through the woods, and he would now have to be even more careful.

He moved off the aurochs' trail and into taller grass nearby, leaving minimal sign of his passing. Squatting down he watched the woods, only his head visible above the top of the grass. To break up his outline he pulled up his hood and wove the stems of some grass clumps through purpose made holes in the material. It was an old but effective practice, and so long as he did not move, or the enemy come too close, he would remain undiscovered.

He waited, and soon a troop of a dozen elugs moved out of the timber and paused. There appeared to be some discussion about where to go, but they soon made a decision and commenced walking. Lanrik grimaced as they came down the trail the aurochs had left and toward him.

He sank deeper into the grass and lay perfectly still. It was bad luck that they were coming this way, but at least they did not appear to be scouts: there were too many of them, and they made no attempt to hide their presence. The army had sent out patrols of ordinary elugs, and this particular group would have swept the timber to ensure there were no concealed enemies.

Lanrik slowed his breathing and peered between the grass stems. He heard their approach before he saw them clearly. They were talking, their boots scuffing the ground and their equipment rattling and creaking. Definitely not scouts, he thought.

They came into view and filed past his hiding spot. Their scimitars were scabbarded on their back as was usual, and their iron-shod boots crushed the grass. That would further obscure his own tracks. He counted a dozen as they passed nearby, and just when he thought the last one had gone he saw another.

The final elug, shorter and thinner than his companions, moved along silently and then stopped and peered at the ground. After a few moments the elug's gaze lifted off the earth and scanned the taller grass. Lanrik went cold. The elug seemed undecided for some moments then called to his companions in their guttural language. Their speech was harsh to an Esgallien's ears, and though the Raithlin learned a smattering of their tongue, he did not understand anything.

Harsh replies came from several in the group ahead. The elug stubbornly shook his head and responded at length. His companions laughed, and Lanrik could tell from the receding sound that they continued to move away. The elug shook his head angrily and trotted off.

Lanrik was relieved. His plans had almost come undone; it was luck alone that had saved him, but he knew he would need still more before the day was done. He waited some time before moving again. The elugs had completely disappeared, swallowed by one of the folds in the plains, and he moved on with speed. The safest place for him now was in the woods. If he reached them, he would find better places to hide until nightfall.

He walked quickly but frequently looked back. That last elug possessed some tracking skills even if the others did not. If he found additional sign, he would be doubly suspicious. What if he doubled back to investigate?

The afternoon waned. The incessant beat of the drums seemed very close but would carry across the plains for miles in all directions. It was like a dirge; a death procession marching to Esgallien and all he wanted was for the irksome noise to stop and to find a place to hide.

The aurochs' trail continued to the east, heading toward lower land and their preferred environment. Lanrik moved off it and crossed the intervening space of perhaps a quarter mile to the woods. There was nothing to obscure his tracks, but night was coming, and that would make it hard for anybody to follow.

It was darker beneath the canopy of leaves. The trees were mostly beech with a scattering of ash, and green foliage roofed the columned trunks. Swathes of bluebells flowered within the shade.

This was a world vastly different from the plains. Galenthern was a lonely place where the wind blew unhindered all the way from the faraway sea. It was a wild land; a land where solitude could weigh on a person as though the immensity of the sky was a crushing weight. So strong was the feeling that some who came to the plains could not endure it and hurried back to the bubbling humanity of Esgallien. But to Lanrik it was a place of freedom.

Yet he liked the woods too. They were places of mystery with unknown vistas around bends in their aisled tracks or where hidden glades opened deep in their heart. They held sights that perhaps his eyes were the first to see, and the earth upon which his wandering feet stepped was the undisturbed leaf mold of centuries.

He had no time to explore today and quickly worked his way to the western eaves. He crept forward, and the light of late afternoon broke through the ragged edge of the timber. Carefully, he snaked on his belly through a thick growth of bluebells that diminished as the canopy thinned and allowed too much light for their liking. He lifted his head a little to see over their deep blue tops.

He saw the army and his heart quickened. The blood in his veins felt like churning ice. A watershed moment in the history of Esgallien had come: the future held either the continuation or destruction of a society that had flourished for a thousand years. Yet it was oblivious. He was the sole witness to the enemy's approach, and a burden of responsibility settled over him.

He squinted against the setting sun and scanned the leading ranks. At least there was no sign of an elùgroth. In Esgallien there would be a lòhren to oppose a sorcerer, but he had no defense and it was a relief.

Striding with a mile-eating gait at the front of the host were lethrins. They stood over seven feet, and though he had never seen them before, he had heard many stories. They were immensely strong and filled with an implacable hatred of their enemies. Esgallien folklore claimed they were born from the stone of the Graèglin Dennath. He did not believe that, but looking at their skin, even from

34

such a distance, he could see that it was tough like hardened leather and would resist the bite of a blade. They were miners that hewed tunnels in the rock beneath their mountain homes with massive picks and unwearied arms. Because of their ferocity and overwhelming strength, they usually formed the vanguard of an army. Over black tunics trimmed with precious stones, they wore silvered chain mail vests that left their arms free. Their mighty hands gripped massive iron maces that glinted dully in the sun's westering rays.

Behind them rode the leadership. This was a small group, and their black horses paced with a graceful stride. The captains of the host, as was common with elug armies, were men from the tribes of the Azan people. They were white robed and stern, and it was these riders who would drive the army on with fear but also lure it forward with the promise of plunder and loot. They were bearded old men; silvery whiskers spilled over their chests, and tulwars in ornate sheaths hung from their sides. Their heads were wrapped in white cloth, protection against the desert heat of their homes near the Graèglin Dennath.

The sun slipped below a cloud-streaked horizon, and its dying rays gleamed like pooled blood on the masses of elugs that seethed behind the captains of the host. Rank after rank they moved across the plains in a heaving multitude, intent on the destruction of Esgallien.

The foremost of the white-robed captains would be the *shazrahad*, the commander of the army, and his headcloth was scarlet to signify his status. He gestured to a man riding nearby who lifted a twisted horn of some strange desert animal and blew a great blast out of its hollowed mouth. A mighty yell rose from numberless elug throats, parched from the day's march. It thundered like the crash of the ocean blasting into a cliff, and the army came to a halt while the tumult rolled across the empty plains. The sun died; daylight turned to twilight and hope died in Lanrik's heart.

Did he dare to enter the army's ranks and try to slow them? Surely the army was unstoppable, and if he continued with his plans he would die for no benefit. But if he broke his promise to Lathmai, could he live with himself?

He was preoccupied, and awareness of a noise behind him only came slowly. He recognized it distinctly now, the soft but clear sound of something moving in the bluebells.

Panic rushed through him and he jerked his body to the right. There was a heavy thud and dirt and plant debris sprayed upward. Rolling to his feet he looked about him with wild eyes.

A lethrin, with silvered chain mail shining in the near dark, heaved its massive iron mace from the pitted ground. Lanrik saw that behind the monstrous figure a short and thin elug circled into view. No doubt it was the same who had been suspicious earlier in the afternoon. Its companions had not been interested in investigating, but it had found other help.

The lethrin swung again, and the mace sliced through the air with astonishing speed and power. Leaping back he managed to avoid the stroke and wondered if his blade would have any effect on the toughened hide. He decided if he was to have any chance of survival he must kill the lethrin swiftly or the elug would maneuver behind him and finish him off.

He edged to the left as the lethrin swung the mace once more, then darting in he stabbed at the creature's neck. For a moment he thought his blade would strike home but the lethrin, for all its mass, was more agile than he expected. It jumped back and the elug came close behind him but then retreated as Lanrik turned his blade toward it. The lethrin seized the opportunity of momentary distraction and smashed the mace toward his legs. He stumbled away and struggled to regain his composure. *Clear like water; cold like ice.*

Breathing steadily and studying his opponents as they edged closer he began to feel that this was an unwinnable fight. He retreated a little more, coming close to the fringe of the tree cover and knowing that if the fight spilled onto the plains it would alert the army.

He realized that he had made a tactical error. He would not be able to kill the lethrin swiftly, if he could do so at all. He must therefore take care of the elug first. As soon as the thought passed across his mind, he recognized its truth and acted.

He moved forward and attacked the lethrin, his sword flashing with speed and striking the creature's arm at least once, but to no effect. As anticipated, the elug closed in behind him and Lanrik swiftly turned and slashed with the blade. Though the elug attempted to back away, he was not quick enough. Lanrik's sword cut lethally into the unprotected flesh of his neck. The elug slumped to its knees and Lanrik darted to the side and tried to turn around to face the lethrin again.

He was not quick enough. Searing pain erupted across his upper back. Groaning, he somehow managed to right himself in time to avoid a follow up stroke.

He gasped as pain shot through his body. It was a bad hit even if it had only been a glancing blow. A cold sweat sprang to his forehead, and he felt nauseous. He could no longer move freely and sensed the lethrin was moving in to deliver a death-stroke. The creature did not speak or show any emotion. The iron mace circled through the air in easy sweeps; no one could survive a full-blooded blow from it, yet Lanrik knew he could no longer trust his body to avoid one. He must turn the strength of the lethrin and the weight of the mace to his advantage.

The creature circled a little more, and then its massive legs propelled it forward and the iron-like muscles of its

37

arms drove the mace toward him with unstoppable force. Lanrik evaded the blow by stepping to the left but stumbled to one knee. The lethrin sensed its moment had come and heaved the mace high in preparation for a mighty stroke.

Lanrik regained his poise quickly, the stumble being a ploy, and lunged upwards with all the strength of his legs. The point of his sword sank deep into the lethrin's armpit. The blow did not have the power that he wished, for his arm was growing numb and his back seemed weak due to his injury. Nevertheless, it struck with considerable force and the creature's weight was coming forward. Dark blood welled and the lethrin recoiled and smashed a massive arm down over the blade that tore it from Lanrik's hand and injured his wrist.

He scrambled to draw a knife. As he did so the lethrin lunged for him once more and he circled sideways out of range. Several times the lethrin attacked but quickly began to show signs of weakness. Its movements became sluggish, and he was able to retrieve his sword.

The creature let out a deep-throated bellow, and Lanrik responded by flinging his dagger which caught it across an arm. It barely scratched the skin but distracted it and Lanrik, now only able to hold the rapier in his left hand, struck it across the neck. The lethrin flinched from the blow but then dropped the mace and rushed forward catching him up in its arms. He felt crushing force against his ribs and grunted as the air rushed from his lungs. He kicked and struggled but to no effect. Yet the lethrin was weakening rapidly and stumbled to one knee. Suddenly the deadly grip lessened and Lanrik broke free and rolled away. Gasping, he watched as the lethrin toppled to the ground and died.

He gritted his teeth while an urge to retch slowly subsided. He would live, at least for the moment, but he would not be able to fight for a while.

He crawled on hands and knees through the churned up bluebells to see if the lethrin's bellow had alerted the army. If so, they would swiftly catch him; and capture was worse than death.

4. Death in Every Glance

The sun had set, and twilight groped across the plains, yet Lanrik could still see the army and the ring of sentries that encircled it. He must attempt to pass through them. His earlier doubts remained, but his promise to Lathmai drove him. He pictured her broken body and the imploring look on her ruined face; an image that would stay with him forever and push him forward even when his courage failed.

He also remembered Mecklar's contempt and itched to show him wrong. The Raithlin had learned their skills from ancient contact with the Halathrin and preserved them all this time; they had value and he would prove it.

No one headed in the direction of the wood, which indicated the lethrin's yell had not been heard. It gave Lanrik time to study the host. Officers of Esgallien's army might question him closely on his return, and he must observe the enemy's numbers, morale, and organization.

The host was some ten thousand strong. The leadership fell back to the center of the group for safety during the night, and servants erected tents to shelter them. They tethered the horses and positioned scores of wagons, used for the transport of food and supplies, nearby. The shazrahad established the camp quickly and set it out well. He knew what he was doing, and morale and discipline appeared sound; but the morale of armies was always capricious, especially elug ones.

The drummers marched at the rear, perhaps sixty elugs who would sleep beside their equipment. An idea occurred to him about how to use them to his advantage, and he decided that he would infiltrate the camp at that point.

He made some swift calculations. Mecklar was half a day ahead. It was about one hundred and forty miles to Esgallien, and an army marched twenty miles each day. It would reach the ford in seven days, but if he could slow it by half a day news would reach Esgallien a full day ahead. That would make an enormous difference.

Marching twenty miles in a day sounded like a lot, but it was even more than it seemed. Soldiers carried not only equipment but also their food. Supplies were in an imperishable form such as grain, cured meat or flour. The elugs would not carry more than seventy pounds, only part of which was food, and therefore had supplies for about ten days.

The wagons would probably carry additional food as well as equipment and would slightly increase the time the army could spend in the field. Hunting would not supply an army, nor in this case could it obtain supplies from communities along the way: none existed. The enemy must establish a supply line to keep the army in the field for any extended period. Food was essential; soldiers needed at least one meal a day, and unfed soldiers could not fight. A supply line was always a point of vulnerability, but there was no way for him to attack it. Whatever damage one man did would be insignificant, and it was upon the morale of the army that he must concentrate; that was the only way he could slow it down.

When full night came, it descended quickly, and he could no longer see the enemy. Regretfully, he discarded his bow. It was different in size and design from the type used by elugs, and most of them did not even carry one. It would draw attention and reveal him as a spy.

He pulled the hood of his Raithlin cloak over his head and walk toward the army. It was going to be a long night, but the sooner he started the greater was his chance of doing what was needed and escaping before dawn.

He walked quickly but quietly. There was no moon yet, but the stars had sprung into the sky, and their glimmering was bright and clear over Galenthern as it never was above the torch lit streets of Esgallien.

In the distance, he heard the lowing of aurochs as they called to one another and felt a breeze pick up from the east. It was cool and felt good on his back, but if it continued through the night it would bring rain from the sea by morning.

He could hear the army as well. Though muted by distance, it became gradually louder as he approached. Sound traveled far over the open spaces of Galenthern, especially at night. He slowed a little and sought lower land on which to approach, not wanting to form a silhouette against the horizon. Looking back, he noticed low clouds in the east blocking the starlight. The breeze sharpened, and he wrapped his cloak about himself more tightly.

He continued to slow his pace, and then finally stood still. The sounds of the army traveled clearly: he heard intermittent barks of harsh laughter, the rattle of cooking pans and saw movement around many fires. He was careful not to look directly at the light in order to avoid hindering his night vision.

Lanrik estimated he was three or four hundred paces from the army and close to the sentries. It was through them that he must try to pass before entering the army, but he would have to wait a little longer. The bulk of the host was still awake, and the sentries would be alert. He must study the darkness and try to locate them and how they operated. Would they remain stationary or rotate around the camp? This was something he must discover, and he settled into a sitting position. If he was close enough, one of the sentries would eventually cough or make another noise and give away their position. If not, he would move a little closer and wait some more.

His back began to ache where the lethrin had struck him, and his fingertips tingled. It was a bad injury, and he would be in no position to fight for some time. What he hoped to achieve did not rely on fighting though. His plan involved something else altogether, but there was no guarantee that he could accomplish it. He would need luck to remain undetected, and the clouds that rolled in from the east was just the sort he wanted. The night was growing darker, and if it rained, he would look less suspicious with the hood of his cloak pulled up.

There were tales about lòhrens who could walk unseen in the midst of their enemies. Many stories were told about them and the powers of lòhrengai that they learned in their fortress of Lòrenta. Lanrik did not believe them all. But he did believe in the Raithlin skills and would prove them. He *must,* for if he failed, the king might disband the organization. The shame of playing a role in that was unthinkable.

Something to the left attracted his attention. Though he did not know what it was, it triggered his instincts, and he trusted them. Moments later, he heard a noise from the same direction. He did not look at the area directly: at night, it was easier to spot something in peripheral vision than by a direct gaze. Sure enough, he saw movement. It began as a deeper shadow amid the darkness, then grew distinct. An elug walked slowly along the perimeter of the picket line, closer than he had anticipated, and he cursed himself. Such mistakes could prove costly.

The elug drew level with his position. It spoke, and his first instinct was that the sentry had seen him, but he forced himself to remain motionless, and another form emerged from the darkness. It was the next sentry in the line, and he realized that had he not stopped where he had, he would have walked straight into him.

The two elugs spoke briefly before parting, and no doubt there was an exchange of passwords. The one he had first seen remained where it was, and the other one moved away. In this way the ring of sentries circled the encampment, and there would be a long while between movements. This was his opportunity to pass through the picket line, and he must do so soon in order to escape before dawn.

He stood very slowly and watched the vague image of the sentry carefully. He was grateful for the increasing cloud cover. Without it, even the shine of starlight would have silhouetted him. He stepped back slowly, feeling his way with the toes of his soft doeskin boots for anything that might make a noise, before easing his weight backwards and then starting the process again.

Moments passed, and the indistinct form of the elug receded into darkness. Lanrik edged back just a little more then moved carefully to the left. He did not know how far apart the sentries stood but decided to move only just enough to stay out of view of the one he had located.

He moved forward again. The wind rose, and he felt raindrops on his hands. He hoped it continued for the noise would help cover the sound of his movements, but the squall died as soon as it started. Warily he walked onwards, continuing to feel the ground with his toes before committing weight to his step.

He passed through the picket line, and because of luck or skill, no sentry saw him. The scattered fires of the army grew bright, and the encampment came into view. Soldiers sprawled haphazardly all over the ground as far as the eye could see, but few were now awake. Yet he felt utterly vulnerable for it needed only one enemy out of thousands to unmask him.

His footsteps faltered. He felt a sudden urge to retreat but Lathmai's face haunted him, and his promise to her ran through his mind. To move stealthily now would only mark him as an intruder, and he forced himself to step forward into the ring of light about the encampment and

44

walk with confidence. He covered the ground quickly but without haste. The drums were a little to his left, and he veered in that direction. There were a dozen, and each was a large construction of sun-bleached animal hide stretched over a wooden frame. Rusted iron rings hung from the sides, and long poles passed through them enabling four bearers to lift and carry the drums. A fifth elug served as the drummer.

The elugs near the first drum slept. Without hesitation, but as quietly as he could, he withdrew a knob of charcoal from his pocket and marked the taut skin with the drùgluck sign. The black symbol stood out against the pale hide, and he moved on. The drummers would refuse to touch the instruments in the morning and the army would not march until they set the pace. It would take some time for an Azan commander to force them to do so.

He finally walked toward the last drum, but as he neared it, one of the elugs stirred. Looking up the soldier stared directly at him, and then spoke in their hoarse language.

Was it a question or a command? Lanrik did not know, but he guessed it to be some sort of query about what he was doing. He muttered an inaudible reply and walked away.

The camp was still, but he did not know if anybody was watching the exchange. The last thing he needed now was a confrontation; it would draw attention to him. But what he dreaded most happened. He heard the elug get to its feet and move toward him. A rough hand grabbed his shoulder and tried to turn him around. Lanrik did the only thing he could and hoped it would work. He did not resist the pull on his shoulder but turned compliantly to face the elug, and in the same movement jerked his knee into its groin. He clamped one hand over its jaw, muffling the scream that was beginning, while his other grabbed the side of its head. He applied all his strength in a twisting motion.

The elug's yell died before it really began, and a crack of bone signaled the end of its life. It slumped to the ground and Lanrik looked around. Nobody had raised an alarm.

With trembling hands and a pounding heart, he bent over and placed some charcoal in the elug's lifeless left hand. Walking back to the drum he marked it then moved away as quickly as he dared. That would give them something to think about in the morning.

He felt ill. His stomach churned, and a cold sweat filmed his skin, but he braced himself for what he must do next. He intended to thread his way through thousands of elugs until he reached the center of the encampment and the tents of the army's leadership. The drums were just the first step in his strategy, and each successive action would be more dangerous than the last. It was going to be a long night, and he wondered if his promise to Lathmai was a death sentence. But the thought of what she had endured for her people strengthened him.

He walked onwards and the army swallowed him. The edge of the encampment was now out of sight, and elugs were everywhere around him. Most were asleep, but some were alert and watchful. He felt death in every glance, yet he made himself walk smoothly and with confidence as though on some errand.

At times there were paths through the host, and at others he stepped over sleeping soldiers. Here and there a fire flickered and about it a group of elugs sat and talked. He caught many of their words, harsh and guttural, but few held meaning for him. He guessed they were no different from the soldiers he knew and were probably telling stories of the great fighters they knew or the exploits of other elug armies. By morning, he hoped they would be talking instead about what had happened during the night and that superstitious dread mired their steps.

He kept going and adjusted his scimitar so that it stood out clearly on his back. It was this more than anything that enabled him to walk through the camp, for it gave him the look of an elug in silhouette. But he quickened his pace for night was passing, and he must be gone before dawn.

Suddenly he saw a group of a half dozen elugs approach. It was too late for him to angle away without appearing suspicious so he looked downward and kept going. The elugs quickly bridged the gap.

He realized that something was wrong, for the elugs kept to a tight circle about one of their own – perhaps a prisoner caught trying to desert or steal equipment. Lanrik moved a few paces to the side, all he could manage without stepping into a group of sleeping soldiers, and waited for them to pass.

They eyed him carefully as they neared, and the prisoner took the opportunity of this distraction to attempt an escape. Like a leaping deer he tried to slip through the circle, but a hairy hand reached out at the last moment and caught his elbow then a steel shod boot smashed into his knee. There was a distinct crack and the elug fell in a wailing heap. The elugs closed round him once more, and their boots flew as they kicked and stomped him. The wailing soon stopped as the creature lost consciousness, but the punishing blows continued for some time. This was cruelty beyond anything Lanrik had seen, and enemy or otherwise, he fought down a nearly overwhelming urge to intervene.

Eventually the elugs ceased, and the largest swung the unfortunate prisoner over his shoulder. They laughed as they walked onward but watched Lanrik closely as they passed. Their eyes glittered in the glow of the campfires, and he knew they could easily turn on him. Though it ate away at his soul, he kept his head down while they walked by and ensured there was no eye contact.

The elugs passed and made their way through the camp, and Lanrik began to move as well. There were too many wakeful eyes on him now, and he wished to get far away from this spot.

He noticed groups of lethrins for the first time, and tents became more common as he progressed. He was approaching the center of the army. He saw wagons and changed direction slightly to avoid them. They would hold food and were therefore the natural target of a saboteur. They would be well guarded and he must do the unexpected.

He reached the center of the camp, and it was a mass of large tents where the silver-bearded leadership of the army slept. Lethrin guards stood to attention everywhere and actively studied their surroundings. A little to the side was a cleared space where some fifty horses were tethered by ropes to sturdy pegs driven into the ground. Even in the dim light Lanrik liked what he saw; these were some of the finest horses in all the kingdoms of Alithoras.

He edged his way toward them. They would provide a concealed spot near the tents from which he could study their arrangement without suspicion. He must somehow find a weakness in the lethrin guard and pass undetected into one of them.

What he intended to do now would be far more dangerous than marking the drums with the drùgluck sign. To slow the army he must instil superstitious dread into the soldiers, whatever the risk, and what better way than to kill the shazrahad in his protected tent and leave the sign there?

It was not something that he wanted to do. The taking of a life was wrong. Nor would he be killing a warrior in battle. He would be doing it in the dark, without warning and merely to fulfil a strategy. Yet was it not right to protect his people from slaughter? Would it not be a crime if he had the chance to save his homeland but did not take it?

The philosophers could spin arguments either way, but in the end they just wove a circle of words. Each argument seemed valid and justifiable. He did not know what the answers were; he had only his inborn sense of rightfulness to guide him and his own conscience to serve as judge.

His people had a right to freedom, whatever that actually meant. The world did not allot freedom or subjugation according to a carefully calculated plan. A community won, or guarded it, by their actions. It was something that could be lost if actions were not taken to protect it. That was what he would do now. The army had *chosen* to invade his lands. Azan men had *chosen* to lead the horde. If they had not done so they would be in no danger from him, and yet they had, therefore it was right to counter them.

He hardened himself for what he must do. Not all choices in life were easy, and not all consequences light. But it was a small thing compared to Lathmai's sacrifice.

He reached the nearest horses and spoke softly to them, moving with sure and confident motions. Some cocked their heads and watched him while others blew wind. He moved among them, talking and stroking their necks.

The horses quietened. A little to his right a stallion eyed him. It was a tall horse for one of the Azan breeds, the alar as they were called, and its coat was black as midnight without a star or even a single white sock. It looked at him with blended intelligence, alertness and curiosity. It was no time to study the conformation of a horse, but he could not help but make his way over for a closer look.

The stallion moved smoothly and freely which promised a good action, and it had wide and flexible nostrils for the drawing in of breath. Its neck was neither

49

too long nor too short, and its legs were set down square and straight. The back was almost straight, having as it should just a slight rise above the hips.

Lanrik moved forward and rubbed a hand along its hindquarters. The forequarters acted more in the nature of balance; it was from the hindquarters that the propelling power came in a series of successive springs. The stallion's rump was rounded, muscled and deep. No one could really judge a horse just by its looks, but they were a guide, and Lanrik realized he was in the presence of a stallion fit to father a breed.

The immortal Halathrin had brought horses with them during their exodus into the land long ago. They named their new home Alithoras. It was pristine and fresh, but they brought much of their old life, marvelous things as they seemed to those who first met them, to ease the burden of their transition. Little was more precious to them than their horses. They were longer lived than men and yet during their lifetime would bond with only one rider and allow them alone to mount. They were the fastest creatures in the land, yet even the Halathrin favored the alar breed and sometimes rode them into battle.

He moved forward for a better look at the tents. Staying in the deep shadow between horses, he looked out over a row of saddles stacked along the length of the picket line.

What he saw did not fill him with confidence. There were many tents, each guarded at the opening by a pair of lethrins. As the tents were set up in close proximity, the lethrins who guarded their own also had a clear view of the back of the tent in front of them. How would he gain entry?

What he needed to do was determine in which tent the shazrahad slept. Perhaps that was not so difficult because the tents were different sizes and of different quality. One of the closest, in fact a tent in front of all the others, appeared larger than the rest. It was certainly large enough for the leader and a number of his servants. The Azan people were haughty, but if the shazrahad had set his tent before the others to show superiority instead of somewhere in the middle for anonymity, he might pay dearly for his pride.

Lanrik looked closely at the two implacable lethrins in front, and then something behind them caught his attention. It was dim in the shadows, but he was sure he could see, propped up against the tent, the faint outline of the horn the shazrahad had ordered blown to stop the march. It was ready to hand for the call to march tomorrow.

So far so good. He had located the right tent. But how could he get inside it?

5. Dark as the Tomb

Lanrik was in trouble. Never before had he faced a task upon which so much depended. His Raithlin training was comprehensive, but none of his instructors would have guessed that he would one day be required to infiltrate an enemy army and steal into the guarded tent of its commander to kill him.

Yet that was what he must achieve. To attempt it he needed to clear his mind, put aside his misgivings, and break things down into their simplest components.

His training *had* included penetration of enemy camps. The Raithlin, though separate from the regular army, were formed to carry out such tasks, and there were methods to follow and procedures to adopt. His greatest obstacle to reaching the tent was the vigilance of the lethrin guards. They would see him. His first consideration therefore was to find the route that would best hide him.

The most obvious factor was that a fire burned to the right of the tent and cast a deep shadow to the left. Also, the lethrins must look in that direction, and the light would hinder their night vision. He considered this in the context of the Raithlin principles of concealment: the eye recognized movement first, silhouette second and color last.

His gray cloak blended with the shadow to the left, and that would help to eliminate any silhouette. The elug scimitar would lie flat on his back and actually help to break up his outline. He could not avoid movement, but by taking his time and seeking a path over the lowest ground, he could minimize its risk.

He felt something on the back of his hand and realized it was beginning to drizzle again. A gusty breeze rose, and he decided to act straight away. The shower would not last, but it would offer some additional concealment and help cover any noise he made.

The grass was slick with moisture, but he paid it no mind as he dropped to the ground. The horses did not like it but made no commotion while he crawled forward in the way of the Raithlin: palms on the earth, elbows close to the body to provide support and reduce silhouette, his weight borne on the forearms and one leg at a time to lift his body just enough to avoid scraping noises.

The grass of the plains was trampled into the earth and provided scarce cover, but at least it did not make much noise. He crept forward until he came to the saddles. From this point he would have no concealment except for the slight depressions in the ground that he must seek and follow. He would have to move very slowly and rely mostly on the shadow cast by the fire. It would take a long time to reach the tent, and he felt that the night, and his chance of escaping the camp before dawn, was slipping away. But haste would only get him killed.

The drizzle continued and he crawled forward. He kept his head down most of the time, for the shine of a person's face often revealed them in the dark, but it meant that he could not see the lethrins. He did not know if they looked in his direction or showed signs of suspicion; he had to trust to the shadow and his skill.

The drizzle let up and he stopped. It was time to rest anyway, because moving this way was difficult. He lifted his head just a little, and the lethrins did not appear to show any interest in the place where he lay. He took some deep breaths and ignored the wetness that seeped into his clothes.

What he must do first was stay out of the firelight. When he reached the deeper shadows cast by the tent then he could change direction. Noise drifted from somewhere far away in the camp, and he moved once again as the guards' attention was momentarily distracted.

He went on for some time, and though he moved slowly, he made good progress. In his current position he could see the lethrin guards at the opening of the tent to the rear and left of the shazrahad's. They were looking in his direction but until now had given no indication of suspicion. For some reason they suddenly appeared uneasy, as though unsure of what to do. Had they seen or heard something?

The tent flap opened and one of the officers emerged. He was a tall and stern man, and he ran his hand through his long beard thoughtfully. He did not speak to the lethrin or acknowledge their presence, and Lanrik lay perfectly still and waited.

The officer looked upward to study the sky. He spent some time doing so, observing first the northern quarter and then the other directions. He was probably trying to determine what weather the army could expect on their march tomorrow and to make plans for it.

Lanrik could have told him: it was going to rain. The wet would hinder the army, making it uncomfortable and lowering its morale. Water would seep into their clothing and equipment, and the earth of the plains, churned by countless feet into a sticky mess, would cling to everything.

Another shower passed over, heavier than before. The officer turned his back on the night with an air of revulsion and returned to the shelter of his tent. His back was stiff with disgust, and he still did not acknowledge the lethrins, nor did they appear to expect it; their expressionless faces remained trained outwards in unbroken watchfulness. The officer's dissatisfaction amused Lanrik, but hoped that by morning the weather would be the least of his enemy's problems.

He continued forward and breathed a sigh of relief when he reached the long shadow cast by the shazrahad's tent. Though he was closer to the lethrin he was now

54

actually harder to see. He angled directly toward his goal and found a slight depression in the ground, which he followed. It was wet and cold, and the slickness of mud covered him, making progress slow and unpleasant.

Time passed, showers came and went, but the fear of discovery was ever present. After what seemed an endless period he finally neared the tent. Was it partitioned? If so, would the shazrahad be in the front or back?

The depression turned and ran near the back of the tent. Entering was the most dangerous moment as he would be at increased risk of discovery. He wanted to be as far away as possible from the lethrins guarding the tent to the rear, as they had a direct line of sight toward him. Similarly, he wanted to distance himself from the lethrins who stood to attention at the front of the shazrahad's tent, as they would be most likely to hear any noise. He decided to move out of the depression and crawl to the middle.

The canvas was heavy with moisture and secured by guy ropes and pegs that held the walls to the ground. He had two choices. He could try to slit the canvas with a knife, though it was strong and would make noise. If he chose this method he would have to proceed very slowly for he did not know who was on the other side or how close they were. It would be risky. The alternative was to pull one of the pegs out of the ground. These were made of metal rods, with the top bent over, and hammered through an eyelet woven into the bottom of the wall.

The peg looked secure and he tested it without result. No doubt a special tool was normally used to remove it, but he would have to rely on his sword to provide the required leverage. This had its own dangers as a drawn blade might reflect some light and reveal his presence.

It was time to spend a few moments in thought. Either choice was dangerous, but levering out the peg was probably the safest. Most of all it had one great advantage over slitting the wall: when he was done, he could replace the peg and hide his method of entry. This would support the sense of a supernatural agency at work that he was trying to engender. He made his decision and acted.

Slowly, and with care to make no noise, he unsheathed his rapier. The elug scimitar was too unwieldy for such a job and more visible. He worked at the peg, taking his time and finding the point of maximum leverage. He was frightened the sword would slip and make a loud noise or sudden movement.

He tried several times, but the peg was firm in the ground. Risking greater force he attempted it once more, and this time it gave way with a distinct noise. It was not loud, yet audible to an alert guard, and a ripple went through the canvas wall as well.

The guards at the front of the tent were the greatest danger. He pressed his body as flat as possible against the earth and kept his face down but watched in their direction from the corner of one eye. Fear gripped him as he saw the enormous bulk of a lethrin step into view. Its iron mace, loose but ready in a massive hand, was dull red in the slow flicker of firelight.

The lethrin took a pace forward and peered closely at the spot where Lanrik lay. Was he visible? He thought not, and yet if the lethrin stepped any closer even the shadows and his stillness would serve no longer. He prepared to surge to his feet.

The lethrin stood its ground. Long moments passed then abruptly it turned and walked away. Lanrik breathed a sigh of relief, but his heart pounded in his chest for some time.

He waited where he was and remained motionless. If he made any further noise now it would be too suspicious, and the guards would investigate thoroughly.

The minutes passed. Rain began to fall quite heavily, but there was no further sign of the guard nor could he hear any movement from within the tent. He steeled himself to move again.

The rapier would hinder him inside and he sheathed it. In its place he drew a knife and carefully wiped both sides of the blade through mud to reduce any chance of its glinting in the darkness. Keeping his head low to the ground, he took the loose section of canvas wall in his left hand, held the knife ready in his right, and slowly lifted the material until there was sufficient gap to reveal what lay beyond.

It was dim. However, a candle shed some wavering light across the interior. It was set on a three-legged table near the front entrance and burned within a large holder of intricately carved horn.

A scent of exotic spices filled his nostrils as he scanned the rest of the room. The abundant luxury of it astonished him. A path of crimson silk led from the entrance down the middle of the room and stopped at a flap in the dividing wall at the last third of the tent. He could see nothing of the other room.

Woolen rugs covered most of the canvas floor. On the near side, silken cushions in an array of colors lay in a circle. Among them was a tall and elaborate chair, nearly a throne, of black walnut polished to gleam like oiled iron. This would be where the shazrahad held council with his captains and where he received messengers.

Woven tapestries decorated the canvas walls. No doubt these told stories of the Azan people or even the shazrahad's own career. Hung as decoration from the bottom of the fabric were gems, pearls and the ubiquitous carved horn that the southern people admired so much.

On the far side of the room three men lay on piled sheepskin rugs beside chests with gold bands and clasps. No doubt they were aides, and though still, Lanrik could not tell with certainty that they were asleep. The shazrahad himself was not there. Anybody who sat upon a throne to talk to his captains would not sleep near his staff. He would use the other room.

Lanrik studied the dividing wall closely. There was a flap at the end of the crimson aisle, the wall unpegged in contrast to the outside, and he would therefore be able to gain entrance closer to where he was.

Delaying further would not benefit him, and he eased himself inside. The carpeted floors helped subdue any noise, and there was no movement from the aides, but it was best to stay low to the ground, and he crawled through the room until he came to the partition. There he lay still and placed his ear to the wall. He listened for several minutes, but there was no sound of movement from beyond.

Lifting the wall just a little he peered within. There was no candle and the room was completely dark. It would not serve to be overly cautious because the longer he delayed the greater the chance the candle light would be seen through the gap he had created so, he slid under the wall and let it fall behind him.

Darkness, black as an unmeasured pit, shrouded him. His skin prickled for he could see and hear nothing; it was dark as the tomb. At the thought of death a shiver ran through his whole body. Its presence was all about him, and he felt that at any time his life could end. Yet he also sensed that he was at a crossroads, and what happened here would change his life forever.

For one of the few times since leaving Lathmai's cairn he felt indecisive. What should he do now? He did not want to grope around in the blackness of the tent. He was far too likely to make a noise.

There was only one thing to do. Regardless of the risk, he must lift the dividing wall high enough to allow sufficient candle light through so that he could see and memorize the layout. Time was slipping away from him, and a feeling of recklessness was growing. He would do what he must and the consequences would follow.

He lifted the wall quite high and wavering light entered the room. It was dim at first but then his eyes began to adjust. It was smaller in here but decorated with the same opulence. At the far end a low pallet stretched across the floor, and on top of this lay the shazrahad. The scarlet headdress that he wore around his head during the day lay on a polished table near the entrance to the chamber. A silver pitcher rested there too, as well as the curved tulwar favored by his people.

Lanrik swept his gaze over the rest of the room, and what he saw in the deeper shadows near the back shocked him. A young girl, dried blood on her face, was tied to a chair. She was cloaked all in black, and a heavy hood hung behind her shoulders. A dark staff lay across her lap. He realized that these were no ordinary items: they were the regalia of an elùgroth. And yet the girl was tightly bound. Most disturbing of all was that a stained hangman's noose hung from the ceiling before her eyes.

He looked closely at her. Even in the dark he could tell she was Esgallien rather than Azan. Her hair was black but her skin milky pale. He could not see her eyes, but they would likely be green. What he *could* see was her expression. She was awake, and her alert gaze scrutinized him, showing neither surprise nor fear. There was merely a sense of waiting to see what would happen.

Lanrik was at a complete loss to understand the scene before him, but he raised his finger to his lips and gestured for silence. Slowly he let the dividing wall close until it was completely dark once more. In the distance he heard a loud commotion. He guessed that far on the edge of the camp soldiers had discovered the slain elug, and the drùgluck signs, and that word was spreading. There were calls of *ghash*, the elug name for a malevolent spirit. Lanrik smiled grimly in the dark. Things were going to plan. Or at least they had been. They were falling apart now though. The calls would soon grow louder, and the shazrahad and his aides would waken. He had very little time left in which to act.

He now faced a dilemma that he could not have foreseen and for which no amount of Raithlin training would prepare him. His whole purpose in coming here was to kill the shazrahad and disrupt the march of the enemy. Yet regardless of the inexplicable elùgroth regalia and the girl's bizarre circumstances, it was clear to him that she was not an elùgroth but a prisoner. And she needed help. The purpose of the hangman's noose, if nothing else, was plain enough: it was to remind her how easily her life could be taken and to intimidate her. He did not know what she had already endured, but her future in the hands of an enemy army was unthinkable.

Should he move to kill the shazrahad? If he did so it could cause a noise and wake the aides, assuming the commotion from outside had not already done so. There probably would not be enough time after that to free the girl and escape. Or should he release the prisoner and abandon his plan? That would mean jeopardizing the future of a nation in order to help one person.

The calls of ghash were growing loud and frenetic; he had just moments in which to make up his mind. Already he might have left it too late.

6. Chance Meetings

Lanrik made up his mind and acted. He did not know if his decision was right, and he doubted that anybody else would either, though many would still judge his choice.

He had seen the room when there was light and knew where the obstacles and clear paths lay, so he moved with purpose and trusted the woolen rugs to obscure any noise.

In the complete dark there was no need to crawl, and he walked at full height. His eyes strained futilely, but his hearing became attuned to every slight noise.

The faint sound of a person's breathing warned him that he had neared his destination. He reached out with his left hand until he felt what he sought, and gripped the knife handle firmly with his right.

"Be easy," he whispered.

The Raithlin blade cut through the ropes that bound the girl. She gave no answer but he sensed her silent nod in the dark.

The cords fell away and she stood, though she was unsteady on her feet. How long had she been tied to the chair? Who was she, and why had she been made a prisoner and not killed? He had no answers and knew he never would unless he got her out of the tent and away from the encampment.

His mission had failed. He had made a choice to save one person that could condemn an entire nation. But would a nation be worth saving if it were willing to sacrifice a girl to captivity among an army of elugs? He did not think so, and he considered that many in Esgallien would agree. They would want him to save the girl, and they would take their own chances. His uncle had a saying that he had never understood. *The good of the many outweighs the one: the good of the one outweighs the many.* It made sense to him now.

His mind turned back to the present problem. Could he still salvage something of his initial plan in the next few seconds? He retrieved charcoal from his pocket and rapidly made the drùgluck sign on the base of the chair. It made a rasping noise but was much quieter than the yells growing like wildfire in the camp.

If they managed to escape, the shazrahad and his aides would know that a person had entered the tent, but the elugs would see it as the work of a supernatural agency, a ghash. It would also ensure the shazrahad lost credibility. What army could have confidence in a commander from whom a prisoner, under his personal guard, had been spirited away? He realized that his mission might not have completely failed after all.

He took the girl's hand and guided her toward the exit flap. Even in the dark he knew where he was going. A brazen idea came to him, and he reached to the left. He found the table where he expected it and quickly took the shazrahad's tulwar, leaving the elug scimitar in its place. He felt for the scarlet headcloth as well. There was noise on the pallet, and the sleep-heavy voice of the shazrahad broke the quiet. Lanrik did not understand and did not answer. He snatched the headcloth and quickly pulled open the flap.

After the blackness of the shazrahad's room the candlelight seemed bright. One of the aides stirred, and feeling panic rise, Lanrik walked the girl straight to the point of the wall where he had entered.

When they were outside he held up two fingers, and then pointed to the front of the tent to warn her about the guards. She nodded her understanding, and they huddled low to the ground while he drove in the peg that secured the wall.

The shadows were leaching away, and the pale light of dawn was growing. Only the cloud cover saved them, for on a clear day they would have been seen. He had taken too long to get into the tent, and even alone the chances of escape were remote: with the girl they were near impossible.

The clamor of the encampment was increasing, and the cries of ghash were coming from all around. Within the shazrahad's room there was a sudden yell. Loud movements followed as the aides scrambled up, and there were questioning shouts from the lethrin guards. A moment later he heard their heavy tread as they ran into the tent.

What could he do? There was nowhere to hide in a camp of enemies, and only moments left before discovery. To make matters worse the girl was looking at him. She had not panicked and seemed to take everything as it came, but there was trust in her eyes, and the thought of letting her down pricked his soul. *To give her hope of rescue and then watch it wither would be worse than failure.*

He made his final choice of the night and wrapped the shazrahad's scarlet headcloth around his head. Suddenly he smiled in the dark, and a wild sense of recklessness flowed through him. He recognized it as a response to intense strain but did not care: it was all he could do not to laugh. The girl caught his mood. She looked at him and her eyes gleamed. She was ready for what came next even though she had no idea what it was. He did though, for a plan had been taking shape in his mind, and though the chance of escape was remote, nothing would stop him from trying.

He took the girl's hand once more and led her along the side of the tent. He had no choice but to trust to the deeper shadows along its edge to hide them. They came to the front where the horn was propped against the canvas; it would be the key to what happened next.

He snatched it up, surprised at its weight. Up close the beaten gold mouth gleamed in the flickering light of the fire, which now exposed them. The twisted horn was detailed with scrimshaw, and there were two gold bands wrapped around it connecting it to a leather carry strap. He flung it onto his back and guided the girl toward the horses. Speed was essential, but running would only attract attention.

It began to rain. There was enraged shouting from within the tent and harsh cries from all over the encampment. Most were indecipherable, but Lanrik repeatedly heard the call of ghash.

They reached the horses. The whole camp was beginning to boil with frenzied activity, but as yet, nobody paid them any heed.

"Take a saddle and choose a horse," Lanrik told the girl. She did as asked with speed and competence and wasted no time on questions.

Lanrik stroked the neck of the black stallion he had seen before and readied his own saddle. He had thought they would have to ride bareback, but as they had not been discovered yet, he would take advantage of it.

An elug worked up the courage to approach the shazrahad's tent and shriek the word ghash at the top of his voice. The lethrin guards emerged and were followed by the shazrahad, bareheaded but carrying the scimitar Lanrik had substituted for the tulwar. He stepped forward and beheaded the elug with a single swift stroke.

Lanrik had seen enough. The girl had chosen a fine chestnut mare and dawn was at hand. It was time to go, and he guided the stallion out of view to the rear of the picket line. She followed and the two of them mounted. In the growing light he saw the army that stood between them and freedom. The soldiers were awake, agitated and alert.

They nudged the horses forward, and a wall of elugs watched them with hostility and suspicion. Only the Azan rode, but Lanrik knew the headcloth he wore was not enough to fool them.

Sometimes the easiest way to hide was in plain sight, and the best way to avoid suspicion was to draw attention. He reached for the horn and drew a deep breath. The sound of it grew as he winded it. It rose in volume and took on a deeper timbre, rolling in a thunderous wave across the entire encampment. It was a noise like no other: the twisted horn, its curves, and the gold mouth, made it unique. It rang across Galenthern and filled him with a peculiar thrill. It was music, a call to arms and a challenge all at the same time. It stirred his blood and fuelled his recklessness.

The sound rumbled and finally ceased as Lanrik ran out of breath. All was momentarily silent except for the splash of rain. He swung the horn over his shoulder, noticed an unreadable look on the girl's face as she studied him, and kicked the stallion into a gallop. She followed without hesitation.

"Ghash!" he bellowed as he rode. He picked no path between the elugs; there was none, but they parted as the horses surged toward them, and fear and confusion spread. Some took up the call themselves, and others fled wildly. The army roiled and seethed, and those who were calm before became infected with panic. Through the turmoil ran the horses, galloping over the trodden earth, leaping the remnants of campfires and discarded equipment while elugs scrambled all about them.

Lanrik laughed as he rode for he had unleashed mayhem on the army. The dead drummer and drùgluck signs had already been found, and word would soon spread about the prisoner who had been spirited away from the shazrahad's own tent. The loss of the tulwar, horn and horses, treasured possessions as they were, and the headcloth symbolizing his rank, would insult him. All of this would make him furious, and therefore susceptible to errors of judgment. Even more so for he would have no superstitious dread: he would know that it was a person, and not a spirit that had shamed him.

Lanrik glanced often at the girl. She was a good rider, but who was she? How had she been taken prisoner when the army was so far from Esgallien, and for what purpose?

He had no answers and no opportunity to think. They reached the edge of the camp, but the perimeter guards gathered to block their path. These had observed but had not been infected by the commotion of the army. They were oblivious to its cause but mindful of their role. They were there to ensure that nothing moved in or out of the camp except scouts using the correct password.

The elugs drew their scimitars and formed a long wall. Lanrik winded the horn once more. The sudden sound rang across the plains and smote the elugs as a weapon. It was something surprising, so far outside their experience that they began to falter. Through a gap the horses leapt and out onto the green grass of Galenthern.

The horses galloped, the man and the girl laughed with the release of enormous tension, and the army receded behind them. Even the opening of the heavens, and a cold downpour of rain that fell in thick gray sheets, failed to subdue them.

Eventually the cold and the wet crept upon their awareness, and the thrill of their flight subsided. They had escaped, at least for the moment, for as yet there was no sign of pursuit.

What should they do now? Before making any decisions Lanrik wanted a rest and a talk with the girl. She was obviously important to the enemy, otherwise they would have just killed her, but now he must find out why.

He pulled the stallion up, and she did likewise with the mare.

"Time for a rest," he said. He dismounted and tied the reins to a low growing bush. The girl did likewise and then flung away the black cloak. She was dressed in pants, and a green tunic belted with soft leather. The only ornament she wore was a bracelet of twisted gold.

They looked at the army, and though obscured by rain and distance, it was clear that it had not commenced to march nor was there any pursuit. He glanced at the girl. She was tall and lithe, and the expression on her face intrigued him. She looked like a happy person resigned to the fact that the world was a sad place.

She met his gaze and grinned. "Now that's what I call havoc!"

Lanrik thought things had turned out well. "That was the plan," he answered with satisfaction.

The girl held out her hand. "I'm Erlissa." Her grip was firm but her skin was soft.

"I won't flatter myself," she said. "You rescued me, but that can't have been what you were in the encampment for. What exactly *was* your plan?"

Lanrik told her of his plan to slow the army. The expression on her face barely changed, but her eyes reflected a measure of astonishment.

"You've been busy," she said

"That's the truth," he agreed.

He ran a hand through his damp hair and explained what he had originally intended in the shazrahad's tent.

She looked at him in silence for a moment. "You would have *killed* him?"

He realized that he had fallen in her estimation, and it stung him. "I would have done what was necessary."

He was dirty and hungry and in no mood to debate philosophies, so he changed the subject.

"How were you captured?"

Erlissa shuddered. "It was my fault. I received a message that old friends of my parents wanted to see me.

The messenger was supposed to lead me to a country estate, but it was a ruse. When we left the city he hit the back of my head and tied me."

She looked as she always did, resigned to the state of the world, but a hint of anger colored her words.

"He changed direction then and headed across Esgallien Ford. I didn't know why we were going onto the plains, but I knew it wouldn't be for anything good."

"How did he get you across the ford?" Lanrik asked. "It's guarded."

"He was a Raithlin. The guards knew him, and he told me that he'd kill me if I betrayed him."

A shiver passed over Lanrik. He had to ask a question even if he knew the answer.

"Did he tell you his name?"

"It was Gwalchmur."

Even though he expected it the confirmation came as a blow. What could motivate a person to commit such treachery?

Something else occurred to him. He had heard Erlissa's name before, but it was the mention of her parents that sparked his memory. They had been remarkable healers who had traveled the kingdom but had tragically died in a small community overwhelmed by an epidemic. This had left their daughter an orphan. Other healers had fled, but her parents had stayed, and children were saved that otherwise would not have lived. They had spread the remarkable story.

She looked at him directly and must have guessed his trend of thought.

"You know who I am now, don't you?"

He nodded. The orphaned girl had become famous as well.

"You're known as the Seeker. You find things for people – things that no one else can." He did not mention the rumors that she was adept at lòhrengai, the power of the lòhrens.

"That's why I was taken. The enemy wanted to use my talent."

"At least you're safe now."

Erlissa smiled. "Thanks to you, but I have more to tell yet. Gwalchmur took me across the ford at dusk and out onto the wilderness of the plains. I thought I knew fear then, but it was nothing compared to what I felt when he led me to an elùgroth."

She paused and struggled to control her emotions. "His menace was beyond description. He questioned me and I dared not give false replies. He wanted me to join their order, to become an elùgroth. I told him it would go against everything I believed in to use my talent to harm people, and that it would defile the legacy of my parents. He pressed me over and over again until I thought he'd kill me. But he didn't. He said I'd join them in the end, and he put an elùgroth cloak on me and made me carry a staff that stank of death. He placed a hangman's noose over my neck to remind me what would happen if I continued to refuse. Then he ignored me."

She looked to the ground as though she did not want to continue. "You told me that the Raithlin stationed on the plains had been slain by an elùgroth. I knew that already. Gwalchmur and the elùgroth took me with them as they did it."

She blinked away tears. "Evil was done that night and the next several – dark sorcery as I have never seen and cruelty beyond imagination. Even Gwalchmur would have fled – if he dared."

Erlissa held her arms loosely by her side, but Lanrik saw that her hands shook. She had witnessed things that no one should ever see and had lived in fear for days.

Gathering herself, she spoke once more. "Even that isn't the worst of it."

Lanrik had a sudden sense that she had been building to this moment.

"After the killing I was taken to the army and left in the shazrahad's tent. I heard his meetings with the army captains. They went to no trouble to prevent it because they didn't think that I would ever return to Esgallien."

She looked as though even she could not believe what she had heard.

"The army marching on Esgallien isn't the only one. The free cities of the east are being attacked by several more, and the Halathrin to the west also. There's a string of armies coming up from the south and attacking simultaneously."

It was the greatest offensive by the enemy in hundreds of years, and Lanrik wondered if there were traitors elsewhere. If one of the other targets fell the enemy might be able to form a base from which they could attack Esgallien from two sides.

"Even that's not all," continued Erlissa. "The free north is in peril, and the armies will try to capture whatever they can. But in the end, it's all a ploy. The greatest opponents of the enemy have always been the lòhrens. They've walked among the races of Alithoras and spread knowledge, offered council and united us all. And they've always combated the dark sorcery of elùgroths. They'll come now to help, and leave their home in Lòrenta vulnerable. The history of the centuries, and the knowledge of nations are stored there. It's the repository of their collected wisdom, and while they're drawn to the south a dozen elùgroths are heading north to destroy it."

Lanrik's mind reeled. If the lòhrens were broken a power of great good would be extinguished from the world. How much harder would it be for the free north to oppose the enemy? How long could they survive without the uniting influence of lòhrens and the lòhrengai they wielded to oppose sorcery? Suddenly he had a realization that all that he knew and loved, the Raithlin, his city and its people, were just a small part of a greater whole that the lòhrens had nurtured for thousands of years.

"Lòrenta might be emptied of lòhrens," he said, "but it's rumored to be guarded by lòhrengai."

"That was discussed with the shazrahad," Erlissa said. "The elùgroths will use an artefact of power. The Azan dared only whisper its name, but I think they called it a Morleth Stone. Many elùgroths were involved in its making, and several of them died. It will act as a conduit of elùgai, to accumulate then focus it under the combined will of the dozen elùgroths. The shazrahad had great faith in it. He was confident Lòrenta's defenses would be overcome, the fortress destroyed, and all the lòhrens eventually hunted down."

Just as it had been urgent before to slow the army, Lanrik knew it had now become imperative to return as swiftly as possible to Esgallien.

"The lòhrens have to be told in time for them to protect themselves."

"True," Erlissa said. "But what of slowing the army?"

Lanrik considered the situation. His first responsibility was to Esgallien, but he had discharged it. Mecklar had begun with a half-day head start, and that lead had now increased. The army should have long since commenced to march but did not show any signs of doing so. The tents were still standing and the soldiers milling around. It would be some time yet before it could begin, and when it finally started the things he had done would continue to hinder it. He was satisfied that he had achieved his goal and fulfilled one of his promises to Lathmai.

His duty now was to see Erlissa safely back to the city so she could give her information to a lòhren. There were several in the kingdom, so they would not prove difficult to find.

It was time to move once more, and they mounted the horses. Lanrik looked at the army; it was too far away to see anything significant, but it remained stationary. He felt satisfied, but then he saw something that sobered him.

"Look," he said.

As they watched, a column of six riders separated from the host and moved across the plains. It was the pursuit he feared. Their tracks would be visible and the column was heading in their direction. They must decide where to flee: straight back to Esgallien or elsewhere? To Esgallien was the obvious choice, but the Azan had rested during the night, and he had not slept for over a day. He must sleep soon, and he saw as well that each of the riders led a spare horse. They would nurse their mounts, but Erlissa's and his own would get no respite. Consequently, their chance of keeping ahead of the pursuit was small. He glanced at Erlissa and read the same understanding in her face.

"What do you think?" she asked.

"We can't outrun them," he confirmed, "so we must hide instead."

She looked about uncertainly. "Where can we hide on the plains?"

Lanrik made a sweeping gesture. "All about us is open space, but scattered here and there are woods and swamps. The woods are small and can be searched, even by riders. The swamps, on the other hand, are thickly timbered and treacherous. They're no place for a horse, let alone a column of riders. In a swamp we'll have some measure of safety, and there are paths of sure ground for those who know the way. If we can elude the search for a while we'll be able to leave when it's done and still beat the army to Esgallien."

"I take it you know such a swamp and its ways?" Erlissa asked.

Lanrik did not reply. His attention was on the column, and at its head was something that he had not expected. Even at this distance he could see that the lead rider wore a scarlet headdress. This meant that the shazrahad himself was leading the pursuit.

He realized it had now become a personal feud between them. The shazrahad had lost face, and the only way to regain credibility would be to personally recapture his prisoner. He could not kill her, for the elùgroth wanted her alive, but he could inflict innumerable punishments. Then he must show that the army's misfortunes were not caused by a ghash, but a man: a man that could be captured and publicly executed. Also, the shazrahad had lost his sword, and it was probably handed down through generations as a family heirloom.

He looked at it for the first time in the light of day. The scabbard was decorated with gold thread and scrollwork depicting a great hunt. At the end of the hilt was a ruby, red as blood, and when he drew it the sword shimmered with the typical appearance of a pattern-welded blade: strong, flexible and sharp-edged. It was inlaid with gold and script that he could not read and was a sword such as even the king of Esgallien would never have seen.

Thinking of all the things he had done to the shazrahad it was no wonder he had come after him personally. It would further contribute to the disorganization and slowing of the army, but it also meant he would pursue them unrelentingly. Even in a swamp they would be lucky to elude capture, and he knew better than most that swamps had dangers of their own.

7. Dead Man Swamp

The stench of the swamp reached out tendrils before they entered it and clutched at them tightly when they passed its threshold. There was no breeze, except in the tops of the trees, and the air was humid and heavy.

They followed a twisted trail, firm but slick with mud, which wound deeper inside this new world. It was dark under the trees, the half-light a haunt of owls and far off unidentified noises.

They dismounted and led the horses. Lanrik chafed at the delay, for to bring word to the lòhrens too late would be a disaster. He was cautious though, because getting killed would mean it never reached them at all.

Tree roots stuck out in knobs and tangles, and the leaves of overhanging limbs dripped with moisture. Gray moss trailed from high branches like the groping hands of ghosts. He knew some of the trees: willow, aspen, ash, elm, birch and oak, but some of these were different from home, and there were still others for which he had no name.

"This place gives me the creeps," Erlissa said.

He searched for the right words to describe his feelings.

"It's different." He looked around as he spoke, but his glance, ever watchful for snakes, did not stray from the path for long. "But think how strange it'll be for the Azan – they come from a land of deserts and dry mountains."

They neared a scum-covered pool that reeked of decay, and Erlissa crinkled her nose.

"I suppose the Raithlin have a name for this place?"

He did not want to upset her, but she had shown that she could deal with the truth.

"It's called Dead Man Swamp."

"You're joking?"

He scraped black mud of his boots. "I'm afraid not. The Halathrin explored these lands long before our ancestors established Esgallien. They found a corpse deep in the interior. The water level was dropping during a dry time, and the body was partially exposed. Whoever it was hadn't died well."

"How did they know that?"

"The mud of the swamp preserves flesh. They couldn't tell when he died – a week or a thousand years previously, but his arms were flung up, hands clawing, and his head upturned with gaping jaws."

"He drowned?"

"They thought he fell, or was cast, into a pit of mud from which he couldn't climb."

Erlissa slapped at a mosquito on her arm. "I thought we were the first people to settle these lands?"

He shrugged. "So most of us think, but there was at least one person here before King Conhain came."

Far ahead in the deeps of the swamp something bellowed. It was the harsh and drawn out hawing of an aurochs, the call they use to communicate over long distances.

"Apart from the risk of drowning in mud, what else is dangerous here?"

"The first rule," Lanrik said, "is to look where you walk. There are plenty of snakes, but the one to watch out for is the black adder. Its bite can kill, and they'll often not move until you step on them."

"Anything else?"

Lanrik shrugged. "The wild cat. They've been known to attack a person if cornered or hungry, but mostly they stay away."

"Charming," Erlissa said.

They continued and it became darker as the afternoon waned. The rain turned to drizzle then ceased. It grew warm beneath the tree canopy, and flies swarmed around the horses until they swished their tails and flicked their ears constantly.

Ducks called suddenly. The urgent noise was stifled by the thick growth, but Lanrik pinpointed its origin to somewhere along their backtrail.

He paused and listened for a moment, but though he heard nothing further, he knew what it meant. "They're following."

"Should we move off the trail?" Erlissa asked.

"To leave the trail is to die," Lanrik said. "The aurochs have made it, and the ground is firm. Elsewhere, you could walk a mile or sink in moments."

"But if we stay on the path won't the Azan just follow?"

"I hope so. We'll lead them into the heart of the swamp and beyond, and when we've taken them through its twists and turns we'll go where they won't be able to follow."

Erlissa waved a persistent fly away from her face. "What's going to stop us from getting lost?"

"The Raithlin know how to find their way, and there are methods to pick a route, even in such a place as this. Besides, I've been in this swamp before."

Erlissa had no other questions and they moved on. The brief afternoon warmth faded, and the path narrowed until they had to lead the horses in single file. Other paths branched off, but Lanrik kept to the original. To their right stagnant ponds had become increasingly frequent, and turning another bend, they formed a watercourse. The flow of water through reeds and rushes was still sluggish though.

Night came on suddenly and Lanrik, with great care, led them a little way off the trail.

"To leave the path in the dark, even just a little, is dangerous," he said. "We'll not be able to move around during the night, but I don't think the Azan will risk pushing on either."

Erlissa nodded and Lanrik was impressed that she had not complained even once about the flies or smells. They were in danger, from both their enemies and the swamp, but she did what was necessary without fuss. It was a pity they seemed totally different types of people. Her disappointment in him when he had told her of his intention to kill the shazrahad still stung.

Night fell as if someone had cast a blanket over the swamp and suddenly extinguished all light. At the same time, the mosquitoes that had been a nuisance before swarmed around them in living clouds. A vast cacophony of noise arose; there was croaking from countless frogs, some with deep booming calls, and others with high-pitched screeches, but all were incessant. Crickets chirped and small animals rustled the undergrowth while they hunted. Occasionally, there came the desperate squeal of the smaller falling prey to the larger.

Water dripped from leaves; it ran through reeds and rushes with a slow hiss, and it plopped and splashed as creatures moved in the watercourse. Everything was damp, including the ground the two travelers sat on, and there was no chance of a fire.

Lanrik shared his water flask and some of the packages of food he had taken when separating from Mecklar. It was a cold and frugal dinner, for the supplies were not intended for two people.

Erlissa took a sip of water. "It must take years to learn the Raithlin skills," she asked.

He yawned, weariness settling over him like a cloak. It had been a long time since he had slept.

"It does," he said, "but most of us have a background from childhood that helps. Many grow up hunting and tracking, and a lot were taught since their early days by relatives who are, or were, Raithlin."

"What about you?" asked Erlissa.

Lanrik hesitated. He did not normally talk about this, but he and Erlissa had shared danger together, and he liked her, even if their attitudes were worlds apart.

"My uncle taught me," he said. "Conrik was a Raithlin for many years."

"Is he still one?"

"Not anymore," he said.

"Why not?"

Lanrik let out a long sigh. "He was once among the best of us. The older Raithlin say he was offered the position of Lindrath and that he could have led them all. The king made the offer, though I never had a chance to talk to my uncle about it."

"What happened?"

"He declined. The king demanded to know why, but my uncle gave no reason. The older Raithlin say Murhain, in a great fury, commanded him to explain. My uncle, who rarely kept his opinions to himself anyway, told him the truth. He said that he had no desire to enforce Murhain's will or impose the changes that he intended. He told the king that he did not think he respected the Raithlin, and that he had no understanding of what they could achieve or how to use them."

"He spoke like that to the king?"

Lanrik shrugged. "So I'm told. He went too far, but there was a strong feeling in our ranks along those lines."

He hesitated and looked at her closely, wondering how much he should say.

"There still is," he added. "Anyway, Murhain was enraged and challenged him to a duel. Conrik laughed at him and walked away. The king called him a coward, but my uncle only laughed louder and said that he had no wish to kill a fool."

An owl hooted somewhere in the distance, and Erlissa cocked her head to listen. She ran her hands through her hair and shook it out.

"Would your uncle have killed him?"

"I think so. There's no doubt that he was a better swordsman. He was one of the finest in the kingdom, and Murhain is only competent at best. Conrik always said that you shouldn't draw a sword unless you had no choice, but having done so, it was a weapon of death and best used to that end quickly."

He could not see what her expression was in the dark.

"The world would be a better place without swords."

Lanrik agreed with the sentiment but thought the reality of the situation was obvious. "Yet they exist and some people won't hesitate to oppress others for their own gain. If the oppressed don't take up a weapon to defend themselves, then the few will always dominate the many."

The shadow of the owl passed overhead as it sought a better perch from which to watch for prey.

"What happened to your uncle after that?"

"No one knows for sure. The story is that on his way home that night he started a drunken brawl with some of the Royal Guard in an alley. He killed two of them but the third escaped. He fled and the king pronounced a death sentence, but he was never found, and how he escaped the city has always been a mystery. The gates were closed, and the Royal Guard searched relentlessly."

"That's a sad end," Erlissa said.

"It brought much shame to the Raithlin," Lanrik told her. "It also shamed our family. Perhaps that's why the Lindrath chose me to demonstrate our skills to Mecklar. It was an opportunity to redeem our name."

Erlissa was silent for a while, seeming to decide whether to speak.

"You said it was a *story* that your uncle got drunk, but no one knows for sure. It seems that you carry shame, but you have doubts that you should."

Her perceptiveness surprised him. The shame of the events was great, but so too was the uncertainty.

"When my uncle was outlawed his friends tried to find out what had happened. The only witness was the guard who'd escaped. The king gave his judgment after speaking to him, but his identity was kept secret, and no one else ever heard his evidence."

Lanrik paused. Some would consider what he was about to say as treason.

"It's whispered among the Raithlin that the king ordered some of his guards to provoke trouble and kill my uncle that night. It's even said that the king disguised himself as the third guard – but who knows the truth?"

He had spoken the words, perhaps words that should not be said, certainly words that had never been uttered outside the circle of the Raithlin before. Erlissa was silent for a long while.

She finally reached out and touched his shoulder. "You're not the simple Raithlin you give the impression of being. It's not enough for you to use your sword for the protection of the kingdom. I think you'd risk everything, even confront the king himself, to discover the truth of things. You must have loved him."

Lanrik was shocked. Erlissa had voiced what had only been a vague idea growing in his mind. Could he use his success in delaying the elug army as a shield to press Murhain for answers? Was that a part of her gift as a Seeker? Or was it the gift of female intuition? Whatever the case, he had somehow revealed more than he had intended. But he was tired. Tired of the shame that his family had to endure, tired of the danger and stress that had been ever present the last few days, and most of all just now, tired from lack of sleep.

He did not answer her, and she did not seem to expect one. Tomorrow would be another long day. He lay down to sleep, and Erlissa did likewise, but the sound of her breathing slowed and grew regular long before he found the rest he needed.

It was a troubled night. A freshening breeze cleared away the showers then stilled, allowing a clutching mist to rise from the sodden earth. The cacophony of frog and cricket rose and fell in tune with some unfathomable rhythm of the swamp. There were strange creakings and mutterings from tree trunks, and insects crawled, swarmed and bit.

Daylight finally seeped into the swamp. They ate a cold and miserable breakfast, and then carefully guided the horses back to the path. A horse neighed along their backtrail, and Lanrik knew the shazrahad had pushed hard and gained ground on them, but he did not mind for the land was treacherous, and to move at speed was foolhardy.

The track now divided frequently into others. These were like cave entrances formed of tree and fern, but the tunnels soon disappeared into mist and half-light. He made no attempt to hide their trail: he wanted the Azan to follow them deep into the swamp.

A gray heron, giving its croaking call, coasted over the treetops. Its long neck was retracted, and its wing-beat slow and ponderous. They looked up and watched it, for the canopy of leaves was giving way, and bright sunlight streamed through the gaps.

The trees, which had crowded round them since they entered the swamp, receded. They turned a final bend and a new landscape opened. A lake, steaming with mist, stretched out before them. It was a thousand paces long and nearly as wide. Innumerable ducks and waterfowl swam its waters.

On the far right trees marched right up to its shore, but the left was covered in sand and beyond that a green plain of grass. On this, aurochs and deer grazed in the distance. White egrets, elegant as always, were prolific. Many of them stalked the ground on long legs while they searched for food, but great numbers roosted in the far fringe of trees.

Erlissa raised a hand to shade her eyes from the sun.

"Who would have ever guessed this existed?"

"It makes for quite a change," Lanrik said. "Swamps are made out to be horrible places but really they're full of life."

Erlissa looked at him. "It still smells disgusting."

Lanrik laughed. "There's no getting around that."

A flight of ducks arrowed over the tops of the trees, and then flew low over the water before landing.

"How can there be a lake and grassland in the middle of a swamp?" Erlissa asked.

Lanrik shrugged. "The way I understand it is that Galenthern, however level it appears from a distance, is covered with folds and undulations. Some areas are low enough to expose a different type of soil. It's dark clay, and water percolates through the earth for many miles around to feed the swamp and fill the deeper lake. The grassland itself is a little higher and the aurochs probably formed it. They're destructive animals, always pulling down leaves from low branches, rubbing saplings and grazing seedlings. Over a long period they can turn forest into pasture."

Erlissa pointed to the grassland. "Is that where we're going?"

"Yes," Lanrik said. "And we'd better do so now, for the Azan are close behind."

They moved into the open and picked their way across the grass. The ground was damp, but not muddy, and they were careful to avoid the more suspect areas. For the first time since entering the swamp they rode, though slowly and with care.

The deer had long since disappeared into the surrounding trees, and as they approached halfway across the little plain the aurochs moved with much noise and backward looks into the fringe.

Lanrik veered toward the lake. He dismounted and handed the water flask to Erlissa who took several small sips and returned it. It was nearly empty. He waded out as far as he dared to reach clear water.

"This is the cleanest, but still dangerous. Later on I'll filter it through sand or charcoal to make it safe."

When he was done they watered the horses. They mounted again and Erlissa drew in a sharp breath.

"They've come," she said.

He saw them. They were mounted, the shazrahad in the lead, his scarlet headdress bright against the green of the trees under which they momentarily rested.

Lanrik smiled grimly. "Not all of them."

Five riders, with their spare horses, watched them bitterly from the eaves of the trees; mud spattered, bedraggled and weary as only travel through swampland can make man or beast. Of the sixth, there was no sign: the swamp had taken him.

The pursuit began in earnest. The shazrahad was close to his enemy, his redemption near to hand, but he had learned caution in the last day. He led the Azan onto the grass, but did not gallop as the rash or foolish would. He took his time, choosing his way with care, and followed his prey with determination whetted by frustrated desire.

Lanrik and Erlissa moved on and did not look back; that would only waste time. With as much speed as they dared, they moved toward the end of the lake where there was a large area of rushes.

The rushes were the haunt of black adders. The snakes, thick and fat, lay on the narrow paths that wound between tall stems. They basked in the sun and were slow to move even when Lanrik, now on foot and leading his mount once more, stamped the ground. The horses were nervous with fear.

They continued. The rushes gave way to trees again, and once more they walked in the half-light of the swamp forest. In places, slime-covered water submerged the path for many paces at a time, though the ground underneath was solid.

Lanrik picked their way carefully, first choosing one path and then another, switching as often as he could. Some tracks remained for the Azan to follow, but it would slow their pursuit.

It grew warm and sticky as the day passed. The sounds of the Azan reached them regularly as they struggled on. They were close behind, but no matter how hard they pushed, they could not quite reach their prey.

Late in the afternoon the swamp changed. The paths and trees faded, and they came to a flat area covered with ankle deep water and vegetation just reaching above the surface.

"This is it," Lanrik said. "The corpse the Halathrin found was here. It's called Dead Man's Flat."

"Then we're trapped," Erlissa said. "It's too dangerous to walk over that."

Lanrik did not take his eyes off it. "There's a way forward," he said. "The Azan won't follow, or at least they'll soon give up if they do."

He looked at Erlissa and saw doubt for the first time. "I'll not lie," he said. "It's dangerous, and yet there's a way for those who know. The soil here is of different types, some the dark clay of the swamp, and some the chalky rock of Galenthern. To traverse the clay is to sink into oblivion, but you can walk on the rest – with care."

"How do you know which is which?"

"Look, and tell me what you see?" he asked.

Erlissa studied the flats and a frown appeared on her face. "It all looks the same to me."

Lanrik chuckled. "Let's hope the Azan think so too. But however it looks, as the soil varies, so does the vegetation. Some plants prefer the black mud, others the chalky soil."

Erlissa looked at the flats once more. "That's so simple, and yet so hard to see."

"The Halathrin are skilled observers of nature. It was they who long ago gave the Raithlin the secret of crossing Dead Man's Flat. Let's hope the Azan aren't as discerning."

He listened for any signs of pursuit, but heard nothing. It could still be some way back, or closing in. Nevertheless, night was drawing on, and they could travel no further, so they spent another unpleasant night in the swamp. Lanrik hated the delay. While they were stuck here the army was marching far ahead of them and getting ever closer to Esgallien. Should it reach the ford before them, it would prevent them from bringing their warning to the lòhrens.

When dawn came they had already eaten a sparse meal and were ready to move.

"Quickly," Lanrik said. "Take off your boots. In bare feet you'll better feel what type of ground you're standing on. And if you step in mud you have a better chance of extracting yourself. Boots act as an anchor."

They pushed forward onto the flats. Lanrik led and Erlissa walked her horse directly behind. The wet ground was slippery, and the water level fluctuated between ankle and knee. Though the ground was soft, they often felt crumbly rock within it. Sometimes Lanrik paused, uncertain of the path. Even though he knew what to look for the variation in vegetation was not always clear.

Behind them they heard harsh cries, and the Azan appeared out of the trees. They mounted their horses, and one of them whooped and yelled. Seeing the shallow water and much green grass, he thought it safe to ride. He kicked the horse into a gallop, and it raced across the flats.

Lanrik was tempted to ride as well. He pushed down the urge and trusted the Raithlin lore. The Azan rider approached without problem and left a trail of splashing water. However, the horse suddenly propped and stumbled, its legs deep in mud, and the rider cartwheeled over its head.

The more the horse struggled the deeper it sunk. Its hind legs kicked and pushed wildly but to little effect. In its extreme panic it heaved too far in one direction, and the right foreleg twisted and broke. It screamed in terror and agony.

Lanrik wanted to close his ears to the sound but could not; nor could he turn his eyes away.

He and Erlissa watched as the rider scrambled and sunk, yelling and trying to reach his horse. The horse quietened and accepted its fate with glazed eyes. The man screamed to the last.

When it was over there was silence on Dead Man's Flat. The antagonists watched each other over the gap, and hatred burned in the shazrahad's features.

Lanrik thought he would turn back, but he did not. He yelled at his men, and with great reluctance they dismounted, spread out, and led their horses forward. He followed them at a distance, monitoring their progress and staying in their safe tracks.

Lanrik and Erlissa pushed on without speaking. He took his time, knowing that their lives depended on the path he picked more than the progress of those who followed.

They were halfway across when one of the Azan yelled. They turned and looked as he struggled. It was a close thing, but he got out of the mud, and then led his horse further to the side. He tried again, but soon succumbed once more. He withdrew, exhausted, terrified and bootless for the mud had sucked his footwear away.

The others fared no better. Only their slow pace enabled them to escape the mud once they stepped in it, but even so they were nearly killed several times. Their luck and strength could not last much longer.

Lanrik and Erlissa drew ahead while the Azan slowed then stopped. The shazrahad yelled, projecting a deep and authoritative voice over the flats.

"Halt," he commanded. The two fugitives turned.

"You must return my sword. Do that, and I shall pursue you no further."

Lanrik's breathing was ragged from exertion, but he still laughed. "You *can't* pursue us anymore."

The shazrahad showed no chagrin. "Will you flee as a mere thief, then?"

Lanrik did not like that. Everything he had done in the enemy's encampment and the tent were acts of war against an invading army, not petty theft.

"Does the sword mean that much to you?"

The shazrahad paused. "Yes," he said eventually.

"Then withdraw your army from the field and I'll return it."

The Azan were a people whose culture greatly esteemed honor. He would not accept the offer, but it was worth a try for if it was, the shazrahad would be as good as his word.

The face of the Azan remained impassive, but his silver beard bristled. "I cannot do that."

"Then the sword," Lanrik said, "will remain the spoils of war."

"You do not understand."

"I understand this," Lanrik said. "Time is short and our conversation is over."

He and Erlissa began to cross the flats once more. There was silence for a moment before the shazrahad spoke again. His voice smoldered with suppressed emotion.

"Then I, Musraka, curse you, and all your line. I will pursue you across the earth all the days of my life. Not desert heat, nor storm or bitter night will hinder it. So shall it be!"

Lanrik kept walking and did not answer. The sword was worth a fortune, but so too was the horn and horses, yet these had not been mentioned. Perhaps if a lòhren interpreted the script on the blade the reason would be clearer.

They reached the end of the flats and looked back. The Azan were gone.

"Can they find a way around?" Erlissa asked.

He shook his head. "The trails wind about in a maze, and it would take them days to find the way, if ever. The quickest thing to do would be to go back to where they entered the swamp and ride north over Galenthern until they find where our tracks will leave the swamp, but they'll never catch us now."

They moved on. The day passed and the trees grew up tall and dark about them once more. The trails wound and turned, but Lanrik knew the way. After some time they followed a path that widened. Though it was dark, they wanted to be out of the swamp and they mounted and rode, but with great care.

Night had fallen when they emerged onto the green grass of Galenthern. The stars were swollen and bright as they only were in the wilderness, and a northeasterly breeze pushed the smell of the swamp away.

"Fresh air!" Erlissa said.

Lanrik thought her smile and the flash of her eyes was brighter than the stars, and it felt good to be alive.

"Ride," he said. "Ride for the lòhrens and all Alithoras!"

And the horses ran, fast and surefooted toward a land they had never known, but to a city their riders loved.

8. A Choice that is no Choice

They sat upon sweat-stained mounts. Green-grassed Galenthern lay behind them, and ahead was Esgallien Ford.

"I don't see anybody," Erlissa said.

"Neither do I," Lanrik replied. "Nobody at all."

He was worried. Esgallien's army was not here, and the way to his home was still open. Had Mecklar given them the warning?

There were other problems. This side of the ford offered concealment for enemy scouts who could attack them as they crossed. And the crossing itself would be difficult. The Careth Nien was hundreds of paces wide at this point; making it shallow, and though the stony bottom gave good purchase the waist-high water flowed so quickly that it could sweep away a rider.

The bank was not steep. It was an inside bend of the river, and there were deposits of sand and gravel. Erosion gullies, sun-bleached tree trunks and flood debris were scattered widely.

He nudged the stallion forward and kept in the open. The angled early morning light helped him to see any tracks. When the sun was high, a trail was harder to spot.

He noticed the imprints of iron-shod boots. Elug scouts were hidden ahead and would attempt to kill anybody returning to Esgallien.

"They're already here," he warned Erlissa.

The ford covered a large area, and the elugs must either be scattered or concentrated. Spread out, riders would have a chance of breaking through, and if grouped together, there was a chance of avoiding them altogether. The horses would be their advantage. They were fast, sure-footed and agile.

The alar were tired though, having borne their riders far across Galenthern. After leaving Dead Man Swamp Lanrik and Erlissa had trailed the enemy host, following its beaten path and detritus.

Eventually they had heard the throbbing of elug drums, ominous and sullen. The rearguard came into sight, and they observed whip-wielding Azan forcing the drummers to set the marching rhythm. The drùgluck signs had worked.

The army was half a day late and struggling to maintain its pace. Lanrik had proven the Raithlin skills, far exceeding the exercise with Mecklar. This was validation, and the king could no longer begrudge their funding.

The riders swung wide of the host, and then looped back to its front. It had cost them a day and allowed forward scouts to beat them to the ford.

Lanrik turned to Erlissa. "We'll have to rely on the speed of the horses. The elugs could be in a number of hiding places, and we can't avoid them all. Our best chance is to surprise them and try to get past before they have much chance to react."

Erlissa scanned the bank and shrugged. "It's a simple enough plan," she said.

Most people would have been tense, but she just accepted that they would get through, or not, as chance dictated. He admired her composure but found her fatalistic attitude disconcerting.

They moved forward at an easy walk, giving no sign that they knew scouts were there, but avoiding places of ambush until they had descended the steeper part of the bank and the ground flattened. The debris and erosion gullies would make the next stretch a treacherous place to gallop.

"Are you ready?" Lanrik whispered.

Erlissa flashed him a grin and by way of answer kicked the chestnut mare so that it bounded forward. The stallion took off after her, and Lanrik drew his Raithlin sword. The horses sped toward the river, veering one way and then the next to avoid sand gullies. They jumped scattered logs, and their hooves alternately churned through gravel and clattered against hard rock.

When they neared the river, ten elugs raced to intercept them from a gully to the right. Lanrik urged the stallion on until he caught up to the mare and placed himself between the elugs and Erlissa.

They made it to the water, and it splashed and sprayed about the horses' legs. One elug, a little ahead of the others, reached them and slashed at Lanrik. He parried with the sword, enough to deflect the blow, but the angle was awkward and the elug's strike tore the weapon from his grip; it spun and fell to the riverbed. The elug swung again, but the stallion surged ahead in a rush of foaming water.

The river deepened, and the elugs milled indecisively behind them. They were afraid of the current, for there were no rivers such as this in the dry Graèglin Dennath mountains.

Lanrik cursed the loss of his sword and muttered under his breath. The water was deep now, but the horses moved on. The force of the current was strong, and it grew stronger as they headed toward the center.

Erlissa looked at him, and he saw understanding in her eyes. She knew what the Raithlin swords meant to those who carried them; everyone in Esgallien did. The Lindrath presented them at the initiation ceremony of a new recruit, who cherished and preserved them for the rest of their lives. He cursed once more. *At least the elugs are no longer a threat.*

The force of the water diminished as they passed the middle of the river and approached the northern bank. When they came to land it was steep, and the horses slipped and struggled to the crest. They halted, for there would be a Raithlin guard.

The Careth Nien was a border: wilderness lay to the south, the tamed and fruitful lands of Esgallien to the north. Ahead were cultivated fields, and hornless red cattle grazed pasture; they were the descendants of animals Conhain brought when he founded Esgallien. Thick hedgerows of hawthorne, blackthorn and hazel bordered the paddocks. Some were left as pasture, others ploughed, the dark earth awaiting a crop; and some, seeded in autumn, were now lush with the green shoots of oat, barley and wheat.

They waited. Several moments passed before a lone man rose from behind a fallen log and strolled toward them. He carried a notched bow and was dressed in Raithlin garb: soft doe-hide boots, gray pants and tunic covered by a forest green cloak and hood. Woven with red thread above his heart was the Raithlin motif of a trotting fox looking back over its shoulder.

Lanrik noticed, despite the man's casual appearance, that his glance was sharp and took everything in; the girl, the horses, the hilt of the shazrahad sword sticking up from his backpack and the horn slung over his shoulder.

The guard lowered his hood. "Well met," he said. "You and Mecklar left on foot, yet you return on an alar stallion and in the company of someone far more beautiful than the king's counselor. There must be quite a story to it all!"

Lanrik laughed. "There is, Gilhain. But I don't want to repeat it, so the others had better join us." He looked around. "I can probably guess who's with you. Come Rhodlin and Rhodmur, where are you hidden?"

Two men, obviously brothers, both heavily freckled and crowned with red hair, emerged smiling from some tall grass.

"There should be more," Lanrik said. "Perhaps also the brothers Arawdan and Arawnus."

Two more men, these with solemn faces, black hair and blue eyes, swung down from the branches of an oak tree and landed lightly on the ground.

The Raithlin unstrung their bows and made a pretense of studying the horses, but he saw their surreptitious glances at Erlissa.

She smiled. "The mare is beautiful, isn't she?"

"Indeed," Gilhain said. "But the rider is fairer still."

Erlissa laughed. It was the free and light laugh of a girl used to compliments and at ease with the men who gave them.

Lanrik realized with a shock that he did not like the attention they were giving her. Was he jealous?

He cleared his throat. "Has Mecklar returned?" he asked.

Gilhain's expression changed. "Oh yes."

"He was as charming as ever," Rhodlin said.

"Charming enough to inform us," Rhodmur added, "that the Raithlin were useless, treacherous and that our days were numbered."

Gilhain slapped his thighs and laughed. "He'll have to eat his words now. By his calculations, the elugs should be here already. He said you intended to slow them down, and obviously you succeeded."

"He also informed us," Arawdan said in his somber voice, "that you would not be able to do so, that in fact you would return soon after him, having thought better of trying."

"The *king* will have to think better of things now," Gilhain said. "The elug army isn't here and the horses, horn and sword show that you've been in their camp and delayed them – a feat to enhance the renown of the Raithlin."

"A feat indeed," Arawnus said, in a voice even more solemn than his brother's. "You will be the Raithlindrath one day."

He used the formal term for their leader rather than the usual abbreviation, and his words gave Lanrik a queer feeling. The predictions of Arawdan and Arawnus were often uncannily accurate. He noticed the respect with which the other men looked at him, and it made him uncomfortable. *I haven't done enough to deserve it.*

"How soon will our army arrive?" he asked.

Gilhain glanced northward. "A horse was given to Mecklar and a rider sent with him. News was taken quickly to the king, and we expect the army by noon."

Lanrik could not help but feel that Mecklar had let him down. He should have returned to Esgallien more swiftly than this.

"It'll be close," Erlissa said.

"Close," Gilhain replied, "but the ford won't be breached."

Irrespective of his words, he glanced worriedly to the north again. After a little while, he guided Lanrik and Erlissa to a small cottage built some way from the ford. He prepared a meal of cured meat, bread and wine while the other Raithlin remained on watch.

The morning passed. Gilhain's mood was one of forced buoyancy; the attitude usually adopted by the nervous. He was moved to tears however when they talked of Lathmai.

"Gwalchmur is a dead man," he said, "if the Raithlin find him."

Lanrik remembered his promise to Lathmai and wondered what Erlissa would say if she knew.

The faint but growing sound of elug drums broke their wait. They left the cottage and returned to the ford, Lanrik strapping on the shazrahad sword and taking the horn. The Raithlin were standing in plain sight on the bank, their bows strung and arrows notched.

Rhodmur acknowledged Gilhain. "Elug scouts began to cross the river so we revealed ourselves. They turned back but more will join them soon enough, I guess. They'll try to force a crossing when there are enough of them."

"Let them come," Gilhain said. "We have arrows and enough blades to stop them."

Lanrik knew this was true. However, the elug army was fast approaching, and a handful of Raithlin would not hold *it* back. He did not doubt their own army, if it arrived in time, would secure the ford against the enemy. It was an adverse place for a hostile force to cross. The swift water would slow them and make it difficult to hold shields in place. Archers would take advantage of this, sending accurate and murderous volleys of arrows repeatedly into their dwindling ranks. And if any reached the bank, they would scramble up the steep incline into a wall of waiting spearmen.

There were no other crossings except those guarded far upstream by the Halathrin and downstream by the free cities. A strong man could swim the river, but elugs had little love of water, and single swimmers were not armies. Armies must carry food and equipment. Food would spoil and equipment weigh down a soldier and drown him. Rafts could be built, though with great labor, as there was no timber near the river. However, the army must receive supplies, and such a bridgehead required strong protection, for a successful counterattack would sever the army from its lifeline and destroy it.

The sound of galloping horses came to the Raithlin, and columns of riders swept along the hedgerow-bordered road coming from the city: a hundred, two hundred, three hundred – a contingent of Esgallien's cavalry had arrived. They thundered up to the ford and dismounted. Their horses would be of little use here, but they carried short-limbed bows and sabers.

Their commander pulled his mount in close to the Raithlin, and Gilhain stepped forward. "It's good to see you," he said.

The officer dismounted and shook his hand. "It's even better to see that the enemy isn't here yet. Mecklar led us to believe we'd be too late."

They talked a little as they waited. The elug army was in sight now, rolling forward to the surge of the drums, but the ford was guarded and Esgallien's army close behind.

It eventually came, marching to the beat of no drum but to the blowing of ancient carnyx horns, the sacred instruments that had been winded in the tumult of battle by their ancestors before the days of the Halathrin. The soldiers strode forward, the forerunners holding high the banners of Esgallien's lords. At their head, brightest and most poignant, was the Red Cloth of Victory that all the kings of Esgallien had used since the founding of the kingdom out of battle and despair.

Lanrik felt a surge of pride. These were his countrymen, sworn to protect the nation, willing to risk their lives to do so. And the king's banner, whatever he thought of Murhain, brought goose bumps to his skin just as it did to all in Esgallien: every farm hand, every weaver, every shepherd, every baker. It represented for them the sacrifice Conhain made to save his people.

The army of Esgallien took up position; the elug army was still a mile distant. The king and his retinue established themselves on a westward rise with a view of the ford. A general would direct the battle as Murhain was not a war leader.

Out of the multitude, the Lindrath walked to Lanrik, and they shook hands.

"You've made us proud," he said.

"I did what was necessary," Lanrik replied, not wanting any attention.

"It was necessary," the Lindrath said, "but it was more than could have been asked."

Lanrik shrugged uncomfortably. "Lathmai gave even more."

The Lindrath looked at him carefully and then nodded. "She'll be honored," he said quietly.

Lanrik knew he meant it. They were simple words, but behind them was the weight of everything that it meant to be a Raithlin. They were a close group, little given to showing emotion but bonded by the hardships of their training and the purpose they served.

Lanrik beckoned Erlissa over and introduced her to the Lindrath. She told him what she had learned of the threat to the lòhrens. His eyes widened as she spoke, and he shook his head as though denying that such a plan could exist, but there was no hesitation in his voice when he spoke.

"Lòhren Aranloth is with the king's retinue," he said. "The last time I saw him though, he'd gone off into a field saying he needed to think. We'd better track him down."

The Lindrath led them through the army and to a place behind the king's banner. They forced their way through the hedgerow and into the open field beyond. It was pastureland, and the red cattle in the paddock looked at them briefly and then continued to graze placidly. It was a repetitive and peaceful sound.

The lòhren was an old man. He sat on a tree stump, his long legs gathered under him. He stood when they neared, and Lanrik watched him closely. His actions were fluid and graceful. Regardless of his appearance, he moved as no old man Lanrik had seen before. He carried an oaken staff but did not lean on it. He was dressed in white robes and his hair was white also. His face was wrinkled but the skin was clear and a healthy pink. A diadem circled his brow, nearly hidden by his hair, and was engraved with some strange symbol that tugged at Lanrik's memory, but he could not see it clearly or recall its significance. The man's eyes were sea-gray: the deep eyes of someone who had seen the highest joy and the lowest tragedy. They were eyes that looked into the hearts of men and read souls as others did the pages of a book. Lanrik had a feeling that his thoughts and nature were being considered as a smith would study the virtue of a new metal.

The old man strode forward and met them. Surprisingly, he spoke to Erlissa first.

"Are you well, my child? A shadow has fallen on you since last we met."

Erlissa had made no mention of the fact that she knew a lòhren.

Her shoulders slumped. "It's as you guessed long ago, Aranloth. The enemy tried to make me join them." She straightened and glanced at Lanrik. "But he saved me."

Aranloth looked at her sadly, and Erlissa turned back to him. "I'll still not join the lòhrens though."

"Peace, my child."

Aranloth turned his attention to Lanrik. "You've done well," he said. "Apart from saving Erlissa, the talnak horn and the shazrahad sword you wear are tokens of success."

Lanrik was surprised. A talnak must be the type of an animal hunted by the Azan to obtain the distinctive horn. It was knowledge the Raithlin did not possess and proved that the lore of the lòhren, even of lands in which it would be death for them to walk, was far reaching.

"How did you know about the sword?" he asked.

Aranloth laughed freely, and it contrasted with the dignity of his bearing. "It was a simple guess," he said. "You rescued Erlissa and took a talnak horn from the enemy. Such a prisoner and the horn would only be kept in the shazrahad's tent. Given that you were there, and observing the scabbard and the ruby on its hilt, the sword must have been his."

"So it was," Lanrik said. "And it must be more valuable than the horn for he was interested only in getting it back."

"Really?" the lòhren said thoughtfully. "Talnak horns are of great ceremonial value to them. Both horns and swords are heirlooms handed down through centuries, and they each represent courage; one for the hunt and the other for combat. Tell me – is there script on the blade?"

"There is," Lanrik said.

Aranloth rubbed his chin. "I'll look at it later and see what it says. But for now, there are no doubt other matters to discuss. You would not otherwise have come to see me when battle is about to be joined."

Erlissa briefly recounted what she had heard in the shazrahad's tent, and the true purpose of the enemy. Aranloth listened closely, and so too did the Lindrath, but he also eyed Lanrik from time to time. That slowing the army had involved entering the shazrahad's tent obviously surprised him.

Aranloth remained calm. His face was serene and showed no hint of disquiet. He must have felt it though, and Lanrik was impressed. This was a man who got things done while others panicked.

"Are you certain they spoke of a Morleth Stone?"

"They used the term several times."

"And it will be taken to one of the mountain ranges north of Lòrenta?"

"Yes, but they didn't say which."

"It could be Anast Dennath or Auren Dennath," Aranloth said. "It's ill news either way. Morleth Stones are dangerous. They offer a way for many elùgroths to use sorcery in unison. Their making is not without cost though: elùgroths would have died."

The Lindrath looked puzzled. "But why take the stone to the mountains and not Lòrenta?"

Aranloth answered, searching for a simple way to explain. "Lòhrengai and elùgai gather energy. It becomes part of us, and bent to our will, is transformed. It cannot be completely changed though and retains much of its original nature. The elùgroths assembling outside Lòrenta will be linked to the energy the stone absorbs from the mountain peaks. The mountains are a different world: not quite of the earth nor yet the sky; bathed in bright sunlight but deathly cold; at the top the world yet littered with seashells. I believe the elùgroths intend to open a way into the spirit world; a place between life and death. Lòrenta will be drawn within, and though not destroyed, it will be cut off from us, and we from it."

"I thought Lòrenta was protected against assault?" Lanrik said.

"It is," Aranloth answered. "The defense comes to life during an attack, but as Lòrenta won't actually be harmed, it won't respond."

Lanrik was not sure what to make of all this. Talk of spirit worlds and the like was beyond his experience, but just because there were powers at work beyond his understanding did not mean that he could ignore them. He remembered what elùgai had done to Lathmai.

Aranloth was thoughtful for a long while before speaking again. "Without lòhrens all Alithoras is vulnerable," he said.

Erlissa looked at Lanrik. "That's why we brought the news to you quickly."

Aranloth nodded in acknowledgement. "Yet the elùgroths have too great a start."

"There must be a way to stop them," she said.

"I have not the strength on my own," Aranloth replied. "And I have not the time to find enough lòhrens. Beyond doubt, Lòrenta will be driven into the spirit world. But it must be kept there some time for the sorcery to bind permanently. If the stone was destroyed before then, Lòrenta could be saved."

"Then there *is* a way," Erlissa said.

"Assuredly," the lòhren replied, and he looked at her with sad eyes.

Erlissa returned his gaze for some moments before hanging her head.

Lanrik knew she had realized something he could not yet see yet. He put his hand on her shoulder. "What's happening?" he asked.

It was Aranloth who answered. "The Morleth Stone could be anywhere in the mountains," he said. "Only Erlissa has the talent to find it in time."

Erlissa's head snapped up. "I *won't* join the lòhrens," she said. "And I'll not be part of this battle. My parents gave their lives to heal rather than hurt. They went where they were needed, whether the people were poor or rich, bad or good; they helped everyone they could without judging. I can do no less than follow their example."

"I understand," Aranloth said. "I do not ask you to join us, but I will say this. You are the only hope of finding the stone in time to destroy it. If that is not accomplished, Lòrenta will be lost. And the lòhrens, scattered and susceptible, will be killed."

Erlissa shook her head. "I want no part of this! Do you think I'm blind? Once I've found the stone you'll be able to destroy it. What then? The elùgroths, linked to the stone, will be killed! Tell me it isn't so?"

"If the stone is destroyed the elùgroths will perish," Aranloth confirmed. "That is a certainty. Its counterpart is that if the elùgroths succeed, the lòhrens will die. One of these will come to pass. You can help, or not help. Through no fault of your own, that is your choice."

Erlissa rubbed her eyes. "If I say no?"

"You must not."

"Why, Aranloth? Tell me why?"

"Because to say no puts all of Alithoras at risk."

"You're giving me a choice that is no choice!"

"I *also* do what I must," Aranloth murmured.

Erlissa was silent for such a long time that Lanrik thought she would never give an answer. She repeatedly turned and twisted the gold bracelet that she wore as though it somehow held an answer. All the while, the old man watched her with eyes that understood and regretted her turmoil.

The cattle grazed contentedly in the paddock, small birds piped and tweeted in the hedgerow recking nothing of the fates of men, lòhrens or elùgroths. In the distance was the clamor of armies and the rumble of elug drums.

"Very well," Erlissa said at last. Her face was pale and her voice listless. "I'll find the stone for you, but the death of the elùgroths will be on your head. I'll have to go to Lòrenta to do it. I must feel the energy of the thing before I can trace it back to its origin."

"I know," Aranloth said. "We'll leave today."

The lòhren turned his gaze to Lanrik. "You also must come," he said.

Lanrik was stunned. He had not expected this. He wanted to help Erlissa; she seemed to need it even more now than she had in the shazrahad's tent, but while Esgallien was being attacked his duty was to it.

"I can't," he said. "The Raithlin will be needed here."

The lòhren hesitated. "I understand," he said. "Will you at least come with Erlissa and me while we see the king? We must tell him what's happening . . . and you may learn something to change your mind."

"Of course," Lanrik said. "But I'll not change my mind."

The lòhren did not answer but glanced at him with an expression that might have been pity. It was a look that worried Lanrik.

9. The Blood of Kings

Murhain showed them little interest. His retinue of a dozen men sat in the shade of a canvas sheet stretched between tall trees. They were the elite of Esgallien society: rich, perfumed and luxuriously dressed. They drank watered wine from polished goblets; gold and jewels flashed from pale hands; and they pretended with calculated failure not to notice Lanrik's disheveled appearance. Mecklar was present, and Lanrik had a feeling that things would not go well. The king's counselor smiled coldly at him.

He had more time and respect for people like Gilhain. He doubted any of these men had ever worked, and while they sat on camp chairs and sipped wine at leisure, soldiers were ready to risk their lives.

Aranloth had told them something about the king on their way here, and the lòhren's words ran through his mind. *The blood of kings can be a curse. Everywhere Murhain looks he sees the achievements of his father and forefathers for a thousand years. Some people have a spirit that thrives on this, and it spurs them to great heights. For him, it is a crushing weight. It forces the worst from him.*

Lanrik's thoughts were interrupted as Murhain spoke to Aranloth sarcastically.

"Nice of you to join us."

Aranloth did not answer. He leaned on his staff and gazed steadily at the king with those sea-gray eyes that seemed to see all until Murhain looked away.

"O king," the lòhren said. "I sensed no elùgroth with the approaching army. This troubled me, for I had expected one, and I went somewhere to think."

104

"You always come and go as you please," Murhain said. "But the rest of my retinue stays with me. That's the kind of loyalty I need as we face the enemy."

Aranloth smiled, but it took none of the sting from his words. "I am not of your retinue, though. I am merely a wanderer in this land, and is not well-spoken counsel worth a thousand ill-conceived whisperings?"

Murhain turned red and the lòhren went on. Briefly, he explained what Lanrik had done to slow the enemy, how he had rescued Erlissa and what she had discovered of the plan to overthrow Lòrenta. The king appeared bored, which made Lanrik angry, but sudden activity in the elug army diverted everyone's attention.

Boom! The war drums of the elugs rang no longer to a marching rhythm but to something more frantic. The vast mass of the enemy commenced clashing sword against shield and stamping the ground with iron-shod boots. The drums strained, and the hideous voices of the elugs rose in frenzied ululation.

Ashrak ghùl skar! Skee ghùl ashrak!
Skee ghùl ashrak! Ashrak ghùl skar!

The chant flowed without beginning or end. All the while the beating of the drums grew louder and faster. The stamping of boots thundered, and a cloud of dust lurched slowly above the horde and dimmed the faltering sun.

The king's voice, trembling and breathy, broke the silence of his retinue.

"What are they saying?"

Aranloth shifted his steady gaze from the elugs to Murhain.

Death and destruction! Blood and death!
Blood and death! Death and destruction!

105

In the dusk-like noontide, there was a sudden boil and swirl of silvered chain mail. Precious stones glinted dully on the black tunics of a hundred lethrins. They separated from the host and surged into Esgallien Ford. In their wake scrambled a thousand elugs; leaping, jumping, stumbling. The Careth Nien, white with froth and foam, churned about them.

Water rose to the lethrins' thighs; to their waist; to their chests, but their mile-eating stride carried them forward. They neared the northern bank before Esgallien's longbows thrummed, and arrows flashed through the air. The lethrins, disdaining shields, lifted high their iron maces and trusted to hard skin and mail vests. Arrows bounced, broke and shattered. The lethrins came on, but a few toppled, transfixed through eye or neck by black-fletched shafts.

Wave after wave of arrows, fired with speed and skill, struck mercilessly. Further lethrins were cut down, and arrows fell all the more thickly on those remaining. The onrush slowed and then stopped. Iron maces fell from massive hands. The lethrins slid into the water, silvered vests sinking deep, and they were gone.

The elugs neared. They carried shields but many lost their balance, and having to swim to regain it, were forced to discard their protection. The current swept some away.

The remainder screamed and cursed, first at the fast flowing water and then each other. The river took its toll, but more than two thirds approached the northern bank. Countless bows released once more, and sure-flighted arrows sped to their targets.

The elugs milled uncertainly. Arrows struck them. Some hissed, uselessly piercing water, others rattled off shields; many struck unprotected flesh. A mass of bodies floated and bobbed downstream.

The attackers had not reached within a hundred paces of the bank, but they had endured enough and turned to flee. The war drums stopped then commenced a slower beat. Their sullen sound filled the river valley, and the flights of arrows ceased.

"Keep shooting!" yelled the king. "Shoot and kill them all!" He turned to his retinue. "Why don't they shoot?"

The luxuriously dressed men did not know the answer. Lanrik did, but it was the Lindrath who answered.

"The commander could have killed more elugs, but he wanted them to know that retreat was safe. That way it will be encouraged in future attacks."

Lanrik did not think there would be too many more attempts though. The enemy had been decisively repelled. Esgallien was prepared, and he had fulfilled one of his promises to Lathmai.

Aranloth spoke once more. "O king," he said. "The ford is well defended, because of the time Lanrik bought us, and there is little chance of the elug host breaking through."

"No chance at all," Murhain said. "That is certain, but the role Lanrik played is less obvious. *Mecklar* brought word of the approaching army. We only have the Raithlin's word for what he did, and that isn't worth much given it was one of their own who betrayed Esgallien."

Lanrik's anger was steadily increasing, but he clenched his teeth.

"Harsh words, O king," Aranloth said. "Erlissa's story confirms the truth."

The king scowled. "I, who am descended in true line from Conhain, will be the final judge of that."

"You are the king," Aranloth said, "but will you not acknowledge the evidence of Lanrik's actions and how the Raithlin skills helped save the kingdom? Will you confirm their ongoing existence?"

Murhain looked toward Mecklar, and Lanrik waited anxiously. There was an undercurrent of tension here, of old arguments lying beneath the surface. What held his attention most though was that a decision about the Raithlin's future could be made.

The king turned back to the lòhren but did not meet his gaze. "I have considered things," he said. "I've weighed them up, carefully reviewed all contingencies and put in place plans to manage risk. The benefits of my policy will unfold over time, and to expedite the process I will communicate my reasoning personally to those affected. People will understand the decision and realize the benefits implicit in change. Communication is the key."

Lanrik went cold inside. He'd heard this kind of talk before. They were empty words, but hidden within them was the outcome the Raithlin feared.

Aranloth leaned on his staff. "O king, what is your decision."

Murhain gathered himself. He straightened in his chair and spoke as though he was giving a well-rehearsed speech.

"I declare the order of the Raithlin disbanded. The maintenance of their organization isn't cost effective in view of the limited benefits they provide. There is now doubt as to their loyalty, as discovered recently by Mecklar, and Gwalchmur is outlawed. Lanrik will be questioned closely by Mecklar to determine if his claims are based on truth or are fabrications intended to prop up the Raithlin."

There was silence. The Lindrath seemed shocked. Only the lòhren was undisturbed; he looked as though he was waiting for something more.

Lanrik took a step forward. "Lathmai died to save Esgallien, and I've risked much. Shall I show you proof?"

He held out the scabbard that carried the shazrahad's sword. The gold thread and scrollwork depicting hunting scenes caught sunlight and gleamed. The magnificent ruby at the hilt was redder than blood, and when he drew the pattern-welded blade from the sheath the metal rang and shimmered. The gold inlay glistened, and the script he could not read flashed in the light. The blade intrigued even Aranloth.

"This," Lanrik said, turning the blade in the air before him, "is the shazrahad's own sword. Do you think I found it lying discarded on the grass of Galenthern? No. I entered the enemy camp, then the shazrahad's tent."

The king leaned forward. His eyes were wide and filled with greed, then he sat back in his chair and veiled his yearning.

"The fate of the Raithlin is determined," he said. "Your own situation is . . . more fluid. You're dismissed for the moment, but leave the sword behind. I'll scrutinize it carefully."

Lanrik was amazed at the calmness that settled over him. He was no longer angry or nervous, though he had reason to be both. The king's desire was clear, and he knew that if he left the sword behind he would never see it again.

"No," he said, and sheathed the blade.

Mecklar reared up, his face red with fury, and his thick fingers wrapped around the hilt of his sword. "Do you disobey your king?"

Lanrik remembered their contest at the Spring Games, and once more had a feeling that he and Mecklar would finish that fight, but not today. He shook his head.

"If you wish to question me or look at the sword please do so. But the sword is mine and stays in my possession."

"Fool!" Murhain said, losing his composure. "Soldiers in Esgallien's army don't keep the spoils of war! They belong to me!"

Mecklar placed a moderating hand on Murhain's arm. "What the king says is true, though soldiers receive a tenth part of the value. You can be assured, Lanrik, you will get what's coming to you."

There were different ways to interpret that statement. Lanrik smiled tightly.

"Your thoughtfulness is touching," he said. "But you're forgetting that I'm not a soldier. The Raithlin aren't part of the army, and by custom established by Conhain, we keep our own spoils of war. It was a reward for the risks we run."

Lanrik felt a sense of satisfaction. The Lindrath nodded in confirmation, and the king turned red. Evidently, he did not know much about the Raithlin, but he was not so easily put off. In his embarrassment, and despite Mecklar's tightening grip on his arm, he lost all discretion. "I don't care about traditions! I want that sword!"

No one spoke after his outburst. His retinue looked uncomfortable, and the Lindrath and Erlissa stared at him.

Lanrik, thinking of his uncle, swallowed and spoke. "Will you come with guards to kill me in the dark, as you did to Conrik?"

"If I must!" screamed the king.

There were sharp intakes of breath among the retinue.

Mecklar tightened his grip on the king's arm, but Murhain would have none of it. "I'm the king of Esgallien – the highest authority in the land. I do as I choose!"

Aranloth stood straight and tall, and Lanrik realized he had been waiting for this moment. He had guessed the king would want the sword and that Lanrik would deny him. He had somehow *known* this confrontation would come.

"O king," Aranloth said. "Long have I counseled you for the benefit of Esgallien, but to little effect. In place of advice, I now offer foretelling. Listen well!"

The lòhren's voice slowed and deepened. It became distant, but relentless like the muttering of a far off sea. His eyes, though open, looked on some vision beyond their grasp. The gray depths darkened. His knuckles whitened on the oaken staff.

"Esgallien is safe," he said. "The enemy will not break through. Yet they will return. In triumph, they will take the ford in the future; and terror will march before them; the walls of Esgallien will then seem thin and weak to its people. Too late will you heed good counsel. Too late will you rue all your choices that went awry. King will you be; descendant of the blood of kings, but in that hour none will obey you. Fate will sweep you aside."

Aranloth ceased speaking. Life returned to his eyes, and they shone bright and clear. Murhain was deathly pale and looked as though he would run.

Mecklar rose slowly from his chair. "None of you will be allowed to leave here."

Aranloth looked at him, and of all things, laughed. "I have foretold the future," he said, "and though that is often painful, it is not a crime."

Then mirth dropped from him like a discarded cloak.

"And who has authority to stop me leaving?" he asked. "As the king noticed, I come and go as I please. I have done so for longer years, and in more places, than you can count."

He did not look like an old man any longer; strength and confidence was in his posture, power beyond their understanding burned in his eyes. He made no move, nor the slightest threat, yet they sensed the might of him, the hidden and deadly strength of lòhrengai.

He gave the king a final look, ignored Mecklar and the rest of the retinue, and strode from Murhain's presence. No one tried to stop him.

"Come," he said, as he passed the others. "Our time here is done and we are needed elsewhere."

Lanrik, his mind in turmoil, followed. The Raithlin, against all his expectations, had been disbanded. What would he do now? What *could* he do? Being a Raithlin was

111

his life; it was all he had ever trained for and all he ever wanted. He felt betrayed and empty of purpose.

They walked in silence. Aranloth was in the front, leading a roan mare that he had retrieved from near the king's pavilion. He was followed by the Lindrath, his expression grim and his eyes a little wild. Erlissa was beside Lanrik, and she glanced at him from time to time. There was sympathy and comfort in those looks, and the occasional brush of her arm against his.

They headed to the cottage where their own horses were tethered, and he knew Aranloth would not waste time in leaving. As if reading his thoughts Erlissa placed a hand on his shoulder.

"Come with us, Lanrik. I need you."

Her green eyes were sincere and concerned. She was reaching out to him, trying to give him a purpose. How had she come to understand him so well in such a short period?

Aranloth, not slowing, looked over his shoulder. "She needs you more than she knows. There will be dangers on the road, and the lòhrengai I must work at times will require all my concentration."

It did not escape Lanrik's attention that the lòhren had said dangers *on the road,* and not just at the end of their journey. At any rate, he was wanted with these people. He admired them, liked them, and could possibly be in a position to help them.

"I'll come along," he said.

He felt relief from Erlissa. She smiled, and they continued toward the cottage. Arriving there, he swiftly collected his belongings and saddled the stallion.

When they were ready, he shook the Lindrath's hand. "Thank you," he said. "You and the Raithlin taught me much over the years. I'm sorry things have ended this way."

The Lindrath mustered a smile. "All things come to an end," he said. "The Raithlin are no more, but our lore will be with us for life. Use it, expand it, teach it if opportunity arises. Who knows where the seed will grow again?"

Aranloth, who had been leaning on his staff and waiting, tensed.

Lanrik unslung the talnak horn from his shoulder and held it out to the Lindrath.

"A final gift," he said.

The Lindrath was shocked. "It's too much," he said. "The horn must be worth a fortune."

Lanrik shrugged. "I've got the sword. This will only be a burden on the journey. Take it for Lathmai, and the others who'll never return from Galenthern. Use it as a symbol of all that the Raithlin have achieved over the years."

The Lindrath reached out. As his hands touched the horn Aranloth spoke, and his eyes were once more deep pools of shadow.

"It will be more than a symbol," he said. "Blow it when Esgallien's need is greatest, and help unlooked for will come."

The lòhren said nothing else, and with more handshakes and well wishes the Lindrath parted. He walked slowly, with head bowed, and Lanrik knew that if he himself had lost all he had ever known or loved, it was worse for the Lindrath.

"He's a good man," Aranloth said quietly.

"The best," agreed Lanrik. "He took the place of my uncle when Conrik fled the city. That's if he survived. I wonder now if Murhain didn't actually find him and have him killed."

The lòhren's eyes were veiled. "It would have been like him. But I think in time you will find your uncle escaped Esgallien and is alive and well."

"I hope so," Lanrik said.

113

Aranloth did not respond, but Erlissa was watching them both. A grin flashed on her face.

"Of course he escaped," she said. "Aranloth knows what he's talking about. Only lòhrengai could have gotten him away."

Aranloth looked at her solemnly. "None in Esgallien need to know that," he said.

Lanrik turned to her. "How did you guess?"

Erlissa shrugged and Aranloth answered. "She did not guess. Her intuition told her it was so. She is not, nor has the desire to become a lòhren – but the talent remains."

The smile faded from Erlissa's face, and she gave no answer.

"Come," Aranloth said. "We have places to go and things to do." He hesitated and looked at Lanrik once more. "We'll meet Conrik on our travels. But you must be prepared – he's no longer as he once was."

The lòhren turned quickly and mounted his horse. Clearly, any questions on the subject were unwelcome. The main thing though was that Conrik was alive, and they would meet again. Lanrik could not imagine him any different from what he used to be, but Aranloth indicated it was so. What changes would time and the treachery of the king have wrought?

As they moved on, it occurred to Lanrik that if Aranloth had helped his uncle escape Esgallien, he was probably living in Lòrenta. If so, he was in danger, and it was yet another reason to join the lòhren and Erlissa on their quest.

10. The Witch in the Wood

Mecklar hastened along the still road. His chestnut gelding was tired, but he pushed it on through the night. It was a poor time to ride, but he had pressing news to deliver; information that should lead to a reward, but that could end in punishment too. He served a harsh mistress.

The elug army would not break through. Even so, it had been difficult to convince Murhain to let him return to Esgallien. But the king was a fool, easily manipulated on most occasions, and oblivious to the forces shaping his own court.

Lanrik was a better opponent. He had a remarkable store of patience, something that he had proven during the testing on Galenthern. The lòhren was dangerous also. The man's eyes seemed to see straight through everybody. It was not a pleasant feeling when you had things to hide.

He nearly missed the turning he was looking for, seeing it late and reefing hard at the gelding's reins. He moved off the main road and down a lane surrounded by open fields. These eventually turned into constricting woods. He went deeper, and then slowed as the lane dwindled and finally disappeared.

Trees grew thickly about him. The wood was dark and secretive, a tangled confusion of ravines and ridges on the hills southwest of Esgallien. It was a treacherous area, chocked with scrub and clinging vines. Even hunters shunned it, and the few who tried found little game, some becoming lost and never returning. He had thoughts on that.

Ebona was a strange woman. She was mistress of the wood, more secretive and dangerous than it. Who she was, and her true purposes were matters to which he had given thought but found no answers. That she hated Aranloth was obvious, though why, he had not discovered.

She was in league with Esgallien's enemies, but he did not think she was one of them. She commanded powers that stilled his heart, powers the lòhren did not display, and though she was not an elùgroth, he feared her. However, he had prospered since entering her service.

He had accumulated gold beyond the dreams of his youth, yet lately his dreams had grown. He exerted authority and influence also. If Esgallien fell, he would lose those, but the gold would buy a lifetime's luxury in another city. The north would not fall to the enemy in his time, at least not all of it. He owed nothing to Esgallien. All it had given him, the fifth son of a farmer, was poverty and hunger: until he met Ebona. Now, people looked up to him, fawned upon him, and he held power over them. It was intoxicating.

He regretted not killing Lanrik when he had the chance. It was ill fortune that they had ventured onto the plains when the elug army marched. He knew it was coming, Ebona had told him so, but not when.

When they found Lathmai on the tor and she spoke of the attack, he knew he must do something to prevent word reaching Esgallien. When he returned with the elendhrot root, he saw his chance. The Raithlin turned around at the last moment though. He had thought he would get other opportunities, but Lanrik's intention of staying behind to slow the army confounded him.

Could Ebona hold that failure against him? Because of it, long developed plans were ruined. Yet always there were plans within plans. It was an unexpected discovery that the attack was part of a greater scheme to destroy Lòrenta. He wondered if Ebona knew. If not, the news he brought would please and surprise her. A rare event!

His return from the plains had posed a dilemma. To travel too fast was to give Esgallien time for it to act: to travel too slowly was to draw suspicion on himself when Lanrik arrived. He had delayed as much as he dared and also given Gwalchmur word and opportunity to escape.

Gwalchmur had done so. He had betrayed Esgallien once, and Ebona would persuade him to act similarly in the future, but there was some doubt that he was fully committed to her. Did he realize that such hesitation risked his life?

Mecklar traveled the rest of the night through the woods. They closed about him, silent and watchful. He knew creatures stalked it that were not found elsewhere. He had seen glimpses of them, or perhaps Ebona had allowed him to see them. Fear, he understood, was better motivation than threat.

Dawn broke and shone through small gaps in the leaf-canopy. He went slowly, picking his way carefully and heading down into a deep ravine. There were several ways to the bottom, but they were all watched. Whether he saw the guards or not, Ebona would receive report of his coming.

He dismounted and led the gelding by hand. It was rough going, and the horse, catching a scent that made it skittish, fought his lead. It took some time, but when he finally reached the bottom the trees thinned. Here, there were several acres of green grass completely cleared of timber. A white dairy cow grazed contentedly, a small herd of sheep bleated peacefully, and a young foal galloped awkwardly near a mare. They too were white.

Mecklar mounted again and rode slowly toward a cottage and barn near the center of the field. The cottage, small and neat, was fenced with wicker, which also enclosed several rows of fruit trees. These were well pruned and heavy with growing fruit. Several white ducks had the run of the orchard and waddled after insects beneath the trees. A vegetable garden, enclosed by its own fence, was near the orchard. It was weed free and productive.

Mecklar reached the barn. He dismounted and tethered his horse to a hook on the wall. As he did so the door opened, and Gwalchmur emerged, his red hair disheveled and his freckled face haggard. They did not shake hands.

"Has Lanrik returned?" he asked.

"He has," Mecklar said, "The king outlawed you."

Gwalchmur cursed but Mecklar merely shrugged. "Ebona will find a use for you, even if it's not in Esgallien."

Gwalchmur did not answer, and the two of them walked to the cottage. There was a gate in the fence, and they went through it, careful to close it behind them.

Ebona waited in the doorway. She was a tall woman with wide set eyes and high cheekbones. She was not young, but neither was she old. Mecklar could not put an age to her, and it disturbed him. He thought she had passed middle age, yet her hair was a luxurious blond, not white, and she wore it long. She was dressed simply in white linen, cinched with a red belt, but the dress draped her full-figured form with grace. She smiled, her teeth beautifully white and even.

"Welcome," she said, and there was warmth in her voice and gesture to enter. They did, but Mecklar was not fooled. His heart beat loudly and his palms were clammy. Ebona, for all her sweetness, would kill him the moment it served her purpose.

It was well lit inside. A log burned in the hearth and sunshine streamed in the windows. Through one of them Mecklar had a good view of the foal which now approached the cottage. It was not pure white, for its long ears were tipped with crimson.

On the back wall were racks covered with root vegetables and dry cheeses. Cured sausages and hams hung from the ceiling. On the table, a neat construction

118

of well-scrubbed timber, lay a dead duck. It had just been killed, and Ebona was removing the feathers. She finished the task, her deft fingers working quickly.

She looked up from her work. "The trick is to dip the bird in near boiling water, and then wrap it in a bag to steam. The feathers come off easily that way."

Mecklar and Gwalchmur nodded but did not reply. Ebona stood, washed her hands carefully and dried them on a clean towel. She brought over a bronze pitcher of water and filled cups for them before sitting down. She waited until the others drank before delicately sipping the water herself.

Mecklar knew she would have heard from Gwalchmur what had happened on the plains. He began by telling her of the failure of the elug army to breach the ford, Aranloth's audience with the king and of Erlissa's information about the danger to Lòrenta.

Ebona listened calmly until he finished. "This would have been prevented had you killed the Raithlin on the tor," she said.

"I know," replied Mecklar, "but there was no opportunity."

She smiled sweetly at him. "You'll ensure that you make an opportunity next time, won't you?"

Her perfect teeth gleamed behind parted lips, but there was a cold look in her eyes.

He swallowed hard. "I'll not fail again."

Ebona reached out and patted his hand. Her fingers were long and delicate, but her thumb was wide and fat like a big toe.

"Of course not. I have complete faith in you."

She sat back thoughtfully, giving no indication of whether she had known of the plan to destroy Lòrenta. The smell of smoke in the cottage was strong, but fresh air came in from the open windows.

"What of the Raithlin? Is he going on this quest with his new friends?"

"He didn't say," replied Mecklar.

"But you know him. What do you think he'll do now that the Raithlin are disbanded?"

"I don't know," Mecklar said. "I don't see why he should go with them. What are the lòhren and the girl to him? He'll likely sulk in the city for some time, too proud to join the ranks of the ordinary army but no good for anything else."

"I wonder. Was the girl good looking?"

Mecklar shrugged. "I suppose so."

Gwalchmur laughed. "You're blind. She's stunning. Too thin for my liking but there's fight in her. She has a sharp mind too."

Ebona ran a hand absently through her long hair. "What do you think, Gwalchmur? Will he go with them?"

"I think he might. There's nothing left for him in Esgallien."

"I think so too," she said, "but there's more to it than that. All three of them are linked now. I feel it."

"What difference does it make?" asked Mecklar.

Ebona looked at him, her glance still cold. "It matters very much. You underestimate him, but I don't. Though you've played down his achievements, it's clear that he's a dangerous enemy. Alone and unaided he defied an army. He penetrated their camp, rescued a prisoner, and stole a shazrahad sword for good measure. Most of all, he slowed them down and ruined plans that had long been in place. No, it just won't do to underestimate him again."

Mecklar nodded. "Well, his luck has run out now. Before I left, the king asked me to arrange things with some of his guard. They have orders to find and kill him, wherever he is, and obtain the sword."

Ebona smiled. "Murhain has a spine after all. I hope the guards won't be obvious about it?"

"They've been cautioned not to, even though it really *is* obvious this time, but what's anybody going to do about it?"

Ebona pursed her lips but said nothing, and Mecklar studied her ageless face. What had she looked like in the first flush of youth? But of her youth, or her past, he knew nothing. That she held a grudge against Esgallien and Aranloth was obvious, but he did not know why. Whatever else, she had been born of the aristocracy. It was evident in her every move and word. The only sign of ill breeding that he saw was her habit of chewing, however delicately, at her fingernails. She was doing it now.

The log burned in the hearth, and neither he nor Gwalchmur spoke while she thought. At last, she broke the silence.

"It's clear Aranloth believes he can stop the destruction of Lòrenta, and this must be prevented. That means he and the others must be killed."

She rose abruptly. "Come," she said, and led them out of the cottage into the bright sunlight. The grass was green and springy beneath their boots. It was a beautiful morning. The sheep and cow grazed peacefully in a far corner of the field while the mare lay in the sun, the foal standing beside it.

She stood in the open field. "Put your horse inside the barn, and then stay back from me," she said.

Mecklar did as instructed, and when he returned to stand beside Gwalchmur she looked at them both. "Whatever you do, do not run."

She lifted high her arms and her chin tilted forward. Her eyes closed and she began to sing. It was soft at first, then her voice grew loud and strong. She drew breath from her stomach, but her chest began to heave with effort. Mecklar did not know the language but sensed it was the forerunner of what they spoke now, the speech of their ancestors that had not been heard since even before Conhain founded Esgallien a thousand years ago.

As Ebona sang the cow continued to graze, and the sheep bleated peacefully. The mare rolled in the grass. The sun shone bright; bees droned as they moved from flower to flower in the garden, and multitudes of black and white butterflies drifted by lazily on a southerly breeze. But even on such a beautiful morning, Mecklar went cold as he heard far off in the woods an answer to the song. It was the howling of beasts.

He glanced at Gwalchmur and saw the Raithlin's face was white. Suddenly, Ebona ceased singing. Her eyes, filled with power and joy, sprang open. The howling stopped.

"They come," she said.

Mecklar waited. He fidgeted on the spot, but Gwalchmur remained motionless beside him, watching Ebona silently.

The minutes passed, like a trickle of water from a crack in a rock wall, slow but unstopping. There was noise in the woods. Something was crashing through them, loud and uncaring of the clamor.

The crashing stopped and there was silence. Ebona tilted her head, and then stamped her foot in the gesture of a little girl.

"Come!" she commanded. "Don't be shy my darlings."

She cupped her hands to her mouth, and her voice throbbed in the glade.

"Come Balert, my little playful one. Come Bilar, who always is aloof. Come Bakert and Bikar, come my little sweetlings!"

Four hounds emerged from the eastern edge of the wood and raced toward her. Mecklar, mindful of her words, stood rooted to the spot and as still as possible. The beasts snarled and growled incessantly as they sped across the grass. They looked like they were fighting each other as they ran, great jaws slavering as they snapped at heels or necks, but he realized they were just playing.

The hounds darted over the field and crushed the grass beneath their paws. They ran to Ebona, circling her and yelping, long red tongues hanging from their mouths. They were massive animals whose shoulders were level with a man's waist. Huge muscles bulged beneath tight skin and a short coat of black hair. The only other color on them was the very tips of their ears. This was crimson to match their tongues. They had little in the way of necks, just massive round heads set on square shoulders. There was something wrong with their eyes though. They were black pits, and there was intelligence behind them, but not the thoughts of dogs.

One by one, her hands ran over their coat, and they stilled and trembled at her touch. She whispered in their pricked ears, and when she was done she smiled at them benevolently.

"Go, my little darlings. Run free beyond the woods. Hunt for me!"

The beasts leaped away. They circled Mecklar and Gwalchmur, a dazzling flash of snapping, snarling and sniffing that tore the grass in a ring, then they raced off and disappeared into the woods. In moments, the noise of their passing ceased. Once more, there was only the pleasant bleating of the sheep, unaffected, but the horses whinnied fearfully in the barn.

Ebona turned to them. Her smile was bright as the sun, and pleasure flushed her cheeks. "I have set my darlings onto the lòhren. They will hunt him down. Ah! I have long wanted to do that! They will set their jaws to limbs and rend flesh. Their teeth will grind bone. Bones will splinter and snap!"

Gwalchmur stepped back but Mecklar asked a question. "They don't have the scent," he said. "How will they find them?"

"Shush," she said, and traced a finger along his lips. "They're creatures of ùhrengai, the old magic; the magic of the beginning. They know the scent of a lòhren. They can smell lòhrengai and elùgai both. Aranloth has probably reached the city now, but my pets will roam the borders of Esgallien at night. They'll find his trail when he leaves and track him, and all who go with him."

"Very well," Mecklar said. "What next?"

"What next indeed," Ebona said, looking at him thoughtfully. "My darlings are strong, yet the lòhren is not to be underestimated. Neither are the other two. What's most vital now, above all else, is their destruction. Therefore, the two of you will follow them. If the hounds fail, you must succeed. My pets will guide you. They have your scent and can find you anywhere. They'll not attack until you're close on the lòhren's trail."

Mecklar was astonished. "I can't leave the king. If I do that I'll be revealed."

"So?" Ebona said.

Mecklar hesitated. He did not think it wise to argue with her, but he wanted to get his point across. "How will the king be influenced if I'm not there?"

Ebona looked at him and slowly shook her head as though she was disappointed.

"Do you think you're the only one I have in his retinue? Perhaps what you're concerned with is yourself though? But haven't you got a great store of gold? Don't you keep it safely in other cities, prepared for the fall of Esgallien and your escape? When this task is completed, we'll start again elsewhere. You'll accumulate more gold and fulfil your desires. Even the ones you haven't yet dreamed."

Mecklar acquiesced. A vast future opened before him. It would not take long, and he would rise once more in service of some foolish king.

Ebona studied them both for a few moments. "Now," she said, "one final thing must be done. I would watch the

124

end of the lòhren. For that, I need not leave here. You will be my eyes, the both of you. In exchange, I'll give you power as you have never tasted before. In order for your efforts to be combined, the hounds will wait for you to attack with them, but don't tarry. They'll only wait so long."

Ebona stepped close. She reached out and placed a palm over each of Mecklar's temples. Her forehead rested against his own, and he felt her eyebrows, coarse like wire bristles, pressed against him. Her long blond hair brushed against his face. It smelled faintly of smoke, and the warmth of her breath was upon him. He felt something stir inside, a connection between them, a rising and joining of his spirit with hers.

He sensed suddenly the power she held, vast as the ocean, and he trembled in awe. A black wave of dizziness engulfed him, and he would have fallen but for her iron grip that nearly crushed his skull. The darkness eased, and he reeled back as she let him go. He watched in a stupor as she turned to Gwalchmur.

When it was done she spoke once more. "We are joined now. I will be with you all the days of your life. Remember it! Serve me well and you shall prosper. Now, retrieve your horses and go to the outskirts of Esgallien. The hounds will find you."

She turned and walked from them, disappearing inside the cottage.

Gwalchmur moaned. "*All the days of my life,*" he said.

Mecklar understood. She had changed them. Their old lives were gone. They would forge new ones, but Ebona would always be in them. He shrugged and walked to the barn. Better to be her servant than her enemy. *He* did not want the beasts hunting him. They were hounds of the otherworld.

11. Esgallien

Lanrik watched the countryside as they rode toward Esgallien. The land was neatly cultivated, contrasting with wild Galenthern, just as the many-towered city was a world of its own.

The fields were changing. Fences of sawn timber replaced hedgerows, and stately villas were the rule now rather than thatched cottages. Carefully planted groves of nut trees, shimmering in new leaf, grew their precious crop, and vines that produced the heady wines of Esgallien basked in the sun of south-facing slopes.

The villas, built of pale stone and roofed with bright red tiles, had wide-arched windows and intricate turrets. Various flags and banners flew from the highest points.

The travelers had ridden until late evening, and then rested through the night. Now they started once more, and the city, ten miles distant from the ford, was only a few miles away.

They were silent, and Lanrik thought of his future. What would he do with his life? It was hard to know sometimes where he began and the Raithlin ended, yet it seemed now that all his training had been for nothing. He would be on his own when this quest was over, and what, apart from the enmity of Mecklar and the king, would be left for him in Esgallien? But where else could he go?

They crested a small rise and looked down on the city. The sun climbed higher in a cloudless sky, and multitudes of butterflies floated past on a southerly breeze.

Aranloth halted and the others did likewise. They were only a little higher than Esgallien, but they saw the network of its streets, its many tall towers and bright domes. Standing out most was the Hainer Lon, the Heroes Way, the main road that swept through the city like a broad river. Along its course armies had marched to war through all Esgallien's history, sometimes to the ford but often into Galenthern, and they had returned the same way in victory.

The Hainer Lon was wide and stone paved. It passed all the important places in the city, allowing people quick access to employment, shops and entertainment. It ended at Esgallien's northern wall, though an unpaved road continued for just over a hundred miles to the gorge of Caladhrist where the city derived much of its wealth. The gorge held deposits of gold, difficult and dangerous to mine from the rocky earth, but abundant. There had also once been gold in the creek bordering the southeast side of the city, the reason for Esgallien's placement, but it was long since depleted.

Aranloth, his staff resting at an angle across the roan's withers, looked at Lanrik.

"Would you like me to translate that script on the sword?"

"Very much," Lanrik said. He drew the blade from its scabbard and handed it, hilt first, to the lòhren.

Aranloth scrutinized the weapon. He started with the ruby on the pommel, which throbbed with color in the sunlight, then passed to the pattern-welded blade. The metal had been forged and reforged from bundles of iron rods, twisted and beaten to give a pliant core on which a hard edge was added. The script glittered as the lòhren turned the sword in the light.

Aranloth studied the lettering. He muttered in a foreign tongue, and a frown grew then deepened on his face. At last, he looked up.

"There are *three* inscriptions," he said. "The language is different in each case, and though I'm familiar with several Azan dialects, I can only read the first."

"What does it say?" asked Lanrik.

The lòhren read it out. *I, Assurah, paramount sword-smith in Azanbulzibar, made this for Hakalakadan. His glory will endure forever!*

Lanrik had heard of Azanbulzibar; it was the capital city of the Azan. Of the other names he knew nothing and said so to the lòhren.

Aranloth shrugged. "I haven't heard of them either. If we were in the Halls of Lore in Lòrenta I would likely find a record of them and discover in what dialects the remaining inscriptions were written."

The lòhren absently scratched his chin. "Actually, there may even be a record in Esgallien. Conhain's grandson, Danhain, was involved in a battle with the Azan. I saw the scroll many years ago in the archives, but I don't remember exactly what it said. I'm sure it mentioned something about an unusual shazrahad and sword though, and it may reveal something to us."

"Do we have the time for that?" asked Lanrik.

Aranloth considered things for a moment. "We'll make time. It disturbs me that I can't read the other inscriptions – they may be important. Anyway, the archives are on our way, and it won't take long to find the scroll."

They rode once more and some time later came to the city wall. It was an ancient though solid structure built of plastered brick and some thirty feet high and ten deep. Lanrik had heard that newer walls further north in Camarelon and Cardoroth were even taller and deeper.

The gate was a different matter. Replaced several times during the history of the city, it was strong and durable. It retained its original name: River Gate, for it led to the ford. Gold Gate, so called because it opened the way to Caladhrist, was on the northern wall.

He looked at the tall towers on each side of the entrance where fifty-foot images of Conhain were carved in high relief. He was clad in war raiment, helm and chain

128

mail finely depicted. In his hand he held a naked sword, ready to strike, the tips of the blades touching above the center of the gate. It was a warning to any army that crossed Esgallien Ford that breaching the walls would not be easy.

Two of the City Guards, over six feet but miniature compared to the carvings, stood watch as the travelers rode through the dim gate tunnel, the clatter of hooves loud in the confined space. On their left the open gate rested against the wall, the iron dull in the shadows, but the bars as thick as a man's arm.

The Hainer Lon, its laid stone thirty paces wide, commenced here. They followed it, avoiding the ruts grooved by the wheels of innumerable wagons through the centuries. On either side were tenement buildings several stories high. They were built of pale stone, and at their fronts were porticoes containing shops that sold the necessities of daily life in Esgallien.

The people of Esgallien bustled on either side and did not seem perturbed by the threat of war. They crowded the footpaths, talking, joking and bantering with friends and strangers alike. They bargained with traders while vendors called out the merits of their produce or wares. They had complete confidence in their army and the defensibility of the ford and thought life would continue as normal, but Lanrik knew how easily it could have been otherwise.

It always jolted him to come here after the stillness of Galenthern. There was a thrum of humanity, and the people were good-natured and happy. The streets, day or night, were full of men dressed in bright cloaks, women in colorful dresses and everywhere were laughing children.

Aranloth's foretelling worried him though, and he broached it with the lòhren.

"You told the king that one day the enemy would overrun the ford and attack the city. Did you really mean that?"

Aranloth guided the roan around a group of children whose playing had spilled onto the road.

"I have little control of when visions come upon me, or what I see, but I can describe them accurately. I saw elugs surging through the ford and marching on Esgallien. There were images of the king too, while the city was besieged, and bitterly will he regret some of his decisions."

"Do you think the city will ever fall?" asked Lanrik.

The lòhren did not answer straight away, and Lanrik looked at his surroundings. If the city were taken what would happen to all these people? Would they be put to the sword, or enslaved? What would be worse?

"It's at risk," Aranloth said. "It has been since the beginning, but the risk is greater with a weak king. The city could fall, but I voiced my foretelling to help prevent that. There are other powers in Esgallien beside Murhain, and forewarned they may avert disaster, or lessen its magnitude."

Erlissa had been quiet for much of their travels but spoke now.

"Nothing lasts forever, Lanrik. Whether it's tomorrow, in twenty years or another thousand, one day all Esgallien's people will be dust and the buildings broken and fallen. Even the Hainer Lon will return to grass."

Lanrik did not reply. He realized that her perspective on life was wider than his. The tragedy she had endured in her youth had shaped her in ways that he could not guess. The need to go on this quest was affecting her too. It had depressed her, but he knew she was extraordinary. She was someone who could plumb the deeps of despair and yet still reach the heights of joy. He noticed Aranloth was looking at her speculatively too.

To the right of the Hainer Lon the ground began to drop away, and they passed at various times the great structures central to Esgallien society. There was the Hamalath, where actors performed plays and brought to life the events of history and popular dramas. Massive columns of intricately carved granite flanked its entrance. Beyond were hundreds of rows of stone benches terraced into the slope overlooking the stage. Five thousand people could sit in the Hamalath and see and hear every move and word of the performers.

Further along was the Merenloth where people gathered to hear the debates of philosophers, declamations of poets and the chanting of bards. The structure was similar to the Hamalath but smaller. Behind it was a many-storied building whose stone threw back the voice of a speaker onto the crowd. Even as they passed the entrance, they caught the words of an ancient lay telling of the exodus of the Halathrin and their arrival on the pine-clad shores of northern Alithoras.

Eventually they came to the inner district. The footpaths were tiled with mosaics of bright color and intricate artisanship. The buildings, larger and faced with decorated marble, flew flags indicating the residences of nobles, the prosperous or the famous.

An extended series of granite arches opened on their right into the Haranast, the largest and most popular facility in the city. A basalt stele dedicated it to Conmur, Murhain's grandfather, who had initiated its construction at great cost and with enormous labor. It could hold ten thousand people who, from the terraced hillside, observed a level field where horses raced. The track was one hundred and fifty paces long and over fifty wide. The riders rode its length, taking a dangerous turn around carved posts at each end.

Near the center of the city the slope on their right became less steep. The oldest facility was built here, the

Karlenthern, where most activities of the Spring Games were held.

The Karlenthern was small, seating fewer people than the other facilities. The benches were no longer level and showed damage from large crowds and long weathering. It had been built in the first years of the city, and the Spring Games held there ever since, though the games had originated earlier. They came from antiquity, before Esgallien was built, before Conhain rode with his people out of the west, before even the Halathrin came to Alithoras. Lanrik felt the history of this place, both the city's and his own. It was here that he had watched Lathmai win the archery contest, and he remembered that one of his promises to her remained unfulfilled. *Gwalchmur is still alive.* He rode past the entrance and noticed Erlissa's uncanny gaze on him.

The Hainer Lon opened onto Conhain Court, the heart of the city, and Aranloth halted. It was a large square, colonnaded on all sides, and it contained bronze statues of all Esgallien's kings and queens. Some were mounted for hunting, some dressed for war, some wore their crowns and royal regalia, some were stern, some cheerful, but all were part of the long history of the city. None more so than Conhain, shown astride his warhorse, suffering and determination fixed in every line of his face as he held high the famous Red Cloth of Victory.

The Esgalliens had learned their architecture, art and way of life from long association with the Halathrin before Conhain brought his people some five hundred miles to the east. But their ennoblement had come at a cost of lives and blood, fighting the Halathrin's enemies. A thousand years had turned those times into legend and myth, a remembrance of blended joy and despair.

At the center of the square was a large and circular dais thirty paces in diameter and raised three feet high. It was a place of ceremony, of public announcements, royal weddings and funerals. It was here, in the oldest and most treasured event of the Spring Games, that he had fought Mecklar in the sword tournament. It was one structure in the city owing little to the Halathrin. It was a relic of a time that was ancient even before they came here and of a distant land where the people gathered at rings of standing stones and man-made hills.

Aranloth led them to a shop selling nuts, dried fruit and cured meats. "We'd better buy supplies," he said.

The lòhren haggled good-naturedly with the owner, an ever-smiling old man in a red cloak, who helped them fill their saddlebags after the purchase. A little further on, they bought hardened leather water-flasks from a young girl in a small stall.

When they left Aranloth pointed with his staff. "That's the building we want. It houses the City Archive."

"Are you *sure* we have time for this?" asked Lanrik.

"It won't take long. I know the place well, and I'll find what we need quickly. There's something unusual about your sword, even for a shazrahad blade, and it troubles me."

They made their way along the edge of the square and tethered their horses to iron hooks set into the building's portico. Aranloth led them up a wide flight of marble stairs, and they passed two City Guards stationed at massive oak doors. The interior had the spacious but dark atmosphere of most of Esgallien's buildings. The roof, a vast dome high above, was decorated with a mosaic of a retreating elug army harried by a combined force of men and immortal Halathrin. The artisan had captured the disorder and panic of the elugs, the straining of men and the grace, vigor and aloofness of the Halathrin.

Frescoes adorned the encircling walls in which private alcoves were built and furnished with tables and chairs. Some, but not many, were occupied. The large space beneath the dome contained aisles of shelves stacked thickly with books.

"This way," Aranloth said. His boots echoed loudly between the stone floor and high ceiling while he led them to the back of the room and to the last shelf, which held scrolls rather than books. They were ordered according to the reign of Esgallien's kings, and he read the dates and titles carefully as he progressed.

He stopped suddenly. "This is the one I remember." He chose a scroll rolled in a ribbon of crimson cloth that had once been bright but was now faded.

The lòhren led them to a table in the nearest alcove. Light entered from a small window covered by translucent alabaster, but he lit a lamp as well. He gently undid the ribbon and slowly unrolled the scroll on the table. The script was small and tightly written, the once red ink brown with age, the parchment brittle and the language archaic.

Aranloth looked it over. "It's headed *Battle of the Tor*," he said. "This is a copy of the original, which was written in the seventh year of King Danhain's reign, the fifty-seventh since the founding of the city. The first part summarizes events of that year."

He skimmed through it, telling them the important parts. "Elugs had gathered in large numbers and tested the ford. They were repeatedly repelled. The Raithlin were withdrawn from Galenthern and additional regiments of the army sent to stiffen the defense. The testing continued through spring and into summer."

Aranloth skipped over much description and began again. "Danhain determined to end the harassment and enforce his authority on the region. He intended to show that the newly founded city was secure by inflicting a heavy defeat on the enemy. He led twelve thousand onto the plains against an estimated army of ten thousand."

Aranloth read silently for a while, and then spoke again. "Danhain wanted to force a battle, but the elugs retreated. Eventually he drew them into combat south of a landmark the Raithlin called the Tor. To the west lay a swamp and on the east flank a forested area."

Lanrik guessed this was very close, perhaps even the same spot, where he penetrated the elug army in his own time.

Aranloth went on. "Danhain considered subsequent events noteworthy enough to personally record his actions. What follows is a transcript in his own words."

I, Danhain, grandsonne of Conhain, sonne of Condred, Kyng of Esgallyen, write these words in the seven and fiftieth year after the Founding.

This summer marauding elugs harried the realme; bolde herdsmen and hunters who had made Galenthern home returned, and the people were afeared of a breaching of the ford.

I levied an army to punish the foe and teach them awe of Esgallyen. Many dayes we marched across Galenthern, receiving word from the Raithlin, that olde and illustrious order, about the movements of the enemie that ever retreated. On the sixth afternoon tidings came that they were nearer than their wont, and by marching during the night we reached them at dawn.

The enemie showed chagrin but did not decamp. Neither host had an advantage of terrain. Esgallyen had superiority of numbers, yet were weary. Thusly balanced, we faced each other.

I attacked. Elugs, with much beating of drums and stamping of iron-shod boots, advanced to meet us. The clash commenced with great cacophony; men's voices were raised in battle cry, and foule was the cursing of the foe. Dust rose in the air; the sky grew dimme; the enemie faltered and fell back.

As it is in lyf so also it is in warr: timing is all. Orders I gave, and men followed to prevent the enemie regrouping. A route ensued and they were destroyed. The remnant fled, yet one rider, proud and fearless, returned. He drew no weapon, and the soldiers suffered his approach. It was the shazrahad, coifed in crimson, and I thought a challenge would ensue. He dismounted, and though I was ready for him, he madeth no strike; neither did he showeth discomfort, alone amid our multitude. He sat himselfe down, at ease in the cross-legged fashion of southern men, and gestured me to join him.

"It was a good battle."

"So it was," said I.

"Thou hast wonne peace for a time."

"That was our purpose," said I, "but for peace or battle we are prepared."

He smiled grimly. "Peace is not fated, and yet it will prevaileth for a while. Know, however, that we shall return. Though sesouns wax and wane, though yeares passe, though those of thy line yet unbirthed sire kings themselves."

He wore a great sword and drew it slowly. It shimmered as do the Halathrin blades; a red jewel throbbed on its pommel, and strange script glittered on its blade.

"This is an embodiment of prophecye. It was made for whosoever of my people becomes Hakalakadan: sovereign of nations, king upon kings, ruler of the olde lands of our fathers and the new realmes of the conquered North."

He trembled in a great passion before lowering his head. "I know now that I am not the Hakalakadan; I am but one of many who will hold the sword for a time. Others will bear it until the prophecye is fulfilled."

Hearing his words I took counsel of myself. Both man and blade alike were now in mine authority, and I bethought to break the prophecye. Yet even for the protection of Esgallyen it would be an ill deed to so treat a man who came free-willed to my presence.

I bowed and let him go, but he had read my thoughts and smiled fiercely.

"The prophecye says also that if ever a kyng of the North should hold the blade the dayes of his lyf will runeth short, and the ruination of his realme shall swiftly follow."

He sprang upon his horse and could have run me down but laughed and rode until Galenthern swallowed him.

Hear now all and one, people of Esgallyen and kyngs yet to be; the sword will return, though different hand wield it. Beware!

Aranloth stopped speaking, lost in thought, then stirred. "So that's it. The word Hakalakadan is a title and not a name. Do you realize as well that while the Azan don't have the sword they'll believe it impossible to conquer the north?"

Lanrik nodded. "I understand, but is it really the same sword."

"Of that I have no doubt," Aranloth said. "Yet still I would know what the other scripts say. There's more to this yet."

Lanrik's hand dropped to the hilt of the blade. "It's hard to believe this is the same sword that Danhain saw all those years ago."

"The very same," Aranloth said. "The Azan will suffer a lack of confidence and drive now, but they will also do anything to regain the sword."

"What can they do from beyond the river?" asked Lanrik.

"Nothing," Aranloth said. "Not themselves anyway, but there are other powers in the world. Anyway, that's all the time we can spare the matter until we come to Lòrenta and decipher the remaining scripts."

Aranloth rolled and retied the scroll, returning it to the shelf.

"Guard the blade well – especially from Murhain," he said. "Some prophecies are nonsense and some come true. I fear to put this one to the test."

They left the building, untied their horses and rode off. Lanrik saw a half dozen of the Royal Guard loitering nearby. He thought they should have been with the king but paid them no further heed.

12. The Wisdom of the Raithlin

Lanrik looked back one last time at the city. It had been his home, the home of his parents who were buried there, the home of his ancestors, some of whom had died in battle while defending it. There were other cities, other places, even other homes: but there would never be another Esgallien.

The Raithlin and Esgallien were all he knew; yet the first had been taken from him, and he was leaving the second in the knowledge that he might never return.

The future was hidden. He had little idea what would happen on their quest, and even less of what may occur after that, but at least he was enjoying the company. That he liked Erlissa he knew, though how deep that would eventually go he was not yet sure. He was also beginning to like Aranloth.

He was travelling with them, going to places he had never been before, and the urge to explore that had once driven his steps over the plains and swamps of Galenthern woke in him again. He yearned to discover Alithoras, to cross its bright rivers, see its snow-topped mountains and dark forests, to walk among its people and experience new ways of life.

He was about to turn away when he saw six riders emerge from Gold Gate. They were Royal Guards, no doubt the same that he had seen in Conhain Court, and suspicion gripped him. He was about to say something, but Aranloth beat him to it.

"I see them. They were outside the City Archive as well. Murhain has sent them for the sword."

Lanrik let his breath out loudly. "I expected better from a king."

"Kings are people too," the lòhren said with a shrug. "There are some that are bad, some good, and many mixed. Murhain belongs to the bad. He'll stop at nothing to get the sword, *but he must not have it*."

"Not only did you deny him the sword," added Erlissa, "you made him look foolish too, and he'll hate you for that."

Aranloth nodded. "We should go. They're not likely to try anything in daylight so close to the city, but we'd better keep ahead. Come nightfall, when they expect us to camp, we'll ride hard and put them behind us."

They continued along the road. It was wide and well made, the middle raised slightly so that the sloping sides drained water. It was covered in turf and good for riding. It could accommodate the army for a swift march to protect Esgallien's interests in Caladhrist, but all that it had ever been used for was to supply the miners with food and equipment, the return of gold laden wagons, and the traffic of farmers and merchants.

Villas lined the roadside once more, but the soil here was less suitable for vines, and there were horse studs instead that bred stock for the races in the Haranast. Esgallien Creek ran through this area; the gold was long since gone, and its flats were cultivated to pasture and deep-rooted legumes.

The road crossed the creek via a stone bridge. It was old, built in the early days of the kingdom, but it was solid and secure. It had survived many floods, and so too had the inn beside it, which was as far north of Esgallien as Lanrik had ever been.

The inn was famous for two reasons. Firstly, the ale was reputed to be the best in Esgallien, a claim that he was willing to support, and secondly, it was said that Danhain had met his wife here. Rhodmai, who had once poured beers for weary travelers, had become queen of Esgallien and after her husband's death ruled wisely for nearly two decades, living to the age of one hundred and one. During that time many of the finest buildings of the city were constructed, and peace and prosperity abounded. The story went that she never forgot her roots and returned to the inn to die. The people loved her, and even today flowers were left at her statue in Conhain Court.

Lanrik kept a surreptitious watch on the Royal Guard, but they did not attempt to catch up. Aranloth was right; they would wait until nightfall, but that was not far away. The sun was low on the horizon, and long shadows from trees to the left spilled across the road.

"They'll get suspicious if we don't set up a camp before dark," Lanrik said.

Aranloth rubbed his chin. "But if we stop they'll draw level with us."

Lanrik made a noise of disgust. "There's nothing for it except to keep going, but we'll have to look casual."

Erlissa looked over at them. "You both worry too much. At the end of the day, we have a lead and good horses. If it comes to a race, we should be able to out distance them."

Aranloth smiled. "I haven't lived a long time without worrying about these kinds of things, but there's truth to what you say."

The thought of a pursuit prompted Lanrik to ask a question.

"How far is it to Lòrenta?"

The lòhren considered for a moment.

"It's over a hundred leagues as the bird flies, that's a journey of two weeks – but we must travel a longer road. The sorcery the elùgroths will use to draw Lòrenta into the spirit world will be a barrier between life and death itself. To pass, we'll need something special."

Erlissa spoke coolly. "I didn't think it would be as simple as you made out earlier. What will we need, and what danger will there be in obtaining it?"

Aranloth shrugged. "The mistletoe plant has long been associated with the threshold between worlds. We must retrieve three berries, but not any mistletoe will do. There are oak groves in the hills of Enorìen that were ancient before the Halathrin came to Alithoras. Ùhrengai is potent there; the old magic, the magic of the making. Eating one each will allow our physical bodies to enter the spirit world, for a time, without harm."

"I see," Erlissa said. "But mistletoe berries are poisonous. I don't suppose these will be any different?"

Aranloth inclined his head. "These are far more potent and poisonous than the ordinary variety. Yet one berry is safe enough, so long as it's picked in the middle of the night beneath the first rays of the rising half moon. Otherwise, it's deadly. So too is eating one but not crossing into the spirit world."

"I've heard of Enorìen," Lanrik said. "It's said to be a special place, but why is that so?"

"The hills are as the world once was," the lòhren answered. "People do not dwell there, nor do travelers or hunters journey to it. The hills are covered by pathless forests that have never felt the bite of an axe or heard the hiss of a flighted arrow. It's a remnant of Alithoras from a time before Halathrin or man, and unweakened ùhrengai flows in its primordial waters, rises in the slow sap of its trees and shines in the bright eyes of the animals that roam its dark tracts."

Erlissa looked at him levelly. "You make no mention of the Guardian."

Aranloth shrugged once more. "There is a Guardian as you say. A primeval creature, a being of ùhrengai. The Guardian keeps Enorìen the way it is, otherwise men would long since have settled there and the ùhrengai been diminished. Guardians aren't dangerous, nor are they safe, but the lòhrens have had dealings with them before."

The long shadows deepened as they talked. Stars glimmered faintly in the darkening sky, and dusk crept over the land. Lanrik glanced back and saw the Royal Guard were still following. Looking ahead, he saw a rise crowned on both sides of the road with trees. Night fell as they reached it, and in the last moments of half-light he dismounted and asked the others to do likewise. It would give the impression that they had stopped to camp.

"Will it fool them?" asked Erlissa.

Lanrik ran a hand through his hair. "For a while, maybe. They have no reason to think that we're aware of them. They'll give us a few hours to eat and go to sleep before they approach. They may outnumber us, but no one in the Royal Guard got there by being foolish. They'll try to take us by surprise – it's safer that way."

It was now dark, and they wanted to rest but could not. They mounted once more and moved off at a slow trot. When they were sure the sound of the horses would not carry they kicked them into a run, wanting to get far ahead. Once the camp was found to be deserted their pursuers would know their mission had been understood, and the real chase would begin.

Aranloth led them, his roan took great strides, and his robes flew behind. The alar horses followed, smaller but surer of their footing, and they showed no signs of tiring. Lanrik began to feel that they could run all night if they had to, and though the roan was a fine horse, the alar had speed and endurance beyond it, or any other horses he had seen.

The stars wheeled in the sky; the air grew still and cool, and dew began to settle over the grass. The night grew old and was quiet except for the regular thud of hooves on turf. Bright Halathgar, the constellation of the Lost Huntress, crept over the eastern horizon and glimmered along their path.

Erlissa rode beside Lanrik, her black hair one with the night-shadows, and her face hidden except for the flashes of the whites of her eyes as she smiled at him in the dark. She at least did not fear pursuit; she worried about nothing and planned for nothing; she was just the opposite of how Lanrik knew himself to be. Yet he had a sense of her wild joy and realized that he did not want to part from her after the quest was done.

Clouds eventually scudded across the sky, and they drew to a halt. There was no sign of their pursuers, and they moved off the road into a grove of trees. They rubbed the horses down and ate a cold meal of bread and dried meat. Then they settled themselves as comfortably as they could and slept. Lanrik wondered if they should set a watch, but the Royal Guard would not have been able to keep pace even if they had followed at once.

It was after dawn when he woke. Erlissa was still asleep nearby, her hair tousled, and her head resting on one arm. Aranloth was awake and had been busy. He had collected tinder and started a small fire over which he was heating water. The canopy of trees dispersed the smoke.

The lòhren looked in his direction. "Nothing like a warm breakfast to start the day."

Lanrik could not agree more. "Warm breakfasts are the Raithlin's delight," he said. Over the years he had eaten more cold and quick meals before the sun had risen than he cared to remember.

He glanced at Erlissa and found that she was awake and looking at him, her eyes were large and dark, but her expression unfathomable. She sat up, yawned, and ran her hand through her hair and frowned with dissatisfaction at what she found. She muttered something that Lanrik did not catch.

They ate their meal within the cool dark of the trees. The road beyond remained quiet; the only movement was of a nuthatch working its way down a nearby trunk in search of insects with its characteristic head-first approach.

When they were done they checked over the horses. None of them showed signs of soreness or injury from the long ride, and they saddled them and moved into the open. The sun was bright, the day was clear, and the turf on the road, though still wet with dew, was springy and fresh. It was a good time to ride, and they would make sure they left the Royal Guard well behind.

They started slow, allowing the horses to warm up, then increased the pace. The countryside around them was changing. The villas of the wealthy were now gone; only farmsteads remained, and those were becoming infrequent and separated by thick tracts of forest. The land was rising into downs, and the ground was rockier, no longer the chalky soil of Galenthern, and the stands of beech that he was used to were replaced by oak.

It was a new type of county for him. He must find a new way of life, too, but what direction should he take? Nothing stood out. The skills he had were not useful except to the Raithlin. Had he wasted his life learning them?

Erlissa rode beside him and looked over.

"What's the matter, Lan," she asked.

He did not like telling people his problems, but there was something about her easygoing manner that encouraged it.

"I'm worried about what I'm going to do when this is over. The other cities have scouts, I guess, but they're not Raithlin, and I don't have the training for anything else."

Erlissa shrugged. "Something will turn up. You're young and determined and could be successful at any number of things."

She looked at him thoughtfully. "I think you already know that. What bothers you isn't the future but the past.

145

You feel it's a shame to let your skills and the traditions of the Raithlin go to waste."

Lanrik pondered her statement.

Erlissa smiled. "I'm getting to know how you think, but tell me this; do you still believe in the Raithlin creed?"

He did not hesitate. "Of course."

He remembered the words he had spoken over Lathmai's cairn. The creed was widely known throughout Esgallien and beyond. He must have said it thousands of times, and he repeated the words once more.

Our duty is to serve and protect
Our honor is to fight but not hate
Our love is for all that is good in the world

"It's curious," Lathmai said, "but there's nothing there about the Raithlin skills. There's nothing about how to track or throw a knife. Instead, what's valued is a way of life. The creed is a code to live by; you can uphold the Raithlin values in everything you do in the future."

Lanrik sighed. He knew she was right, but it would not be the same. "I'll think on it," he said. "And thank you."

She gave him a smile.

They rode all that day, and there was no sign of pursuit. The road was a lonely strip of civilization in the wilderness, traveled by few this far away from the city, but they still saw the occasional farmer who preferred to live in the wild and drive fattened cattle into Esgallien once a year.

The land continued to change; the patches of oak forest grew larger, wolves howled in the distance, and the road still climbed.

They camped late that evening in a stand of trees by the roadside. A cool wind blew from the west, and they sheltered comfortably in the lee of a small but steeply-sided hill. A hollow had been gouged out of its side by wind, rain or human intervention. It was not deep but offered shelter and they used it. A small fire-pit, lined with blackened stones, and obviously the remnant of other travelers, was set in the middle.

They ate another quick meal and settled down to sleep early. The wind moaned over the hillcrest through the night; the boughs of the oaks creaked, and the wolves howled against the dark. Clouds skimmed low and thick, blocking out the stars and bright Halathgar, but brought no rain.

Lanrik slept poorly. In the pre-dawn darkness, when the wind stilled and the trees grew silent, he lay still and thought about what had brought him to this moment. It seemed a long time ago that he had buried Lathmai and his life had been forever altered.

Something else troubled him though, and he was not sure what it was. The horses were silhouetted nearby, and at first he did not know what it was about them that disturbed him. Then he realized their ears were twitching, responding to sounds that he could not hear.

Swiftly he rolled to his feet and drew his sword. The noise woke the others, and they looked at him groggily as he surveyed the darkness. He saw nothing and began to feel foolish. Then he noticed in the slowly growing light the pale glitter of naked steel. Someone had crawled within twenty feet of the camp.

"They've found us," he said.

Aranloth, staff in hand, came to stand by his side.

The steel blade flickered. There was a shuffling noise, and a voice came out of the dark.

"You're surrounded," it said. "Don't do anything foolish."

The speaker stood up and came into view. He was tall and dressed in the uniform of the Royal Guard. He walked forward calmly, sword in hand, and as he did so five others followed. Their swords were drawn too, and Lanrik did not like the eager expressions on their face.

The tall man was their captain, and he spoke again. "This is a dangerous situation, but it needn't be. You're outnumbered, and there's no point in fighting. You know who we are and where our orders come from."

He paused a little then added, "And you know we must have the sword."

Lanrik detected something about the captain that he liked. Prudently, he had not mentioned the king directly, and his hesitation indicated distaste of the task set for him.

The light was increasing, and Lanrik looked him in the eye. "And if I give it to you, what then?"

The captain returned his gaze steadily. "I'll not lie to you. My orders were to kill you and take the sword, but if you give it to me freely, you can go. I'll not kill an unarmed man."

One of the guards behind him grunted. "*You* may not, but the rest of us will. We didn't enjoy that long chase. It was the hardest riding we've ever done, and we want some entertainment for our troubles."

The other men laughed, but the captain turned to them coolly.

"Remember that you're Royal Guards, not gutter criminals, regardless of the tasks that you're sometimes given."

He turned back, and Lanrik felt a sense of desperation. There was no way out of this. The captain was a good man, but he was sworn to serve the king and would not leave without the sword. And he might not be able to control his men even if they got it.

Lanrik could not give him the sword. He did not especially believe in prophecies, but on the other hand he had seen some strange things. And Aranloth, who knew about such matters, had warned him Murhain must never get it.

148

If he had to fight it would be one against six. He did not know what help, if any, the lòhren and Erlissa would be able to give. He looked at the captain and felt sick. He liked the man, but he was their leader. If he was killed quickly it would surprise and confuse the others. It was clear that he was the thinker of the group, and without him they would be leaderless.

Lanrik looked at Aranloth. He seemed a picture of calmness, giving no indication of what he would do, but he read in the lòhren's expression that he knew what would happen next and was ready for it.

Lanrik suppressed his reluctance and turned to the captain. "I'm sorry," he said.

He saw perplexity in the man's eyes and then sudden understanding, but Lanrik was already whipping out a throwing knife. Draw and throw were one motion, and the blade hurled into him. It ripped at his throat and bright blood spurted into the air.

The other guards were dismayed. Lanrik leapt at them, sword drawn, but before he reached them Aranloth was there, his staff swinging wildly among them, and the crack of wood on bone was loud as he struck one on the head.

He joined the lòhren and another man went down, the shazrahad blade having slipped easily through his defenses.

The three remaining guards fled into the trees and crashed through the undergrowth. In moments hooves thudded southward on the road.

Lanrik quickly glanced about him. Two guards lay dead. Erlissa was kneeling over the captain, but there was nothing she could do: he was dead too. She looked up at him. Blood was splattered over her hands and arms from trying to staunch the wound, and tears brimmed in her eyes, but she said nothing.

He cleaned the blood off his sword and walked through the trees onto the road. The other guards were

149

gone, and the clouded sky was red with dawn. He gulped in fresh air and tried to steady his hands.

A few minutes later the lòhren joined him. They watched the slow surge of the sun over the horizon in silence, a sun that three other men would never see again, and Lanrik felt bitter. He had killed the captain, a decent man who had dutifully obeyed his orders. He did not know his name, and would probably never discover it, or if he was married or a father.

Aranloth leaned on his staff and waited.

"Why?" asked Lanrik. "Why did it have to be that way?"

Aranloth seemed to know what he meant. "It would have been easier had the captain not been a good man. But he was. He was following the orders of his king, and it wasn't his fault the instructions were wrongful – yet he paid the price."

"A heavy price for another man's greed."

Aranloth nodded. "That's so, but it's often the way of things. The world teems with injustice, hate, greed, envy and incompetence. A man can only pick his way as best he can, trying to choose right from wrong."

"And what of *my* choices?" asked Lanrik.

The lòhren looked at him for the first time. "I know what choices you made and why you made them. I made my own, as the guards did also. If you thought your actions wrong, you would not have committed to them. Had you reacted differently the sword could be on its way to Murhain as we speak. The ruination of the realm might be at hand, and we would probably be dead. The other five wanted to kill us even if their captain was willing to let us go."

Lanrik kicked the ground. "Was there nothing else I could have done?"

Aranloth sighed. "I'm old, Lanrik. Older than you know. I've seen many decisions go awry; just as many of

150

the good as the bad. Sometimes there *are* no good choices, yet life forces us to act anyway. But you're not the first to experience this. The Raithlin before you have done so, back to the days of Conhain, and even before when they served the Halathrin. They found their way to an understanding, and you will too."

Lanrik thought of the long history of the Raithlin, of his own teachers and the words of advice that had filtered down through the generations. The Raithlin creed that he had recently discussed with Erlissa came to mind. It was the wisdom of men who had been forced to kill, or see those they loved killed instead. It was an expression formulated by people who had endured worse than he had. He whispered the simple words and found they had new meaning:

> *Our duty is to serve and protect*
> *Our honor is to fight but not hate*
> *Our love is for all that is good in the world.*

13. They Have Many Names

It took the travelers over a day to reach Caladhrist. The road, arrow-straight all the way from Esgallien, twisted like a writhing snake on descending the gorge.

The landscape was barren. Massive boulders and sweeps of shattered rock littered the steep sides. Loose stones clattered beneath the hooves of the horses, and a cacophony of noise came from the miners: shouted instructions, yells of encouragement, curses and raucous singing.

They followed the road to the bottom. The air, heavy with smoke and dust, made them cough, and the ridges that hemmed them in cast groping shadows.

Erlissa shuddered. "It feels like the bottom of a grave."

Aranloth lifted his gaze from the barren ground and looked about.

"Many men *have* died here. Caladhrist has been mined since Conhain's time, and over the years, there have been accidents. But it was mined even before that. The Halathrin were here long ago, though even they weren't the first. They found the workings of other people before them, their tools and excavations, and their bones too. Not men killed by mishap they say, but sacrificed. They believe the gorge is haunted by the spirits of the restless dead."

"The Halathrin discovered bodies in the swamps of Galenthern too," added Lanrik. "It's said that they found the traces of a strange and cruel civilization all over eastern Alithoras."

"Strange and cruel are matters of perspective," Aranloth said, guiding his horse around a pile of rubble. "Who knows what those people would think of us and our ways? Of their existence though, there's no doubt. Nor of the men who died here. The miners claim that on some nights they can hear dead men's voices in the hiss of the wind over the ridges. Superstition, of course, and yet it's not a favorable place for lòhrengai."

They continued along the bottom of the gorge in silence. Much of their travel since the fight with the Royal Guard had been quiet. Erlissa was withdrawn, and Lanrik thought she was avoiding him. That she was upset over the killing of the captain he knew, but he did not know how to heal the breach between them. Necessity had forced his actions, but he would not be able to convince her of that. Perhaps it was better not to try.

They slowed to skirt a massive pile of rubble, and Aranloth chafed at the delay.

"We have to hurry," he said. "It's a hundred miles to the nearest oak grove in Enorìen, and the mistletoe berries must be picked when the moon is midway between full and dead. That's only three nights away."

Lanrik thought something else was making the lòhren uneasy, for the time constraint had been there since the beginning. He wondered what it was while the road meandered past old workings, piles of broken stone and washes of gravel and sediment. There were miners and soldiers all about, but most were on the valley sides and few at the bottom.

Erlissa looked about her in disgust. "It's hard to believe that something as beautiful as gold comes from a place like this. How do they do it?"

"With back-breaking work," Aranloth said curtly.

It seemed as though that was all he was going to say but then he expanded.

"Veins of gold are scattered through the sides of the valley but finding them is difficult. The labor of digging by hand to seek them would be enormous. Instead, they divert water from a creek several miles away and hold it in

153

clay-lined tanks at the tops of the ridges. When they're ready to explore a particular place they release a wave of water. It sweeps away the overburden of soil exposing the bedrock and any gold-bearing veins."

Erlissa looked around her with new understanding. "No wonder it's such a mess here. What happens then?"

"If a vein, or lode, is found they attack it with fire-setting. That involves building a fire against the rock and when it's hot, quenching it with water. That makes it easy to break up, and the barren debris is swept away with another release of water."

"What happens if the lode runs deep into the bedrock?" Lanrik asked.

"It often does," Aranloth said. "In Caladhrist the veins are usually horizontal, and the miners drive adits, a kind of tunnel, to follow the lode right into the sides of the gorge. The adit is made at a slight angle to dewater it, and sometimes shafts are sunk from above to provide better air movement."

Erlissa lifted her hand and exposed her twisted gold bracelet. She turned it back and forth in the light, admiring it.

"All the hard work is worth it," she said.

Aranloth looked closely at the ornament. "A remarkable piece," he said.

"It'd be worth a lot of money if you ever sold it," Lanrik said.

Erlissa shook her head sadly. "Perhaps, but it was my mother's, and I'll never part with it."

Lanrik felt stupid. Of all the things he could have said . . .

They soon passed beyond the middle of the valley and approached two miners seated around a ring of burnt stones, the fire long since cold. They had the faces of rough men; people who had worked hard all their lives for little profit and had endured hardship. Dust and grime covered their hands and clothes; their yellowed fingernails were cracked and chewed short, but they were well-mannered.

As Erlissa neared, they stood and tipped their hats, the oldest coughing behind his before speaking. He had a jutting beard that might once have been red like the remnant of hair on his head, but was now yellow-white.

"Afternoon, miss."

Erlissa smiled brightly at him.

"Taking a pleasure ride?" he asked.

"Of a sort," she said.

"Not many folks come down this way. Specially in the company of a lòhren and a Raithlin. We watched you ride in and got a notion that things must be happening in the city."

Lanrik realized that these men hungered for news. They lived isolated lives and wanted to hear about things that were happening in the wider world.

Aranloth seemed to have great sympathy for this. Anxious about time as he was, he still dismounted to talk to them. Who, thought Lanrik, would understand better? The life of a lòhren was one of wandering from city to city, town to town, region to region. He must have spent much of his own life alone in the wilds of Alithoras, starved for company and news.

"There's been war," he said. "Elugs have crossed Galenthern and attacked at the ford."

The old man nodded his head solemnly, and his beard jerked up and down. "We heard rumor of that yesterday. A young boy comes here time to time to sell knives, but he didn't know how things turned out."

"The army met them at the ford and barred their way."

The old man looked as though that was what he expected; nevertheless, there was a hint of relief in his expression.

"I soldiered once," said his younger companion. "Spent some time there, and I reckon it's hard enough just to stand in the current. Crossing with an army waiting on the other side is a good way to collect arrows."

The old man lifted his hat again, this time to run his hand through the thin hair on his head.

"That's big happenings, but there must be more going on. Leastways, I should think so, otherwise you'd not be coming through here."

Lanrik realized that for all the old man's appearance and quaint speech he was shrewder than many who wore the king's livery and earned high wages.

"You're right," Aranloth said. "The king has disbanded the Raithlin as well."

The old man tilted his head in thought. "Now why would he do that? Seems to me that the Raithlin have always been needed and likely always will."

"Costs too much money," Aranloth said.

"Figures!" the old man said, coughing again. "There's more than enough gold coming out of here to fund a thousand Raithlin and run the city for a hundred years, but the king never seems to get enough. Spends it on all the wrong things, I reckon. He'll come to a bad end, that one."

Aranloth answered quietly. "That he will."

They talked a little more, the old man not pressing further on what brought them to the gorge. Aranloth was a font of information, even gossip, on the happenings both small and large in Esgallien before they rode on.

Not long after, they came to the northern end of Caladhrist, and the road climbed steeply. They struggled up it, the horses finding it difficult to get purchase on the loose stones, but eventually they reached the top.

The countryside could not contrast more with the barren valley. It was a land of downs, sloping grasslands, rivulets and thick belts of trees. Before them, a road ran west to east, straight as the one from Esgallien, though it was wider and better made.

Lanrik looked at it closely. It was ancient and rarely used, yet its construction was superior to any in Esgallien.

Aranloth noticed his curiosity. "It's one of the old Halathrin roads. Follow it a hundred leagues west, and it'll take you to their home of Halathar. Follow it forty-five leagues east, and you'll end up at the coast north of the city of Camarelon. But we're not going that far. We'll turn away before then and strike into Enorìen."

They moved onto the road, enjoying the level ground and lack of obstacles that marred Caladhrist, and made good ground eastward as the afternoon progressed. Aranloth's sense of unease now seemed to infuse Erlissa as well, and she became even more introspective.

Lanrik rode behind them. He wanted time to think and clear his head. So much had happened lately, and he had come to grips with so little of it.

The riding was hard but it freed his mind to think, and he enjoyed the sensation of the miles being eaten up and put behind them. Each moment that passed brought them closer to their ultimate goal of saving Lòrenta, and when that was done, he would try to find a way to get on with his life.

Dusk swept along the treed downs, and Aranloth called a halt. They cared for their horses, and then began the usual chores of setting up camp. It was a routine for them now, and they did their jobs quickly and efficiently.

Lanrik prepared a fire-pit and Erlissa, apt at finding dry wood, searched beneath a stand of trees. Aranloth collected water from a nearby rivulet and would also cook the evening meal. He was, Lanrik thought, the best camp-cook he had ever known. No doubt a lot of practice was the reason for it; he had said himself that he was old, older than they knew, and that got Lanrik thinking about him.

Stories about lòhrens were many and varied. In some they had great power, yet Aranloth had not shown any. Certainly, he had not used lòhrengai against the Royal Guard, but only his staff as a physical weapon.

Children grew up in Esgallien hearing tales about the exploits of a lòhren called Aranloth. In one cycle of ballads he was portrayed as a mythical hero of antiquity. In a group of adventure stories he was head of the Lòhrenin, the Council of Lòhrens. In yet another group of poems he was just a kind-hearted vagabond wandering Alithoras and helping those in need. A Raithlin instructor had once insisted the name Aranloth was actually an inherited title used by successive leaders of the Lòhrenin.

When they finished their meal, Lanrik determined to find out something of the truth.

"You know how to fight well with that staff," he said.

Aranloth shrugged. "You learn as you go. Travel far enough, live long enough, and you acquire useful skills."

"Where did you learn it?"

"I've spent much time among the Cheng tribes in the far west of Alithoras. They call me a sage, rather than a lòhren, but it all comes to the same thing. Theirs is a warrior nation, highly skilled in combat, with or without weapons. Some of their masters are extraordinary."

"Why use the staff to defend yourself instead of lòhrengai?"

Aranloth cocked his head in thought. "An interesting question. Some, and by that I mean elùgroths, use sorcery indiscriminately. But there's a price for each use of elùgai and lòhrengai. Something of the user, however slight, is lost. Likewise, something of the energy that is gathered and transformed becomes part of them. Power should be used sparingly, only just enough to achieve the goal, and only when it can be accomplished in no other way."

"That's why an elùgroth is inhuman," added Erlissa.

Aranloth looked at her. "They would argue that freeing themselves of love, sympathy and compassion makes them stronger."

"It does," she said. "But what's the point of strength if there's no higher purpose to use it for?"

Aranloth did not answer. Erlissa had endured the presence of a sorcerer and knew what she was talking about, but Lanrik had not, and hoped never to do so. He had learned something though, even if there was more that he wanted to discover. But they were all growing tired, and soon after lay near the fire to sleep. The howling of the wolves started again, and this time another pack answered from the north.

Lanrik went to sleep listening to the wolves, but he woke some time later to silence. Hours must have passed. There was no noise at all. The fire had died to embers and all was still, but something had woken him.

Aranloth was kneeling near the embers, his staff in his hand, and his head tilted to one side, listening. He looked over, but said nothing.

Minutes passed, but Aranloth did not move nor was there any noise. Yet the uneasiness that Lanrik had sensed in the other two all afternoon now infused him.

Erlissa woke suddenly and looked at them but did not speak. The silence continued, then far away they heard the baying of dogs. It was the sound of a hunting pack, of a team used by a great lord, but nobody lived here nor would they hunt at this time of night.

"The wolves have gone," Erlissa said.

Lanrik knew the howling had long since stopped, but now the baying came again. The sound carried eerily over the otherwise silent downs then ceased.

Aranloth stood. It was the easy rising of a young man, not the old man that he was, and there was anger in his features.

"I've heard those hounds before!"

He stamped the end of his staff into the ground and strode to the horses.

"I didn't think to hear them again, but they're on the hunt and we're their quarry. We have other enemies this night than the Royal Guard. Ride! And don't look back!"

Lanrik and Erlissa did not ask any questions. They had not seen him like this before, and Lanrik wondered what could disturb him so much when the attack of the Royal Guard had left him unperturbed.

They had saddled the horses and moved onto the road before Lanrik spoke.

"What's hunting us?"

"The hounds of Ebona. The hounds of the otherworld. Creatures of ùhrengai. They have many names: all of them mean death."

Aranloth urged the roan into an ever-faster gallop, and the others followed, the baying of hounds loud and excited behind them.

They raced along in a wild chase. Nighttime shadows flitted past, and the light of stars cast wavering shadows. It was a perilous ride where to misstep or fall would kill, but Halathrin roads were wide and even, and they trusted that there would be no potholes to break a horse's leg or tree roots to trip them.

Lanrik was surprised when Aranloth slowed. He appeared to look for some landmark and then moved off the road. They now went at a slower pace, moving southeast over stony ground, shallow rivulets and through a river ford.

The lòhren turned to explain. "Even hounds of the otherworld must hunt by sight and scent. This will slow them."

"But didn't we have a better chance of outrunning them on the road?" asked Lanrik.

Aranloth ran a hand through his hair. "Perhaps," he said. "These hounds are not as others though. Few horses

160

in Alithoras could outrun them – and only when they were fresh."

"Then what are we going to do?" asked Erlissa.

"The only thing we can," Aranloth said. "We must find a place to make a stand. But we'll have time to find somewhere to better our chances."

They pushed on. The baying and yelping of the hounds rose in waves of excitement behind them, and Lanrik noticed after a while that they were on a road again.

Shortly, the baying turned to whines and uncertain barks. The hounds had evidently lost their trail, but Lanrik knew it would not be for long. They would cast around until they found it again then chase once more.

Ahead of them was a mass of trees. It was a dark smudge extending as far as they could see in either direction.

"The Woods of Alonin," the lòhren informed them. "Long did a group of Halathrin dwell here. Some say a remnant still does. If so, they're deeper than we can go tonight."

Aranloth ceased speaking and listened. The baying of the hounds intensified into a fury of excitement and noise. "Ride!" he said.

He kicked the roan into a gallop, but when they passed beneath the trees they were forced to slow again. It was very dark, and the smell of leaf mold and forest was strong.

They did not have to travel far to reach Aranloth's destination. The road led toward a mass of jumbled stones covering tens of acres of ground. It was only as they neared that Lanrik realized the stone was not natural: the piles were formed by broken pillars and walls. This was once a city. Not as large as Esgallien, but a city nevertheless. He recognized a pattern of streets, even parks where trees grew thickly. In the center was a tower, overthrown and dilapidated, and Aranloth led them with

161

a clatter over cracked flagstones and down a shadow-haunted street toward it.

Scattered all about the tower was a ring of fallen and shattered stones. The foundations on one side were intact though and formed a half moon of wall some twenty feet high.

They tied the horses near the wall and moved to face outward. The baying of the hounds drew close and filled the forest. Lanrik noticed that flame had once swept the tower. Masses of charred timber littered the ground, and black scorch marks defaced the walls.

"It's a good place to make a stand," he said. "Our backs are shielded."

Aranloth nodded. "There's another reason. The hounds are creatures of ùhrengai. These ruins will confuse them and reduce their strength. They won't like the regular pattern of the streets, the flagstones beneath their paws, or the very scent of civilization that still lingers in the air."

Lanrik was nervous. Talking might take his mind off what would shortly come.

"What civilization? I'd guess it to be a Halathrin city, but I've never heard of it before."

"So it was," confirmed Aranloth. "You haven't heard of it because it was destroyed before Conhain founded Esgallien. The Halathrin warred with elugs in these lands long before your ancestors came, even before they befriended the Halathrin in the days that are legend to your people. But this city, and the Tower of Haladhon in which we now stand, is remembered by some."

Aranloth paused, his eyes searching the outer ruins, but his mind seemed elsewhere.

"It was in this tower that the lady Alonùradth wed Lord Carandùr, and on that day there were no shadows, no charred stones, no ruins, but rather the Woods of Alonin lay beneath a gentle midsummer sun. More gentle still were the eyes of Alonùradth. But neither gentleness, nor the bravery of her husband, saved her from the curved swords of the elugs when the city fell."

Lanrik thought of the passing of time in this place. A city had risen; men and women had walked these streets while his ancestors had gathered at standing stones and celebrated the birthing sun in midwinter. And stone and people had fallen before Conhain even came to Esgallien.

He had no further time to ponder for the hounds were upon them. They growled, snarled and moved like swift shadows behind piles of stone and ruined walls. The elusive movements drew closer, and here and there, they caught a glimpse of the beasts. Their shoulders stood waist high to a man; their frames were massively muscled, and they were bigger than any dog Lanrik had ever seen.

The horses whinnied in fear. A beast appeared to the right. It rushed toward them, jaws slavering, massive body straining, paws slamming against the stone paving. White flame burst into it, and the hound twisted sideways and tumbled behind cover. It whined in the shadows.

Aranloth lowered his staff. "They'll be more careful now," he said grimly.

Lanrik kept his eyes on the outer perimeter and did not respond. But he had seen the lòhren-fire, and it seemed Aranloth had power after all.

The hounds grew quiet. Far away in the night, there was the sound of fast-ridden horses. Lanrik glanced questioningly at the lòhren.

Aranloth shook his head. "It's not likely to be help. Probably just the remainder of the Royal Guard."

Lanrik knew he was right, but they were still hard words to hear. The lòhren-fire had given the hounds pause, but Aranloth could not be everywhere at once. Lanrik held the shazrahad sword tightly, but sweat was making his grip slippery. He would soon find out if naked steel was a match for otherworldly flesh. But the legends of Esgallien suggested that it was not.

14. Even the Earth Remembers

The hounds roamed the shadows. They came closer, their massive paws loud on the flagstones. They allowed themselves to be glimpsed, and their growls and snuffling breath possessed the night. Lanrik felt a wave of malevolence and sensed their purpose: they were trying to instil fear in order to panic their quarry into flight.

He took a deep breath. *Clear like water; cold like ice.* Remaining still, he noticed that Aranloth also waited patiently. He heard Erlissa move, and turned to see that she was calming the terrified horses.

The hounds came closer. They were now in full view, and their muscles bunched and rippled beneath sleek coats as they padded. He sensed a change in their mood; a direct attack was imminent.

He prepared for their rush, but at that moment Aranloth swept his staff in a wide arc. White flame sprang from the broken foundations of the tower and joined the remaining wall behind them to form a continuous ring. Tongues of lòhren-fire, tinged red as once the embers of the destroyed building had glowed, danced and leaped in a man-high wall. Yet not so high that the beasts could not jump it.

The hounds backed away at first, and then they pressed close to the flame. They had been baulked, but their hunger to rend flesh grew into a frenzy, and they cavorted madly, growling and snapping at the air.

One of the beasts bunched its hind legs underneath it. Muscles bulging, it leaped over the ring of flame. It would have sailed clear, but a single tongue of lòhren-fire licked up and around its arched body. The hound twisted in the air. Landing awkwardly, it rolled on the ground to rid itself of the pale fire on its dark coat, but it adhered like burning oil.

The hound bit at the flame and came to its feet in rage. Its lips retracted hideously as it growled, and the red-tipped ears flattened. It prepared to attack, but Aranloth was quicker and he strode forward and thrust his staff toward its chest. Flame burst in a stream of white lòhrengai. It caught the hound squarely and drove it backward until it was knocked off its feet. Aranloth did not relent. The hound tried desperately to gather itself, but its growls turned to tortured yelps. The stench of burning hair and flesh filled the air, and in moments the creature was a mass of flame. When the lòhren-fire ceased, only ash remained.

There was no respite. The other hounds leaped over the barrier. As with their leader, tongues of white fire wrapped around them. They landed inside the ring and turned and snapped where the flame burned them.

Aranloth unleashed a spray of lòhren-fire. It caught two beasts and knocked them back, pinning them against the ring of flame. The wall flared at their touch, and they yelped while their massive bodies strained against the forces burning them. Lanrik saw that for all the damage being inflicted they could yet break free, but he had his own problem. The fourth hound approached him.

The creature pulled back its lips, exposing predatory teeth and a monstrous jaw capable of snapping bone. Growls, throbbing with enmity, rumbled from its throat. It almost unnerved him, but he forced himself to step forward.

The hound leapt at his throat, and he swung his sword and slashed with all his strength. The blade struck fur and muscle but did not cut as it should have. It drew blood, and the creature flinched, but what would have killed a normal dog only wounded a creature of ùhrengai.

166

The sword was battered from his hands as the massive weight of the animal hit him. He staggered and fell. He had achieved something though, for the hound had twisted to avoid the blade, and its head was buried against his shoulder whereas otherwise the great jaw would have already ripped out his throat.

As he fell, Lanrik gripped the beast. One hand locked around a foreleg, and another took hold of an ear. He strove to roll sideways; to fall with the animal on top was to die.

They landed side by side with a thud. The hound scrambled to get its legs beneath it, its jaw opening and closing, seeking Lanrik's throat. The creature was getting on top, one massive paw repeatedly ripping his leg as it tried to find purchase. In moments, it would kill him, and there was nothing he could do.

He saw swift movement as Erlissa hurled herself through the air. She smashed into the creature with her shoulder and dislodged it from him.

He rolled forward and grabbed the sword as he surged to his feet and stepped between the hound and Erlissa's sprawled body. The creature snarled, a ruff of fur bristling on its neck, and its hind legs bunched to leap.

But it never did. White flame erupted all around it, knocking it down. Lanrik saw its fur catch fire. He watched as its pelt shrank and blackened, exposing flesh and bone. The smell of burnt hair was putrid. It yelped until its throat burned away, and in moments there was nothing left but ash.

Lanrik was nearly sick, but he forced himself to look around. Aranloth had killed the other hounds, so he turned on shaky legs toward Erlissa. She sat on the ground, a trickle of blood coming from her temple but otherwise unhurt.

He held out his hand and helped her up. "That was one of the bravest things I've ever seen. I can't believe you did it – especially the way things have been."

He watched as Erlissa felt her face gingerly and managed a smile. "For someone so smart you can be really stupid. Just because we don't agree on some things doesn't mean we aren't friends. You saved me from an elug army and an elùgroth. You and I will *always* be friends. No matter what."

Lanrik was astonished. *Will she ever cease to surprise me?* He hesitated, searching for the right reply, then heard the approach of riders and the moment was lost.

Aranloth, the diadem on his forehead glinting, came to their side and they looked through the flames, which lessened in height and intensity. Four riders appeared. They came to a halt and looked at them over the dying flames. Two of them, as Aranloth had guessed, were Royal Guards. The others were a shock.

A low hiss from Erlissa voiced a name. *"Gwalchmur."*

This was the traitor responsible for the deaths of Raithlin, including Lathmai. Lanrik felt the full force of his promise to her. He remembered her broken body, the blood and wounds, her eye burned from its socket; images that would haunt him all the days of his life. Now, he had the chance to fulfil his promise, but the words of the Raithlin creed ran through his mind as well.

The other man was Mecklar. What was he doing in the company of a traitor? What was he doing here at all?

The flames ebbed and Mecklar spoke. "It's a long way from Galenthern. Had I known you'd cause so much trouble, I'd have ensured you never returned to Esgallien. But I can fix my mistake. You won't cause further problems. Ever."

Lanrik did not know what to say. Mecklar was a traitor too, in league with Gwalchmur, and working toward the destruction of Esgallien.

168

Aranloth answered. "Not all mistakes can be remedied. They can be repented though. I sense the mark of Ebona upon you, but even she cannot force you against your will. Turn aside, Mecklar. She's a harder mistress than you know."

Mecklar looked at the lòhren. Finally, arriving at some decision, or merely responding to a thought that amused him, he laughed.

"Is that the best you can do, lòhren? I'll take my chances with Ebona. She has power, real power. And what of you? You managed to kill her hounds, but what's that achieved? It's only delayed you enough for us to catch up."

"A circumstance you may regret."

Mecklar grinned. "A *threat* from the great and wise Aranloth?"

"Merely advice. Something for which I'm often asked and rarely, in the end, reproved for."

"Spare me," Mecklar said. "Neither advice nor threats will help you now. Whatever power you have, even if you can use it on normal men, was spent on the hounds. And we outnumber you."

Aranloth looked at him solemnly before shifting his gaze to Gwalchmur.

"Don't you know? You're no longer normal men. The mark of Ebona is on you, and eventually you'll discover what that means. But remember, you can repudiate her should you wish to."

"Enough!" Mecklar said. "The time for talk has passed."

He drew his sword, as did the others, but the flames had not quite died.

Lanrik looked at them all. This would be a fight to the death, and Mecklar alone was as much as he could handle. It seemed as though his feeling that one day the fight of the Spring Games would be finished was true. But while

169

he contended with Mecklar, the other three would be free. What help Aranloth would provide, he did not know, though it was obvious that he was weary, and Mecklar might be right. The lòhren seemed reluctant, or unable, to use power against men.

Aranloth leaned on his staff, seemingly exhausted, head drooped and resting on frail hands that gripped the top of the staff. Yet something in the set of his mouth suggested intense concentration.

The ring of white fire wavered again, and the riders edged closer. Lanrik thought he heard noise somewhere in the ruins. He heard it again, this time louder, and he identified it as drumming. Not the beating of a single drum, but many, and they were elug drums. War drums.

The fire weakened, but the riders now looked behind them. The drums grew louder. They were not beating a marching pace, or a warning to invoke fear, but a battle rhythm.

As well as the drums, Lanrik now heard shouts and screams. There was fighting in the streets, and it was coming closer. Fires sprang to life, buildings burned, and vague forms moved in the flickering shadows.

A mass of elugs pressed hard against a small band of retreating Halathrin. They were badly outnumbered but gave way grudgingly. The elugs screamed curses but the Halathrin fought silently. They were white-clad and fair-haired, tall and proud. Their pale swords did bloody work, in which they took no joy, nor did they show anger. There was suffering on their noble faces though, for their city burned about them.

The battle drew close to the tower, and Mecklar shouted in frustration. He stabbed his sword toward Lanrik. "I'll kill you yet!"

He would have said more, but the other riders had already hastened away and he followed them. They disappeared in the shadows and headed toward the opposite side of the city.

Aranloth lifted his head from the staff. He was pale and weary, anguish in his expression.

"Quickly," he said. "We must get back to the Halathrin road."

The ring of fire darkened to the color of cold embers then flickered out while they mounted their horses. Aranloth led them onto the street. Halathrin warriors were all about them, and just ahead was the pressing mass of elugs, their faces cruel and vicious. The flagstones were slick with blood, corpses littered the ground, and the stench of death was strong. But Lanrik realized it was all an illusion.

Neither Halathrin nor elugs heeded them as the horses walked through the battle.

"It's not real," he said. "How can that be?"

Aranloth said nothing but Erlissa answered. "It's real enough in its way. This is what happened all those years ago when the city was destroyed. This was part of the battle."

Aranloth spoke, his eyes fixed ahead. "The city remembers. The stone remembers. Even the earth remembers. Nothing will forget. Not even when the ruins are swallowed by the ground and tree and grass grow over it all."

The lòhren, his face pale and gray, rode onward. For once, he looked the old man that he was.

Erlissa followed with Lanrik. "It taxes him," she said. "It's the nature of lòhrengai. He's giving life to all that you see around you; the blood-lust of the elugs, their glee in destruction, and the torment of the Halathrin. But it's flowing into him as well."

A lone Halathrin staggered down the street, and Aranloth averted his gaze. Blood dripped from his sword, and his white raiment was gore-splattered. Alone of all the

171

Halathrin they heard him. "Alonùradth!" There was such anguish in his voice that they wished they had not. He looked at them unseeing, his eyes wide and bright, tears on his high cheeks. "Alonùradth," he said again, this time a ragged whisper, and he stumbled on and disappeared among the shifting shadows.

Aranloth kicked the roan into a gallop, and they sped down ancient streets where the past walked in the world of the present.

It felt to Lanrik as though the night would never end, but eventually they made it to the Halathrin road and dawn came. They plodded forward without pause, for they knew Mecklar would not have given up the pursuit. He had been stymied, but only temporarily.

Yet they could not continue without rest indefinitely, and at midmorning, they stopped at the wooded crest of a down that had a long view of the road behind them. There they sat and ate a cold meal.

"We could try to lose them," Lanrik said. "It would be difficult though. There are few trails that Gwalchmur couldn't follow, and it would cost us time."

"Too much time," Aranloth said. "We have swift horses and the road is good. Our best chance is to stay on it and travel fast. Anyway, once we reach Enorìen the influence of the Guardian will prevent pursuit. No one enters the hills without permission."

"Are you sure?" asked Erlissa.

"It's my belief," Aranloth said shortly. "We'll find out for certain when we get there."

"And when we leave Enorìen?' asked Lanrik.

"No doubt they'll be waiting for us, but they won't know where to start the chase. That will slow them down but the power of Ebona is in them. I think they'll find us. We'll need to be rested and prepared. For now, however, I have to sleep."

The lòhren lay down in the shade cast by a stand of hazels, and it seemed as though he slept instantly.

"Last night still troubles him," Erlissa said. "The lòhrengai he used was dangerous, and he's not as he was. He has a depth of compassion that I've seen in few people, and the fall of the city weighed on him. He felt it in his heart as though he were there. He *was* there."

"Who actually is Ebona?" asked Lanrik.

"She's the witch in the woods. I know little about her except that she holds great power and is something from Esgallien's past. To be honest, I thought her nothing more than a story, but Aranloth obviously knows better."

Lanrik knew they should set a watch but it was impossible. They were all weary and had to sleep. He lay down and Erlissa did likewise. He realized a little later that her words about lòhrengai could be taken two ways. Had she meant that it made things real for Aranloth, or had she suggested that he was actually present? Nothing except the immortal Halathrin lived that long though, regardless of the legends.

He woke a little later. He was not refreshed but some strength had returned. Erlissa was speaking animatedly, perhaps even arguing with Aranloth near the hazels, but he was pleased to note the lòhren had regained color and energy.

The two of them came over. "We must leave soon," the lòhren said. "Ebona's influence on Mecklar and Gwalchmur will soon be apparent. She'll extend her power through them, and it may be that I cannot always contend with it. We were lucky with the hounds, but may not be so again. Erlissa will be targeted, for without her there's no hope for Lòrenta. Ebona will have perceived that, if not the very nature of our quest, but steel is no match for ùhrengai."

"Steel is all I have," Lanrik said.

"You have courage, also."

"It wasn't enough against the hound. It would have killed me if not for Erlissa and the lòhren-fire."

"If you would have more than steel and courage, draw the shazrahad sword."

Lanrik hesitated, then did so. The pattern-welded blade glimmered in the air.

"The sword is steeped in history and prophecy. I don't want to add to that, for lòhrengai can have unexpected results, and already too much rests on the blade. Yet, if you wish it, I will. I can infuse it with power."

"What do you mean by unexpected results?" asked Lanrik.

Erlissa interrupted. "Don't even think about it, Lan. He means it's dangerous."

"You saw what happened with the hounds," he said. "I merely slowed one of them. It could easily have killed me, or you. I can't risk that again."

Erlissa turned to the lòhren. "Don't do it."

Aranloth looked at her kindly but shook his head. "I do, as always, what I must. The danger Ebona poses is more than a man can deal with, however courageous. And she will seek to separate me from both of you. It's for him to choose."

The lòhren spoke once more to Lanrik. "If I infuse the blade with lòhrengai it will give you some defense against ùhrengai, and elùgai too, which may be needed before the end. There is risk, but I would not offer to act if I thought it too great."

Aranloth looked at him intently. "Understand this. With lòhrengai, nothing comes from nothing. It may infuse the sword, but it must draw force from somewhere. You will be its source – your courage, mind and spirit. It will draw on your strengths and weaknesses alike, and you must be careful. The choice is yours."

Lanrik thought quickly. There was obviously risk, even if he did not understand it fully, but the benefits were necessary. The hounds would have killed Erlissa, and he had a feeling her life would be threatened again.

"Do it," he said.

Erlissa turned away, and Aranloth looked him in the eyes. "Hold the blade out and keep steady. Whatever happens, don't let go."

Surprisingly, the lòhren laid his staff on the ground and traced his fingers along the sword, across script, blade and edge.

Light glowed at his fingertips. It strengthened until white flame burned on the blade wherever his fingers passed. The pattern-welded metal shimmered more than usual, and lights were trapped within the blade like fish swimming beneath the surface of a lake. They moved of their own accord.

The flame intensified. The script flared, bursting into argent light. Aranloth clamped his palms against each side of the sword's tip, and flame roared to life. Lanrik could feel it in the blade like a living thing. It filled it until bursting, and then it surged up the hilt and into his hands.

He nearly let go, but the flame did not hurt. He tightened his grip, and white tongues ran up his arms, to his shoulders and neck, and engulfed his head. He could see and hear nothing. All he could feel was lòhrengai. It tugged at him, pushed at him and entered his mind. It roared inside until he could no longer think.

The lòhrengai faded then retreated down his arms and back into the blade. The light flickered and was gone. But Lanrik still felt its presence.

"It is done," Aranloth said solemnly. "For good or for ill."

Lanrik sheathed the blade. He felt strange; not unwell, but somehow different. The feeling faded swiftly though, and by the time they mounted and rode it was gone.

He did not regret what he had done. He would do anything for Erlissa and pay whatever price was asked. But he knew that the power of the sword would be a reflection of his mind. His desire to protect Erlissa was good, and he cherished the Raithlin code, yet he had other thoughts as well. He burned to finish his fight with Mecklar, and irrespective of the Raithlin code, he must fulfil his promise to Lathmai. Gwalchmur had to die. How would those things shape the power of the sword, and in turn, affect him?

15. The Eye of the Storm

The man was called Lonfar. It was not his birth name.

He dragged his gaze from the book he was reading to the banging on his door. He was a librarian who wanted quietude, but his past was violent. Although these days his hand was accustomed to a writing quill, it had once hefted naked steel. And though he had come free willed to Lòrenta, it was a prison, for elsewhere his life was forfeit.

"Come in," he said.

His acquiescence was redundant. The door jerked open even as he spoke.

One of the students hurried into the room, but flustered by the urgency of what she had to say struggled to speak.

Lonfar encouraged her. "What is it, Carèthlath?"

Like him, a Halathrin name had been given to her.

She composed herself. "Lòhren Aratar is at the gate-tower and wants to see you."

He thought she was finished, but with a rush she delivered the important part of her message. "An elùgroth has come!"

Lonfar slowly closed his book. Carèthlath was wide-eyed with excitement, but all he felt was fear. It was best not to show it though. Neither she nor the other students were ready for what he knew about elùgroths.

"Did Aratar say why he wants me?"

The girl, struck silent once more, shook her head vigorously.

The lòhren might not have told her, but Lonfar could guess what they would ask of him.

He sighed and dismissed her. She turned on her heels and dashed through the door; no doubt to seek out her friends and tell them about her adventure.

He left the room a few moments later. It was small and sparsely furnished, but it was his home now, and he liked it. His duties as librarian were not onerous and left him time for study. He spent many hours just reading and forgetting his old life.

Lòrenta's library overwhelmed him with choice, and at first, he did not know what to read. He had followed his inclinations though, first studying his own nation, and then the wider expanse of Alithoras and the history of its lands and peoples.

He strode through the library. Lore was gathered here that would stagger the most learned in Alithoras, and a lifetime of study would not encompass a hundredth part of it. There were histories of realms that had long since ceased to exist or been transformed by the chances of time; there were treatises on the diseases of livestock and their effective treatments as well as discourses on topics as variable as the habits of nudaluk birds or the building of ships. Nothing was too grand or too small for the lòhrens' thirst for knowledge. All life, learning and history was precious to them, and the body of lore constantly expanded for they frequently returned from many lands to record their experiences.

He walked down a long corridor that had aisle after aisle running off it, each containing innumerable shelves laden with closely-packed books and scrolls. It was only one of many; the Halls of Lore were massive.

Lòrenta was a fortress, walled and many-towered, though ùhrengai rather than soldiers guarded it, and its ramparts were symbolic rather than practical. The stronghold represented the lòhrens' undertaking to protect knowledge and defend the people of Alithoras.

The walls were rendered with white marble, and the slender towers pierced the air. The battlements were both high and deep, but it was the ùhrengai that would repel any sorcerous attack. He doubted the elùgroth intended such a thing, though his purpose would nevertheless be malevolent.

He exited the library and entered the great courtyard at the heart of the fortress. Trees, gardens and soft-grassed lawns covered it; sunlight streamed down from the square of open sky high above. Students, many of them otherwise homeless or orphaned, sat on the ground or on wooden benches discoursing with their teachers. These were often not lòhrens but former students who excelled at their own studies.

He reached the middle of the courtyard and stopped momentarily to observe the fountain that dominated it. It was constructed of white granite, and the centerpiece of the basin was a tall statue of a lòhren. The figure thrust his staff in the air, and water shot out its end before falling in a frothy cascade over his shoulders and splashing into the pool.

This was one of Lonfar's favorite places. It was calm, and tranquility seemed to settle everywhere with the gentle mist of water that wafted from the fountain. Ringing it were white benches where the lòhrens often met, even sometimes the Lòhrenin itself when its members were recalled from abroad.

It was at this very spot that Aranloth had offered him a permanent role in their community. It was here that he had renounced his old life and turned to the new. He had found a friend here, and the serenity he often lacked elsewhere that caused him to say what should not be said. Aranloth called it the Eye of the Storm, for deep in the earth whence the water sprang was also the source of the ùhrengai that protected Lòrenta. When provoked, it could wreak destruction on enemies outside the fortress, but within it emanated harmony.

With regret, he continued across the courtyard until he entered the fortress's corridors again. As elsewhere, they were wide and well lit by many windows, and he walked them for what seemed a long time. The distance to the gate-tower did not worry him; he was not a young man anymore, but he retained the fitness of his youth, and he could walk from sunup to sundown. He hoped some of his other talents remained too: he would need them.

He eventually came to the tower and climbed its spiral stairway. At the open aired top, he found Aratar and the other half dozen lòhrens currently resident in the fortress. In winter there would be many more, but during summer they were dispersed to the far reaches of Alithoras.

They turned and looked at him but did not speak. He sensed their unease and broke the silence himself.

"I understand an elùgroth has come?"

Aratar pointed a long and bony arm over the battlements. "See for yourself."

Lonfar stepped close and looked over the stonework. Hills surrounded the fortress; the higher slopes were moorland covered with ling and bracken while a scattering of stunted trees and dwarf shrubs hunkered low to the ground. He spotted several kestrels that hovered and wheeled, their keen eyes seeking the movement of mice or voles.

He drew his gaze nearer and saw the elùgroth. A large birch wood covered the lower land in front of the fortress. The sorcerer stood outside its eaves, his black cloak in stark contrast with the silver-white trunks of the trees. He was not trying to hide; he merely waited.

Lonfar knew what would happen next, and he took a few moments to compose himself. His gaze wandered to the moorland, and he sought the peace that he had often found exploring those lonely slopes. The ling was not yet in flower, though when it commenced later in summer the hills would blaze with purple. In autumn, deer would begin the rut, and the roaring of stags would carry across the wastes. The soil, shallow and acidic, promoted little growth except for the ling, and on lower slopes birch trees.

Fog often blanketed the wild hills, and they were perilous to traverse because of the many waterfalls, crags and deep tarns.

As much as he tried, he could not find the tranquility he sought. Memory alone did not serve, and he turned his attention back to the elùgroth. The sorcerer was motionless. He gave no sign and made no aggressive move, but the malice in him buffeted the fortress in waves. This was not any elùgroth, but one of their masters. He was adept in lore that would crush the soul of an ordinary man.

If they wished to find out what he wanted, someone would have to leave Lòrenta and speak to him.

Lonfar knew the lòhrens would ask him to do it, and he did not blame them. He had no lòhrengai and could not defend himself; but likewise he was not a threat, and in that manner a fight might be avoided. Also, they would want him to check if there were others, a task for which he was better suited. After all, he had the skills of a Raithlin. He had renounced his old life for good reason, but it seemed fate was determined to thrust it back at him.

"Do you want me to talk to him?"

"Yes," Aratar said. "You're the logical choice."

"And if he attacks?"

"We don't think he will. We're mindful that you've sworn an oath never to draw a blade again – but we ask what we must. No one here will think worse of you should you be forced to try and defend yourself."

Lonfar looked at the old men around him. They were kindly people and uncomfortable with what they were doing. He did not suppose Aranloth would have asked it of him. Or would he? Necessity was a hard taskmaster.

Aratar was waiting patiently for a response. He looked at him serenely from bright eyes below the diadem that all lòhrens wore.

"I'll do it."

The old man nodded, and Lonfar sensed a release of tension in the others.

"Come around from behind him," Aratar said. "We want to know if there are others."

"How long has he been there? Lonfar asked.

"He was first seen at dawn and hasn't moved since. You'll have time to scout; we don't think he'll go anywhere until he's said what he's come for."

Lonfar nodded in agreement and turned to walk back the way he had come.

"Good luck," Aratar said.

Flashing the lòhren a tight grin, he descended the stairs. He returned to his room and pulled out a pine chest stored under his bed, then opened it.

On top was his Raithlin cloak, neatly folded but worn and travel stained. The trotting fox stitched into its breast brought back memories, but he pushed them aside. Now was not a time for reverie.

Underneath the cloak lay a polished aurochs horn. It was old, a family heirloom that had passed through the hands of generations. It reminded him of the wild spaces of Galenthern that he loved and yearned for. Perhaps that was why he liked the moors so much. They were both wild and free places where a man felt infinitesimally small and yet an integral part of things.

He put the horn aside; it would serve no purpose in his mission. What he needed was his sword. It lay beside its sheath, untouched since the day he had entered these walls, but coated with oil and rust free.

He reached for it, took hold of its hilt, and paused.

It felt good in his hand, and he might need it, but what he needed most was diplomacy. He would have to ensure he said nothing to provoke the elùgroth, but that was his weak point; that was why Aranloth had brought him here in the first place. He had a habit of saying what he thought, and it had always got him in trouble. His words to

Murhain were the worst though. They had put a price on his head. And the price remained. Assassins were still looking for him. They had found him often enough, and he was tired of the killing. Aranloth's suggestion to come to Lòrenta and leave the name of Conrik behind had been good.

The sword was part of his old life. It had always come to his hand as easily as cutting words to his mouth. Either could get him in trouble. But the sword had spilled blood, killed people, and he had no wish to do that again. He had sworn to end the days of his fighting, and he would keep that promise.

He threw back the blade with a clatter and slammed down the lid of the chest. He would not carry it again, no matter that the lòhrens approved. They might not judge him, but he would judge himself. It was stupid to face an elùgroth without it, even if its usefulness against a sorcerer was doubtful, but he had made his oath for good reason, and it was a promise to himself that he would not break.

He put on the Raithlin cloak and left the fortress through a rear entrance and skirted the birch wood. Moving with slow purpose, he studied the terrain as he walked. He chose the route of maximum cover and watched the ground with care, looking for spoor.

For a long while, he found nothing but the pear-shaped tracks of foxes and traces of the shy but ubiquitous deer that roamed the hills. A fog rolled down from the moors and swept over the wood. He came to rocky ground and a mist-topped tarn, its water dark and still. The periphery was thick with reeds and swathes of bracken that dripped with dew, and it was here that he discovered the elùgroth's tracks. The heel imprint of his left boot, marked with a drùgluck sign to warn people against following, was clear. The tracks were well spaced, the paces of a tall man who stepped with purpose and made no effort to conceal himself.

183

He traced them back for some half an hour, looking to see if others had come with him and split away before reaching the wood. He found nothing. The sorcerer was alone, and now he must face up to his hardest task: to speak with him and discover what he wanted.

He retraced his steps to the birch wood. Entering it, he walked easily and quickly. The wood was open, far more so than the woods of Esgallien, and though it provided cover he chose not to use it. He did not wish to surprise the sorcerer; that could lead to a misunderstanding and would be a mistake. Instead, he sang a song with a rousing chorus that was once popular in Esgallien's less reputable taverns and boldly declared his presence.

As he approached the end of the wood, he caught blazing glimpses of Lòrenta's white walls through gaps in the timber. He walked wide of where he had earlier seen the elùgroth and came out into the open before he swung around toward him.

He was still there. The lòhrens, mere figures in the distance, watched from their high vantage on top of the gate-tower. He could sense their anticipation. He fancied he could also feel their relief that it was not them out here. He did not blame them; this was a high-ranking elùgroth, likely beyond even their combined power, and their logic that he had the greatest chance of survival, though unfortunate for him, was impeccable.

It was unlikely the elùgroth had come to attack them though. Lòrenta's defenses would render an assault against the fortress futile, and there would be little to gain from killing an ordinary man outside its walls. Nevertheless, the skin along his spine grew cold and tight while his palms dampened with sweat.

He breathed deeply and tried to calm himself by logically working through the situation. The pivotal question was why the elùgroth had come. He could not think of a specific reason but knew his purpose was malevolent. Whatever the sorcerer said he must keep his reaction to it unemotional and give nothing away about what he thought. His job would be to listen carefully and pass on any message for the lòhrens.

The elùgroth was unnaturally motionless. He was a towering figure, seven feet tall, though some of that was attributable to his knee-length boots. They were iron-shod and midnight black, as were his robes. His head was deeply cowled, and his face obscured; only his hands showed where they gripped a dark and supple wych-wood staff. They were bone white and blue-veined.

Lonfar halted ten paces away. That was close enough.

The sorcerer's body did not move, but the cowled head pivoted toward him with purpose, and he felt the pressure of a chill gaze from the shadowed face. When the figure spoke, his voice was remote like the rumble of slow thunder on Galenthern and cold as storm-driven rain.

"They sent a servant?"

The elùgroth leaned slightly forward and scrutinized him. The skin of his face became visible; it was pallid and bloated but the eyes remained hidden.

"Perhaps I should kill you to demonstrate my displeasure?"

Lonfar felt a sudden rush of temper but held it in check. *Pompous fool.*

"That would let the lòhrens know what you think. The only problem is that afterwards they wouldn't send anyone else."

"Are they cowards that they come not themselves?"

Lonfar shrugged. "Does it matter? None of this brings us to the point."

The elùgroth's expression sharpened, and Lonfar understood why people sometimes fainted in their presence. But he could play games as well as anyone and looked where the eyes would be and waited silently.

185

The elùgroth laughed, low and cold like the grinding of river ice in the spring thaw.

"I will not kill you. I, Elù-Randùr, shall give you simple words to repeat to your masters instead . . . if you can remember them."

Lonfar's temper got the better of him, and he replied with sarcasm. "I'll try my best. If I forget, I'll improvise."

Elù-Randùr was still and silent for so long that Lonfar feared he had gone too far. He gave a slight shrug. He would treat the elùgroth the same as anybody else and damn the consequences. His hand itched for a sword hilt though.

"You have an insolent tongue."

"I've heard that before. But the sooner you give me your message the sooner you're rid of me."

The elùgroth raised the wych-wood staff in his left hand and levelled it at him. Blue veins ran spider-like up his pallid forearms, but the muscles underneath were hard as iron bundles.

"My message is this," the elùgroth said. "Listen carefully, for I shall only say it once."

Elù-Randùr spoke briefly and explained what he wished the lòhrens to know. When he finished Lonfar backed away. His mind reeled as he turned and walked to the fortress. He listened for any sound behind him indicating treachery, but if the elùgroth was going to kill him he would already have done so.

Each step that brought him closer to the lòhrens became harder for he bore a burden that weighed him down. What he had learned could be a ruse, but he did not think so. He had heard both satisfaction and expectation in the elùgroth's voice, and he was convinced.

He reached the portcullis, and it lifted smoothly allowing him admittance. The lòhrens had come down from the tower, anxious with curiosity, but he dreaded to relieve it. The metal grid dropped behind him with a mighty clamor.

"Well?" Aratar said.

"The elùgroth is alone."

"What did he say?" asked one of the others.

Lonfar answered with reluctance. "Lòrenta, the elùgroth told me, will soon be ruined. He offers us a choice. If we give him control of the ùhrengai that protects it, he will permit us to leave safely. Stay, and we will be sent to oblivion."

The lòhrens were confused and spoke all at once.

"He can't be serious," said one.

"The fortress is impenetrable," said another.

Aratar seemed less sure and wanted more information. "Did he say anything else?"

"He knew you would doubt him. He acknowledges the fortress cannot be destroyed, but he claims it can be forced into the spirit word. They have discovered a way to use a Morleth Stone to do so. Our choice is to yield Lòrenta, and all that is in it, or face doom when he is joined by others of his kind."

The lòhrens fell into debate. Some thought it was a bluff; others, chief among them Aratar, thought it might be possible.

Lonfar had no doubt. The enemy had devised a way to get around the defensive ùhrengai. He did not need to understand the whys and wherefores to appreciate the fact. In the end, the lòhrens could not risk anything other than to work on the basis that it was true and choose a response accordingly. Should they hand over the fortress and save the children, or should they hold fast?

He had already made up his mind. Ultimately, the decision rested with Aratar though. He was the highest authority in the fortress. He had a brilliant mind and was a strong-willed man, but Lonfar worried about the trusting side of his nature.

16. Light of the Half Moon

Lanrik was weary beyond exhaustion. His eyes were dry and gritty from lack of sleep, and he shifted continuously in his saddle to find a more comfortable position. But he could not rest, for time was running out. They had ridden hard and slept little for the two days that it had taken them to reach Enorìen. The mistletoe berries must be harvested tonight: the next half moon would be too late.

The rolling hills in front of them were overgrown with dense forest. The angle of the afternoon sun turned the hillcrests yellow-green and the valleys below into pools of shadow. The land seemed wild and impenetrable, yet Aranloth assured them it could be traveled.

The gently sloping downlands lay behind. They had not sighted Mecklar and his followers until this morning when they saw distant riders. After they left the road and struck southeast toward Enorìen, the riders followed suit.

Lanrik was tempted to wait for them. He had scores to settle and promises to keep, but he controlled the sudden urge. Aranloth and Erlissa needed him.

They entered the forest and he sensed something different about it. Unlike the small woods that he was used to, it was vast and old. He saw no tracks of people or livestock, no sign of timber-cutters or hunters. They were in a land that was remote and untouched by man.

Erlissa looked about her with wonder. She was sensing something that he did not feel himself. She was more sensitive than he was, perhaps because she was a woman, or maybe because of her instincts as a Seeker. She always seemed to know how he felt too, and when he needed help. He wished he could do the same for her.

Aranloth found paths where at first there did not seem to be any and brought them to forest glades and open tracts where they could ride with speed. The afternoon grew old, and in a clearing with short green grass they came across a small group of deer. Though they had ridden with noise, and their scent would have drifted ahead on the wind, the animals merely watched them, heads held high and ears pricked. They had never been hunted or learned to fear man.

Lanrik noticed Erlissa looking at him with shining eyes and a bright grin. She appeared very young, too young for someone who had endured what she had, but her joy of life and the wellspring of her kindness seemed unlimited. She was remarkable and heartbreakingly beautiful.

He remembered her words in the ruined tower of Haladhon. *You and I will* always *be friends. No matter what.*

The friendship of a woman like her was irreplaceable. Would there ever be more though? He had feelings for her and they were growing. He recognized that trying to save Lòrenta, and his uncle, were not his only reasons for coming on this journey.

How did she feel? She had called him a friend, but could she see him as something more? A lot stood between them, not least an opposed attitude on how to live life, but he wondered if any of that mattered.

Aranloth slowed and dismounted near a massive oak that dominated the clearing and the deer picked their way into the cover of nearby trees.

"Why are we stopping?" asked Erlissa.

Aranloth handed her the reins to the roan. "The Guardian will have sensed our presence when we crossed into Enorìen, and it's unwise to travel too far into the hills without performing a special ritual. It's the lòhrens way of seeking permission."

Lanrik glanced behind him. "How long will it take? Mecklar and his followers can't be far away."

The lòhren gestured dismissively. "Mecklar is no longer our greatest threat. Men aren't kept out of Enorìen by its reputation alone. The Guardian is all-powerful in this land and will come to us soon."

He walked to the oak and touched its gnarled trunk before gripping his staff with both hands. He stood very still, and the diadem on his brow gleamed within the deep shadows of the leaf canopy. He lifted the staff slowly, one end pointed to the sky and the other earthward.

He struck the tip with sudden force into the leaf mold and lòhren-fire ran along the staff's length. Once more he raised it, then struck again with greater power. Fire flared to life from both ends; it speared deep into the earth and spumed upward. Slowly he lifted it again, then slammed it against the ground.

The earth rumbled and lòhren-fire traced millions of oak roots. The dark soil glowed and power surged up through the tree. It flowed through trunk, branch and twig. Each leaf shivered and then flashed with brilliant light. It flickered out as quick as it came and left the whole tree astir as though caught in a breeze, but not a single leaf fell.

Aranloth came back to them. "It is done," he said formally.

"What now?" asked Lanrik.

The lòhren took back the roan's reins from Erlissa. "The Guardian will come and give us the permission we need, though some sort of bargain will be involved. We cannot wait here though. Darkness is coming and we must be in the oak grove by midnight."

He mounted and led the way again, picking a path uncannily through the tangled growth.

Lanrik noticed that the lòhren was right. Darkness was coming. Already it was dim in the forest and travel would soon be harder. What worried him most though was

Aranloth's statement that a bargain with the Guardian must be struck.

They did not stop to eat or rest. They maintained a steady pace even when darkness fell and the forest woke to life all about them. There were weird grunts and barks, screeches and hoots, and there were thumps and unidentifiable noises that came from near and far. It was not a place that Lanrik would have liked to travel by himself, but Aranloth seemed to know where he was going and Erlissa enjoyed it. As long as he was with her, he did not really mind where he was.

He had begun to think that they would have to dismount and lead the horses by hand when the forest opened. They were deep and high in Enorien now; the hills had become steeper, and rocky outcrops regularly broke the ground. The stars glittered through the canopy, and the half moon would soon rise above the skyline. When it did, their time would swiftly run out.

Aranloth stopped and dismounted. "The Guardian has come," he said.

Lanrik and Erlissa secured their horses before standing beside him. A massive hill bulked in the dim light to their left. To their right was another, not as large, but covered with boulders and tangled scrub. Between the two ran a narrow cleft and a path hemmed by trees. It led downward, but he could not see far in the darkness.

He watched and waited for a long time before a figure came into sight. It strode down the right hand hill with the easy gait of someone who walked all day. There was confidence and purpose in their bearing as well as surety of power.

The Guardian swiftly approached and stood before them.

Lanrik had kept an open mind about what to expect, but he was still surprised. That the Guardian was female was likely enough, but that she was not human took him aback. It hit him suddenly that he had left his homeland, the Raithlin, and all that was familiar behind. He was groping about in a world of lòhrens, dark sorcery, enchanted swords and creatures of whom he knew nothing.

The Guardian had a disquieting presence. There was authority in her posture, the tilt of her head, and the broodiness of her dark glance beneath coarse eyebrows.

Her eyes were deep pits, but the starlight revealed them as nut brown. So too was her skin, though it was paler and tinged leaf-green. Her long hair spilled over broad shoulders in wild cascades like a dark waterfall, and her limbs and body were slick with taut muscle. When she bent her glance upon him he felt her power. In this land she ruled; all things bowed to her will or were broken. And yet there was a hint of shyness about her too, something of the wild animal.

She turned her eyes to Aranloth. "Long has it been since last you came, even by the reckoning of my kind. Yet ever you want something, and it will be no different now. Speak!"

Aranloth showed no offence at her abruptness. "I do as I must, Carnona."

She flashed him an unexpected grin. Her teeth were very white and her deep eyes glittered.

"Few use my old name. It is good to hear it."

Her smile came and went swiftly, and Lanrik realized she could change mood in a heartbeat.

"What do you want?" she said.

"Lòrenta is in danger and—"

"I care nothing for Lòrenta or the affairs of lòhrens," she interrupted. "Tell me your request and I will consider it. That is all."

Aranloth was unperturbed. "Very well. I need three berries; three fruit of the mistletoe that grows in the oak groves and waxes ripe under the summer half moon."

193

Carnona eyed him for a long time without speaking.

"There are such groves of oak and such berries as you seek. Yet they are potent. Do you understand their power?"

"Yes."

She studied him again. She was like a hawk that cocked its head and searched for food.

"Why should I let you take ùhrengai from my land?"

"Because I need it."

Carnona laughed and the sound was like the bark of a wild animal. "As good an answer as any. And what of Ebona? I sense her influence in Enorìen. Does she also covet the berries?"

"No. She wishes to obstruct me."

Carnona folded her arms. Fat thumbs pressed and twitched against the bulge of her muscles while she contemplated the situation silently.

Lanrik noticed that Erlissa fidgeted next to him and he too was alive with strain. He had not realized that so much depended on the will of the Guardian or that success or failure was under her sway.

Aranloth, who had most to lose, was surprisingly calm. He leaned on his staff in the casual posture he often adopted, but Lanrik was not fooled. Just as the lòhren made no outward show of power, he was adept at veiling his emotions during a crisis. Erlissa had said that he was a man who felt deep compassion for others, and Lanrik believed it. Irrespective of his appearance he would be thinking of the people in Lòrenta and the consequences should he fail them

Carnona reached a decision.

"I will allow you to harvest the berries."

Aranloth nodded gravely and waited. Lanrik's relief at the Guardian's answer was washed away when she went on.

"But a price must be paid."

"That is expected," the lòhren said. "What do you wish of me?"

"It is not only you who must pay." She pointed toward Lanrik and Erlissa. "So too must they."

Aranloth straightened. "These are merely my companions, Carnona. They have nothing to do with our bargain."

The Guardian went rigid; her muscles trembled like a horse whose flesh shivered at a strange touch.

"They have everything to do with it."

"I will do what you require of me," Aranloth said, "but they have only come because of me."

"Do you not seek *three* berries? And will your companions not use the land's ùhrengai, just as you will?"

Aranloth was still for a moment. "It is as you say, but— "

Erlissa interrupted him. "What Carnona says is fair, Aranloth. If there must be a price, I am willing to pay it, if I can."

Carnona flashed her a sudden grin from bright teeth, but by the time her glance flickered to Lanrik it was gone. She looked at him intently, and he felt the strength and authority of her gaze. She was queen of this land, and no other power, even lòhrengai, held sway.

Lanrik was overcome with doubt, but Erlissa had shown him the way. "I too will do as I must."

Carnona studied him for a few moments then turned her back on them all and walked away.

"Follow!" she commanded. "I will consider the prices as I lead you to the nearest grove."

"What of Ebona's servants?" Aranloth asked.

"My sister and I strive toward different goals. She had her own realm. Her presence in mine is neither needed nor wanted, and those who bear her mark will be cast out."

Carnona strode ahead and they led the horses after her. The Guardian was short, but she took them swiftly to the steep trail that descended the cleft between hills. They were forced along a path that snaked between rocky outcrops, but she gracefully gathered herself and leapt from stone to stone as delicately as a deer that picked its way between tree trunks.

The trees grew close together and blotted out the starlight. It was still and quiet. Lanrik wondered if they were the first people to tread this path. Lòhrens might have been to Enorien before, but certainly not often, and he doubted they had explored even a fraction of it. A thrill of excitement ran through him, and he walked with eagerness. His eyes were alive to each new plant or tree that loomed in the dim light. At the same time, a deep-seated anxiety gnawed at him. What price would Carnona demand?

The night wore on. Shadows and trees closed about them as they passed deep into the cleft. Lanrik wondered if even during the day sunlight filtered into this remote valley.

It was oddly silent. Nothing moved or drew breath here except them. There were only trees; oaks so old that they might have seen the first dawn of Alithoras.

There was something about the vale that made Lanrik nervous, a feeling that humans were not meant to defile it, and only the presence of Carnona, the embodiment of the land itself, protected them.

Who was she? *What* was she? And what was the history between her and Ebona? He understood little of what was happening but began to be aware that there were powers in the world to which men were oblivious. Nevertheless, they were at work and shaped the land and its life in ways he could not grasp.

The steep descent into the cleft slowed and stopped. It was not so much a valley as an opening through a long ridge of high hills. Oaks rose all about them, mountainous trees bigger than he had ever seen. Their trunks were so large that a dozen men joined hand to hand would scarcely encircle them. Huge boughs weighted with the growth of countless years drooped to the ground. Carnona came to a halt. Her feet sank deep into the earthy remnant of ancient leaves, and she lifted her arms, stiff like tree branches.

"We are come to a sacred place. Few men have walked Enorìen, and none has seen this grove. Here, ùhrengai is strong. It courses deep below the earth, and the tree roots tap it. It rises in their sap. It flows through their trunks into branch and twig. It glistens like dew on the leaves when the full moon waxes."

Her solemn voice took on a note of reverence as she pointed toward a branch.

"There is the mistletoe you seek. It is not of earth or air. It is green of leaf but not rooted in the ground. See how the berries shine in the starlight?"

Lanrik followed her gesture. The mistletoe, like a bird's nest in the oak's branches, had small berries that glowed palely in the shadows.

Carnona dropped her hand and spun to the lòhren. "I have considered the price. It shall be paid or you will not have the berries."

"What is it?"

"Each shall give according to their measure. You have walked the lands of Alithoras as I once did before the Halathrin came. I wandered far and wide before Man or Elug, Dweorh or Lethrin. I traveled the dry south and endured the cold north. I beheld the rain-drenched coasts to our east and the far westward cliffs where the sun sets in red glory. I walked all the land, and everywhere the ùhrengai was strong. Now it is weak. I would have things as they were in my youth. I would have trees again in the

197

southern mountains that are now called Graèglin Dennath."

Aranloth looked at her. "No one, not even a creature of ùhrengai, can recapture the past that is gone," he said gently. "It is the fate of all who live that they yearn for what they have lost."

Carnona barked her hard laugh. "Do you think me a fool? I know that, better even than the lòhrens, even the eldest of them. I do not seek to have what cannot be, yet trees can grow once more in those mountains, even if only in places where there lingers a remnant of the power that was. Such a place you must seek and plant the seeds I will give you. Even you might be surprised at their hardiness. They will not flourish, not while the shadow of the enemy gropes over the mountains and stretches to the north. Yet they will survive in readiness for a time when the shadow is no more and they can thrive."

Aranloth ran a hand through his hair. "Yet while the shadow holds sway in those mountains, it is perilous for such as me to walk them."

"And yet you have done so in the past."

Aranloth bowed his head gravely. "It is as you say. And I will pay your price."

Lanrik felt uneasy as the dark eyes of the Guardian turned on him. She studied him for some time, her gaze stripping bare his thoughts much as Aranloth had done at their first meeting. Carnona was different though. Aranloth had seen a vast store of humanity, the good and the bad, and he knew what people felt and why they did things. Carnona had no interest in people; she was only interested in how they could serve her purposes. He did not think she was bad, it was just her nature, but he sensed that not only would it be futile to try to deceive her, it would be deadly.

"You are marked by Alithoras," she said. "The sun and moon, heat and cold, day and night, the dry and the wet of the wild lands are stamped upon you."

Lanrik gave a nod of affirmation but did not speak. He noticed that her gaze lingered on the trotting fox motif of his cloak.

"You are a Raithlin." She stated it as fact rather than a question, but Lanrik answered.

"Yes."

"My price is this. You must teach your kind, the Raithlin yet to come, the love of the land that is in you."

Lanrik's spirits dropped. "I would if I could. But I cannot. Their long history of more than a thousand years has ended. They've been disbanded."

Carnona laughed. "A thousand years? What is that to me? If you had lived as long as I, you would see the future thrust forward like a shadow of the past. But the Raithlin will return in your time. If you can not believe that, it will be enough that you make the promise to pay my price should I be proved correct."

Lanrik looked to the lòhren, but Aranloth's eyes showed nothing of what he thought.

He turned to Carnona. "I will do it."

As suddenly as she had focused her attention on him she withdrew it and scrutinized Erlissa. A long time she looked at her, as if in doubt. Erlissa waited patiently, enduring the force of her attention dispassionately and seeming not to care what price would be asked. She would pay it if she could, otherwise she would not. Lanrik was getting to know her, though not as well as she knew him.

Carnona folded her arms once more and reached a decision. "A price must be paid, though you are not ready to fulfil it. I will accept this. You must return and speak with me again. At that time, I will tell you what I want."

"What if it's something that I won't do?"

"You will do it, I think." For the first time Carnona's gaze held a hint of compassion, and Lanrik wondered if he had misjudged her. "You would not now, but you will change before your journey with the lòhren is ended. It will be enough if you promise to return."

"Very well. Though how will I know when to do so?"

Carnona regarded her with dark eyes. "You will know. Follow your instincts and you will hear the call."

She turned away and toward the east. "It is time!"

Lanrik glanced at the horizon. The half moon was rising above a jagged line of distant hills. Shafts of moonlight stabbed through the canopy, and Carnona shivered at the caress of each silvery beam. Lanrik realized that the time to pick the berries was now, and it would last but moments.

17. All that I Desire

Aranloth dropped his staff and sprang toward the oak. He was an old man, but he moved with the quickness of youth. He leapt effortlessly onto one of the low-hanging boughs, gripped a higher branch with his arms, and swung his body up and over it.

He repeated the same action several times and was half-way up the tree in moments. Then, taking slow and precise steps, he walked along the branch until he reached the mistletoe.

The berries had responded to the rays of moonlight with a pulsing glow but were already starting to fade. Aranloth knelt, mindful of his balance and the long fall to the ground, and plucked three of them. He slipped them in a pocket while the light of the remainder diminished and finally blinked out.

He descended the tree with the same ease but less haste than he had used on the way up, and when he was close enough he jumped smoothly to the soft leaf mold below. He returned to the others, not even out of breath.

"Now we have a chance!" he said. "The elùgroths won't have everything their own way."

Carnona observed him with her nut-brown eyes. "They pose less threat to you at the moment than Ebona. Not lightly did her servants leave my domain. And they still wait for you without."

Aranloth ran a hand through his hair. "I'll deal with them if I must."

Carnona considered them all briefly. "We will meet again." Her gaze lingered on Erlissa. "For now, I have other tasks and you must rest. Sleep in the grove tonight, and do not leave it until the sun rises. Elsewhere, Enorìen is dangerous."

She looked at Aranloth. "When you wake in the morning you will find the seeds. They will last a long while – but plant them soon!"

Without waiting for an answer, she turned and strode away. The moonlight glistened on the dark shadow of her hair until she passed from view.

Erlissa let out a long breath. "So that was the Guardian."

"One of them," Aranloth said. "Our meeting could have been worse . . . they have little love for our kind."

Lanrik rubbed his eyes. "Her advice was good though. I feel like I haven't slept in weeks, and it's time to rest."

They shared some food and then got ready to sleep. It was difficult though. Not long after Carnona left, noise and movement commenced in the dim light at the edge of the grove.

After a while, a mighty stag came into view. His flared antlers were only part grown, and at times he gave a deep-throated roar even though it was not yet the rutting season.

An old and solitary aurochs bull moved in the half-shadows as well. His horns were swept forward, and he loosed shattering bellows from his enormous bulk. He used his front hooves to gauge deep scrapes in the ground and flung the loose earth behind him in fury.

A wickedly tusked boar came last of all, and he grunted in the darkness and thrashed his tusks against root and bush.

"Pay them no heed," Aranloth said.

He followed his own advice and fell asleep quickly. Lanrik and Erlissa found it harder, yet none of the beasts ventured into the grove, and Carnona's word was true. They were safe within it, and they slept, albeit fitfully.

The half moon sailed high overhead and faded at the arrival of a hushed and golden dawn.

When they woke, they were more refreshed than they expected to be. Carnona had returned through the night and silently left a small bark container near the lòhren's staff. Of the beasts, there was no sign.

The travelers retraced their steps through the cleft, and then headed out toward the fringes of Enorìen.

"What of Mecklar?" Lanrik asked the lòhren.

"He and his followers will be waiting, but whether they will try to find our trail or head us off is hard to say. Either way, Ebona will aid them, and we won't be able to hide for long."

They continued until dusk came. Aranloth led them to the northward edge of the hills.

"We'll camp here and in the morning strike toward where the Erenian River forks from the Carist Nien. Between the two is an island and a good place to cross."

Dawn of the next day found them leaving both hill and forest and riding across the open and flat lands between the two rivers.

Aranloth swept his arm in a wide arc. "The land in front of us is called the Angle," he said. "Near the fork itself the ground is sometimes flooded by one or both rivers."

They crossed the road that led around Enorìen and down to the coastal city of Camarelon. It was the same road that led back to Esgallien, and Lanrik had a sudden feeling as he passed beyond it that he was leaving his old life forever.

"Ahead and to the east are the cities of Menetuin and Faladir," Aranloth continued. "They were founded by tribes related to Conhain's people."

"I've heard of them," Lanrik said. "Esgallien trades with those places, but more so with Camarelon."

"Where's Cardoroth from here?" asked Erlissa.

"Red Cardoroth is much further north," the lòhren said. "It's near to Lake Alithorin. It too was founded during the great migration of people from the west. But we'll be veering to the left. One day you may both see those other cities, though you'll find none better than Esgallien."

They traveled on, and Lanrik warmed to the new lands that he was seeing and the names of places that were mere rumor to him, or better yet, never heard of like Cardoroth. He would like to see them one day. Aranloth knew so much, but he sometimes explained little. How had a city come to be called red?

There was no sign of pursuit, and several peaceful but tiring days passed. The land was deforested and fertile. People had lived here once, though there was no sign of them now except for hints of old roads and the many fruit trees seeded from ancient orchards.

Two nights out from Enorien, they established their camp and risked a fire. They used deadwood from a long fallen apple trunk and enjoyed the fragrant smoke as well as the warmth.

Aranloth took the first watch and woke Lanrik sometime before midnight. The lòhren settled behind him, and Erlissa remained asleep off to the side.

The fire gradually died to shimmering embers as the night passed, and a chill seeped into the air. Lanrik placed a branch on the coals and sparks suddenly flew. The fire flared, and a tongue of flame rose high in the air and twisted into a human figure.

Lanrik jumped back and drew his sword. He was going to yell to wake the others, but the blade was so reassuring in his hand that he felt himself equal to any challenge.

The flame-figure spoke, its voice soft and tenuous like a wisp of smoke.

"Why do you draw cold steel?"

The apparition made no threatening move, but Lanrik was unwilling to sheath his blade.

"Come closer," the voice asked. "Let me see you properly."

He took slow and careful steps with the sword-tip held high. He saw now that the flame-figure was a woman. He could not tell her age, which disturbed him, but she was tall and long haired and wore a white dress cinched with a red belt at the waist.

She tossed her hair and sparks flew. "Why so untrusting?"

"Who *are* you? And what do you want? Speak truthfully, and I'll trust you more."

The flame-figure peered at him closely. After a moment, she nodded.

"I think you have grown much in the last few weeks. But it is not so easy to discern truth from falsehood."

"Perhaps. But I'll judge as I can."

"Very well! I shall tell the truth!"

She pinned him with wide-set eyes that flashed fire. "I am Ebona. Some call me a witch. I suppose I am that, too, but once I was something else, someone of greater power. And I will be that again, and more."

Her breathing quickened as she spoke, and her chest rose and fell as the fire writhed about her.

"I see recognition in your eyes. The lòhren has spoken of me."

Lanrik took a pace back. "Do you deny that you sent Mecklar and the others to kill us?"

Ebona laughed, and sparks shot from her mouth. "I deny nothing! I bade my servants to kill you, yet even as we speak, I regret it. I am inclined to change my mind."

"Why would you do that?"

She leaned toward him. "Because of you."

"Me? What does that mean?"

"Are you always so modest? No! Do not answer. I can tell that you are, so I will say what you will not."

205

Ebona drew herself up. She looked regal; power was in her glance and beauty in her figure that made him tremble. She seemed the queen of the world.

"Are you not smarter, braver and more handsome than Mecklar? You have shown determination and resourcefulness beyond his reach. You have rare and valuable qualities, but what have they earned you? You have fled your homeland. The Raithlin are disbanded. And Mecklar, a lesser man, prospers."

Lanrik thought on her words and did not answer for a moment.

"He's done well. What of it?"

Ebona pursed her lips. "Are you always so direct? No matter! I am direct myself when it suits me. *What of it?* Simply this. Mecklar is under my influence. You, who are a better man, could achieve more. In truth, I do not think there is anything you could not achieve. As I have helped Mecklar, I could help you."

She looked at him, and her eyes were alight with emotion. "Would you like to return to Esgallien? I can make it so! Would you like the Raithlin reinstated? They can be! I can bend the king to my will, weak-minded fool that he is. He attained the position by birth, but he has not earned the right. You, who by your deeds have proven yourself, would make a better king. I, Ebona, could make it so!"

She raised herself even taller, and fire flashed from her eyes. Lanrik felt hot and sweat beaded his face.

"Do you doubt me?" she asked.

He shook his head.

"Then join me! Leave this business of Aranloth's behind you. He has dragged you into events that are of no concern to you. What are you doing here, a plaything for lòhrens when you could rule the lands of your birth . . . with me by your side?"

206

Her voice softened. "Would you like that, Lanrik? Does the prospect excite you?"

He wiped sweat from his forehead with the back of his hand. Suddenly swaying with dizziness, he gripped the sword more tightly. He had a sudden urge to leave the camp, to go back to Esgallien and find Ebona. If he did so he knew that they would become allies. And with power such as hers to help him, he could achieve anything. But something at the back of his mind worried him. *What would Erlissa say?*

He turned and looked at her. She was asleep; her dark hair was ruffled, and she rested her head carelessly in the crook of her arm. He knew what she would say, heard in his head the very tone of her voice. He felt a sudden and piercing love, sharper than steel and hotter than flame.

He shifted his gaze back to Ebona. She was waiting for him, her arms crossed against her chest, and thick thumbs pressed against her milk-white flesh.

"I have all that I desire," he said.

Ebona stood still for a few moments, and then stretched a long arm toward him.

"If you are not with me, you are against me. Would you make me an enemy? I do not wish to kill you, but I will if I must."

"I won't join you," he said.

"Then you will die!"

Ebona towered above him, and her eyes burned with fury. Fire twisted and spun around her, and sparks streamed into the sky.

Lanrik stepped back and heard a movement behind him.

Aranloth had sat up. "Do not fear," the lòhren said. "It's only Ebona's image, and it has no power in the camp. She is nothing but smoke and fire."

The lòhren did not look sleepy, and Lanrik wondered if he had been awake all along.

207

Ebona fixed Aranloth with fiery eyes. "No power? Once you made it so. But I endured. And now I am strong enough to take my revenge!"

The witch gathered herself, and then stepped out of the fire and into the camp.

Aranloth snatched up his staff and sprang between her and Erlissa.

"You surprise me," he said. "But your image still has no power."

Ebona paced like a stalking cat. "She must die, lòhren. It is my will, and it shall be accomplished."

Lanrik had heard enough. He lunged forward and thrust his sword into her, but it passed through harmlessly. He withdrew the blade and saw a flicker of firelight where there should have been a wound.

She spun on him. "Fool! I offered you everything. Now you shall have nothing! Did you think you could injure me with a sword?"

She turned her back on him and stepped toward Erlissa.

Aranloth raised his staff. "You cannot contend with me, Ebona. Not while you are so distant from your body. And not in this land where I am strong."

She smiled at him. "Are you really so sure, lòhren?"

Lanrik desperately wanted to do something, but he was at a loss. The witch took another step forward, and Aranloth looked as though he was about to bring lòhrengai to bear. If he was forced to do so, Erlissa could be hurt in the confrontation.

A thin tendril of smoke linked Ebona to the fire, and an idea occurred to him. Instead of attacking her, he slashed at it with his sword. She flinched but continued forward and the smoke rejoined.

Aranloth raised his staff higher, and white flame ran along its length. The diadem on his brow glittered, and his eyes narrowed with concentration.

Lanrik knew the smoke somehow connected Ebona to the fire. It was in it that she had first appeared and must be the key to her presence, but what use could he make of that knowledge?

The witch moved forward. Her arms lifted, and her fingers formed claws in the air.

Lanrik raced to the fire and kicked away the branch he had put in it earlier, and then dropped the sword and kneeled. He used his hands to frantically fling dirt over the flame.

The fire sputtered and went out. Ebona screamed and turned toward him. She flung out her long arms, but her image turned to smoke and drifted apart in the air.

Lanrik tried to stop himself from shaking. "Did I kill her?"

"No, but destroying her image will have caused her pain." Aranloth slowly lowered his staff. "If she was your enemy before, she is doubly so now."

Erlissa came to stand beside the lòhren. "What's going on?"

Lanrik told her what had happened.

"Could she really have hurt us?"

"I don't think she could have done anything," Aranloth said. "Her power has grown greatly since last I saw her though."

"What *is* the history between you?" Erlissa asked.

The lòhren shrugged. "Ebona was once a power in the world. She wished to maintain authority over the tribes that worshipped her, but Alithoras had other needs, and I broke her influence."

"When was that?" Lanrik asked.

"A long time ago," the lòhren said. "What matters now is that she has found us. I should be able to prevent her from entering our camp again, but she will soon put Mecklar and the others on our trail."

"There's nothing to be done about it tonight," Erlissa said. "We need rest, and so do the horses. I suggest you both get some sleep. I'll keep watch until dawn."

Lanrik knew she was right, and the lòhren's expression showed he was done talking, so he lay down and made himself comfortable. He ensured his sword was close to hand and drifted to sleep with his fingers curled around its hilt.

****

The next few days of travel passed without incident, and whatever steps Aranloth took to ward off Ebona worked. He was withdrawn and tired though, even more so than could be accounted for by the six days of hard riding since he had harvested the mistletoe berries.

The effort had been worth it, however. The fork where the River Erenian split from the Carist Nien was now before them, and they had crossed a great stretch of land that had separated them from Lòrenta.

Ahead, there was an immense escarpment. It was a steep ridgeline of ragged cliffs and stone buttresses, barren of vegetation except for dwarfed bushes that clung to life against wind and sun.

The two rivers were visible to either side. So too was the beginning of the Angle, and at its center where the rivers diverged was a great waterfall a quarter of a mile wide that cascaded over the escarpment with a roar and spume of white water.

Lanrik looked at Aranloth. "Are you *sure* there's a way to the top?"

"I know this land as you know Esgallien," the lòhren answered. "I've explored every nook and cranny, witnessed every splendor and danger, trod every path. There is a way."

They continued, and the two rivers hemmed them in. Each had their source from a lake below the waterfall that churned and frothed perpetually. At its center was an island, all shattered rock and tumbled boulder that was cluttered by flood-deposited driftwood. A many-arched bridge of ancient stone spanned the roiling water toward it.

Aranloth dismounted and hand-led the roan onto the bridge. Lanrik and Erlissa followed suit. It was wide enough for them to ride, but the roar and swirling spray from the waterfall made the horses skittish.

Lanrik looked closely at the slick stone beneath his feet. It was rutted and crumbled like the ruins in Alonin, and he guessed it had been constructed before the founding of Esgallien.

They reached the other side and stepped onto the island. His tracker's eyes noticed heel marks from a boot in the gravel, and he realized that someone had been here recently. The land was isolated, and he had a sudden idea who it must be.

He drew his sword. Even as the blade cleared its scabbard he saw two Royal Guards, weapons drawn, break from a pile of sun-bleached timber to his left. They raced toward Erlissa. At the same time, Mecklar and Gwalchmur emerged from behind broken statuary to the right and closed on Aranloth.

The shazrahad blade sang to him, and the urge to fulfil his promise to Lathmai raged to life. He would kill Gwalchmur for all the things he had done. He stepped toward his enemy and then halted, caught by indecision. *What about Erlissa?*

18. We who Mastered the World

Lanrik spun around and stepped between Erlissa and the guards who rushed toward her. He thought of his throwing knives but wanted to use the shazrahad sword. It leapt like a tongue of flame in his hand, and its power ran through him.

The first guard slashed wildly. Lanrik stepped back half a pace and allowed the blade to pass without attempting to block it. Just as its tip went by, he lunged and drove his sword into the soldier's unprotected armpit. The guard jerked away and staggered, then rolled to the ground and screamed. His part in the fight was over, though the wound would not kill quickly. Lanrik paid him no further heed and concentrated on his remaining opponent.

The second guard approached more warily. He wove the tip of his blade in figure eights, and Lanrik noticed he was allowing his defense to drop just a little too low. It was a ploy to encourage a high attack that he would be ready for, and practiced at countering.

Lanrik obliged and slashed toward his opponent's neck. The guard dropped to one knee and prepared to thrust upward, but Lanrik was already changing the direction of his stroke, and his blade hammered down. Its edge struck between helm and mail coat, and bright blood spurted from a severed neck artery.

Lanrik wasted no more thought on the guards. He turned, wild-eyed, toward his true enemies: Gwalchmur and Mecklar. But Aranloth had done something unexpected. He had used lòhrengai to gather the water spray that flurried across the island and hurled it at his attackers with concentrated force.

"Ride!" he yelled.

Erlissa mounted and followed the lòhren. The hooves of their horses clattered over the rocky ground, but Lanrik hesitated. The driving spray flew like daggers into their enemies. Mecklar struggled to stand while Gwalchmur turned and fled.

Erlissa drew level with Lanrik. "Ride!" she yelled.

He was caught by indecision once more. He must fulfil his promise to Lathmai: Gwalchmur must die, and Mecklar with him. But Erlissa was already riding away, perhaps into danger, and he had to help her. The warmth of the lòhrengai in the sword infused his body, but he slammed it home in its sheath. He followed Erlissa, suddenly cold to the marrow of his bones.

The island ran parallel to the waterfall, and it took them several minutes to reach its further end. When they did so Aranloth took them quickly onto another bridge that arched over the churning water. They crossed, and the howling wind of lòhrengai and water faltered, which allowed their enemies to mount and pursue them.

To the left of the bridge, the great falls thundered in their ears, and Aranloth urgently waved them on. Ahead, a steep ravine led to the top of the escarpment. It was hard to see through the spray of water that clouded its opening and the dark shadows of its interior. Yet, as their eyes adjusted, they saw it was narrow and treacherous with scree and unstable boulders. A ledge was cut into the buttressed cliffs on the left side, and Lanrik repressed a shudder at the thought of the climb ahead. It ran arrow-straight to the top of the escarpment above a deadly drop to the broken rocks below.

Aranloth reached the end of the bridge and dismounted.

"One at a time!" he yelled.

Lanrik let the lòhren and Erlissa go first. He walked slowly behind them and spoke calm words to his alar stallion. Words that he did not feel himself. He steadfastly refused to look at the ever-increasing drop to his right, and he hugged close to the wall. He forced himself on and was a little relieved as they progressed, for the overwhelming noise of the falls diminished as the rushing water passed out of sight behind the edge of the escarpment. Mecklar and Gwalchmur were coming into view though. They had reached the ledge and dismounted.

"They're following!" Lanrik cried.

Aranloth yelled over his shoulder. "Quickly! There's a place ahead where the ledge widens into a recess. We may have to turn and face them."

They moved on in a slow but deadly race. Their pursuers showed less care, or less fear for their lives, and gained.

To the right, on the cliffs of the opposite side of the ravine, was a series of giant carvings hundreds of feet high. Time and weather had blunted and cracked the images, but they were perhaps more powerful for the aura of antiquity upon them.

There were groups of farmers who worked together in unison to harvest wheat with sickle-shaped blades before they threshed the chaff from the grain. Some of the seed was stored in underground silos, and the rest ground to flour in stone querns turned by oxen.

Hunters with long spears, tall and aloof, left a village with their heads bent in the search for the spoor of game animals. There were miners with long-handled picks and shovels, smiths and masons, dancers and storytellers. And there were warriors too: hard looking men in leather armor with round shields and short swords. At the end of the long procession was what must have been a king and queen. They were stern and fearful to look upon, and there was an edge of cruelty in their stony glance. They wore no crowns; instead, great diadems encircled their brows.

Lanrik was amazed at the artisanship, and had never seen anything like it before. It was not as refined as the stonework in Esgallien, but the scale of the achievement was stupendous. It must have taken decades, even hundreds of years, to carve it all into the hard rock. And it would have been dangerous work too. Men must have sometimes fallen to their deaths on the jagged teeth of stone below, and he shuddered at the thought. He took his gaze away from the carvings and concentrated on looking ahead and just placing one foot in front of the other.

The ledge rose higher above the floor of the ravine, and his stomach churned with cold fear that seeped into his limbs. He was scared of heights, but Aranloth and Erlissa were not so afflicted. They drew ahead as the minutes passed and turned and waited for him when they reached the recess.

He was embarrassed when he got there.

"Sorry," he muttered. "I'm no good with heights."

Aranloth placed a hand on his shoulder. "Think nothing of it. I've met many brave men in my time. They all feared something. Only the stupid are without it."

The lòhren turned and intensely studied the wall of the ledge where it joined the recess.

Mecklar was not far away, and Gwalchmur was close behind him. Lanrik looked out beyond them both. He had a better view of things now. The Angle was visible between the two silver bands of river that formed its sides. Between was a green and fertile land that rose to a gentle-sloped hill near the middle. It seemed to him that there were buildings on it, all over its crest and far down its sides. They appeared toppled and broken, but it was too far away to be sure. He guessed that it was the city of the people who had built the ledge on which he now stood and carved the great figures opposite. He could not help but wonder what it was all for, and what had happened to them.

Mecklar and Gwalchmur were coming closer, and he drew the shazrahad sword. At last he would get the chance to kill his enemies and avenge Lathmai. Something about Mecklar disturbed him though. As he advanced, Lanrik had the momentary feeling that it was actually Ebona approaching. Her image seemed to flicker over Mecklar's features, and the king's counselor paused, a contorted expression on his face. Suddenly he stretched out a stiff arm, and blood-red fire spurted from his fingers toward Aranloth.

Lanrik had no time for thought. He lifted his sword and stepped in front of the distracted lòhren. The warmth of the blade filled him, and he no longer feared either falling or the enemy.

The streaking fire blinded him, but he felt it drawn to the blade and the lòhrengai within surge in response. Both powers gathered and roiled at the tip of the blade. He thrust it forward instinctively, and white flame shot through with red arced like a bolt of lightning at Mecklar.

The image of Ebona flung up an arm in defense, but Mecklar was nevertheless knocked off his feet and into Gwalchmur. They both went sprawling dangerously on the ledge.

"Back!" cried Aranloth.

Lanrik reluctantly retreated into the recess. The lòhren had decided what to do, and he raised his oaken staff and struck its tip into the stone overarching the path. Lòhrengai erupted, and with a groan and sudden crack the stone shattered, and Aranloth leapt back.

With a deep boom that echoed throughout the ravine a huge mass of rubble slid down. Some of it plummeted into the chasm and clattered far below, but the ledge was blocked.

Aranloth wiped stone dust from his face and looked at Lanrik.

"Thank you!" he said. "I knew Ebona's influence was growing on Mecklar, but I didn't expect that attack. If not for you, I might have been killed."

Lanrik grinned at him. "You saved me from the hounds of the otherworld. Let's call ourselves even."

"What now?" asked Erlissa.

Aranloth studied the destruction he had caused. He seemed almost remorseful.

"There's no chance of them getting through for a while," he said. "They'll have to move the rubble piece by piece and with great care or more will pile down on them. Either that or they'll go back and try the ravine. There's a way, even if it's dangerous and slow. We can have a short rest, but this is no place to linger."

Lanrik sheathed his sword. He quickly stepped away from the ledge and began to look about him for the first time. The recess they stood on was a large half moon shape, perhaps forty feet long and just as deep at its furthest point. In the center was a squat and ugly stone. It was as tall as a man, and wider than it was high. Each of its four faces was inscribed with strange writing.

He went over to look, and Erlissa went with him. Aranloth, subdued, trailed behind.

The marks on the stone were odd. They were a series of slashes, dots, and half circles, obviously some kind of script, though it was different from anything in Esgallien or any document written in Halathrin that he had ever looked at.

"Have you ever seen its like before?" asked Lanrik.

Erlissa shook her head. "Never."

He turned to the lòhren. "What about you?"

"I've seen it before," Aranloth said shortly. "There's more of it in other lands too."

Lanrik looked back at the stone. It was ancient and had a brooding presence.

"What does it say? Who made it?"

The lòhren appeared reluctant to answer, but at last he let out a long breath and spoke.

"It's the writing of that same race of people who first mined Caladhrist. The stone is very old. The gap between now and the founding of Esgallien is but a tenth of the time since this place was last used. The Halathrin named those people the Letharn, the Stone Raisers, or sometimes just Arn, the builders. An apt name, but even the Halathrin, gifted with tongues, have never been able to translate the writing on the stone."

Erlissa tilted her head in thought. "But *you* know what it says." She stated it as a fact.

Aranloth shrugged.

"Tell us," she insisted.

The lòhren looked at her with a pained expression.

"It's better that some things are forgotten."

"Is it really that bad?"

"I'll tell you this," he said. "The whole area around us was a place of worship and ceremony. The island, the ledge and the carving. It's also a place of death. The writing on the stone marks it as such, and where we stand on this recess, and the tunnel beyond, is at its very heart."

Lanrik had not even noticed the tunnel, but when he looked in the shadows of the far wall he saw what at first he took to be the mouth of a cave. Looking closer, he realized Aranloth was right; it was man made. It was buttressed with slabs of stone, and the lintel was inscribed with the same curious writing. Now that his attention was on it, he thought he could detect a faint odor of decay drifting from the black entrance.

"What does the writing above the tunnel say?" asked Erlissa.

Aranloth did not look at it. He appeared lost in thought, but when he spoke his voice was assured, though reverent.

Attend! We who mastered the world are become dust. We possessed the wealth of nations. Gold adorned our hands; priceless jewels our brows; bright were our swords. The world shuddered when we marched! Now, our glory lies unheeded in the dark of the tomb. Servants mutter secret words as they walk the hidden ways. Death and despair take all others!

"That's charming," Lanrik said.

Erlissa slowly shook her head. "Don't make light of it, Lan."

"Death and despair take all others? It's an empty threat," he said. "Any riches would have been stolen long ago."

Erlissa looked at the entrance and quickly averted her gaze.

"The words aren't empty. Can't you feel it? There's something inside. It hates the living and it kills them if it can."

Lanrik shrugged and looked at Aranloth. "What of the Halathrin? I bet they entered and found whatever treasure there was."

Aranloth was still subdued and leaned tiredly on his staff.

"Yes. A group of them once entered. And they found riches undreamed of."

Erlissa looked at him carefully. "But did they return?"

He closed his eyes. "No. Their bodies still lie within."

The lòhren suddenly turned away and walked to the horses. "We've rested enough. Now we'll have to make good time. Our enemies will either clear the road or find another way up the escarpment. Either way, we won't have much of a lead."

219

Erlissa turned back to Lanrik and placed a hand on his shoulder. "The tunnel is a place of death," she said. "Promise me something?"

Her earnestness and the seriousness of her gaze startled him.

"Of course," he said, without hesitation.

"Whatever happens in the future, promise me you'll never go inside it. No matter what."

"Why would I ever want to?" he said.

"I don't know. But the lòhrengai that gives me the Seeker sense gives me other gifts as well. Sometimes . . . I can see hidden things . . . even things that haven't happened yet. And I have a bad feeling about it. Just promise me. *Please.*"

He looked at her and was amazed at her intensity. Could she foresee his future as some lòhrens were supposed to be able to do? It did not really matter. She had asked him to do something, and he would do whatever she wanted.

"I promise," he said simply.

She nodded, accepting his answer but not making any move to follow Aranloth to the horses.

"There's something else," she said.

He looked to the cave, wondering what else she would ask, but she shook her head slowly and did not take her eyes off him.

"It's not about that." She hesitated, searching for the right words. "It's the sword."

His hand reached down toward its hilt as she spoke.

"What of it?" he asked.

"It's dangerous, Lan. Already I sense the effect it's having on you. And I don't like it."

He laughed. "Now you're worrying about nothing. The sword isn't dangerous. I just saved Aranloth's life with it."

Erlissa kept looking at him. "I'm not saying that it isn't useful. You might have saved his life, but what about your own?"

He did not know what she was talking about. "My life isn't in any danger. Mecklar and Gwalchmur, even Ebona, can't get to us now. Not for a while anyway. And if they do, the sword will protect us."

Even though he had not actually touched the hilt he felt a warm flush of power run up his arm and infuse him as he thought of it.

"What of the Royal Guards?"

Lanrik was at a loss. "What do they have to do with anything?"

"You killed them," she said.

"So what? It's not the first time you've seen me kill."

Erlissa bit her lip, but she did not look away from him.

"No, you've killed before. When you thought it unavoidable."

"So what's the difference?"

Aranloth glanced over because of his raised voice, but Lanrik did not care.

"Well? What's the difference?"

Erlissa's face reddened, but she spoke calmly.

"The difference is simple. This time you paid them no heed. You killed them . . . and then gave them no further thought. None at all."

He threw his hands in the air. "They got what they deserved," he said. "Let that be an end to it."

He walked away from her.

"Think on it," she said, and her gaze followed him.

He did not answer, and Aranloth led them the rest of the way to the top of the ledge in silence. It levelled out and left them on flat land again. The escarpment stretched out to either side behind them, and the Carist Nien on their left flowed toward it, slow and graceful compared to the roar of the falls below.

221

"Now we must ride as we have never ridden before," the lòhren said. "The danger of Ebona grows behind us, and the threat to Lòrenta gathers ahead!"

19. All the Days of his Life

Lonfar's attention drifted away from the lòhrens' debate about how to respond to the elùgroth's demand. Aratar had convinced them that the sorcerer might be able to fulfil his threat but could not foster an agreement on how they should respond.

There was only one answer as far as Lonfar was concerned. It seemed obvious to him, even if the others did not see it.

He was on the outer edge of their gathering and sat on one of the white granite seats that ringed the Eye of the Storm. Water sprayed from the fountain, and he tilted his head to watch it. He felt its peace and was content to wait until the various arguments had run their course, and then offer his own comments when they would have most effect.

This was a change in attitude. Only a few years ago he was as reckless of his words and their consequences as he was of the blade that he had carried. His new life was improving him, both the influence of the lòhrens and the confidence he gained from keeping his vow not to wield the sword again.

Sunlight filled the courtyard and played over its green lawns and many-flowered gardens. It was beautiful and calm, but the students' lessons had been suspended, and it was now empty. The students, no doubt uncertain and frightened, were inside the fortress, and the courtyard was a lesser place without them.

He noticed a sudden quiet and belatedly realized Aratar had addressed him.

"Lonfar?"

"I'm sorry, Lòhren Aratar. What did you say?"

Aratar showed no sign of irritation. He never did. The hands of his long and knobby arms remained peacefully clasped on top of his lap.

"I was telling the others that I invited you because you've encountered elùgroths before. You've also spoken to this one personally, which we haven't. What do you suggest we do?"

Lonfar knew he might not get another opportunity to speak. Aratar valued his opinion more than the others did, but he had not helped his cause by being inattentive. It made him look disinterested.

"The facts are simple," he began. "The elùgroth likely has the means to carry out his threat. If not, no harm can come to the students unless we lead them out of the fortress. The elùgroth cannot be trusted to keep his word about safe passage."

One of the lòhrens interrupted. "What's to stop us from using a back exit and slipping out unobserved during the night?"

"Nothing," replied Lonfar. "Remember though, that while there's only one elùgroth now, there'll be more later. We won't deceive them for long. We're surrounded by wild lands and far from any protection, and we'd be hunted down and killed."

The lòhren frowned. "But if the elùgroth can carry out his threat, then to stay here is to suffer the same fate as the fortress."

All the lòhrens looked uncomfortable.

"We're at an impasse," said one. "No course of action is better than another."

"That's one way to look at it, Carangar," Lonfar said. "It's not how I do, though. To accept that is to remove our ability to act."

Aratar leaned forward. "And how can we do that?"

224

Lonfar knew he had their attention. They were listening carefully, but he guessed that only Aratar had an idea of what he would suggest.

"We have to hold fast and hope for help from outside. And we must take the fight to the elùgroth and attack him before the others arrive. He's their leader, and to harm him is to disrupt their plans."

The lòhrens looked at him in dismay, but Aratar gave a slow nod of approval.

"Lonfar is correct."

"We're no match for an elùgroth master!" Carangar said.

The lòhren gathered himself and went on more slowly. "There aren't enough of us to challenge his power. Let's be honest – only the weakest are left here. That's why we're teaching instead of wandering over Alithoras."

"What you say is true," Aratar said. "Yet it doesn't lift the burden that chance has laid on us. We cannot stay idle while our enemies work to destroy Lòrenta. We must hope for help from outside, but in the meantime do what we can to resist. If we delay too long, the elùgroth's brethren will arrive and deprive us of our opportunity."

Aratar surveyed them all with the dispassionate gaze of a leader. Lonfar could almost see him calculating which of them would give the venture the greatest likelihood of success. The old man's glance fell on him, and an unvoiced question hung in the air.

He had vowed not to use his sword again and kept that promise despite temptation. His decision to lay it down was a symbol of his new life, and if he picked it up now, he was scared that he would never be able to put aside his old ways. But the idea to act was his, and he could not let others risk their lives while he remained safe.

He nodded his acquiescence at Aratar, wondering if there was a solution to his dilemma.

"It's settled," Aratar said. "Some of us will attack the elùgroth and some remain with the students."

His gaze swept over them again. "I'll take on this venture, but I'll need five volunteers to go with me."

Two lòhrens put their hands up straight away, and after a few moments thought, another did as well.

Aratar waited a little while longer. "Anyone else?" he asked gently.

His words were unanswered until Carangar cleared his throat.

"I'll go," the lòhren said.

Lonfar was surprised. Carangar always seemed fonder of talk than action, and he appeared timid and nervous. It proved that you did not really know people until they were put under pressure.

He sighed and stood up himself. "I'll go too, if you think I can help."

"Your help is welcome," Aratar said. "You may not have lòhrengai, but you're a survivor."

The lòhren tilted his head, and his eyes went vacant as though his words had triggered an inner vision. He then dismissed the remaining lòhrens with instructions to mix among the students and offer comfort and guidance.

When they were gone, he looked straight to Lonfar.

"You have the most experience with this sort of thing. How exactly should we go about it?"

A weight of responsibility settled over Lonfar, but he had guessed the question would be asked and prepared for it. He leaned forward and explained his plan in detail.

****

Lonfar waited nervously with Aratar and Carangar near the portcullis. They had been there for a long time, but when the signal from the tower finally came that the gate was going to be opened, it seemed too soon. All of a sudden his heart raced, and his skin prickled coldly.

The portcullis rose, and they sprang through the dark opening and onto the brightly lit ground between the fortress and the birch wood. The elùgroth saw them and straightened. He gripped the wych-wood staff in his pale hands and raised it high.

They sprinted ahead. The lòhrens' robes flew wildly, but Lonfar's Raithlin cloak was tight about him. His plan was working so far. As intended, the elùgroth's attention was focused only on them.

Lonfar was surprised at the speed of the lòhrens. Old they may be, but he struggled to keep up. He ran as fast as he could, his breath ragged from fear as well as physical exertion.

He caught a quick glance behind the sorcerer of fog rolling down from the moors and filling the wood. It was no accident. It was called by lòhrengai, and its seeking tendrils spilled out toward the elùgroth.

The other lòhrens who had volunteered for the attack had exited the back of the fortress and swept around behind the birches. It was their task to summon the fog. The strategy relied on the elùgroth reacting to the frontal attack while they assailed him from the rear. By forcing him to face one group at a time, they hoped to reduce his advantage. Everything depended on timing though, and on the lòhrens getting close enough under cover of the fog before being detected.

Lonfar felt the plan was without honor, but he had devised it because it was all they had. The elùgroth was too strong for them otherwise, and they had to do whatever they could to protect Lòrenta. What was the good of honor if it cost innocent lives and imperiled Alithoras? And as the elùgroth's own actions had put him in this position, was not anything that happened to him consequently his own fault? Yet it still rankled, and Lonfar wondered why doing the right thing felt wrong.

The wych-wood staff was pointed in his direction like a finger of death. A blast of wicked red flame seared the air. He and the lòhrens dived and rolled, avoiding the bolt that scorched the green grass. They came to their feet and ran again while smoke drifted up from the ripped and blackened earth.

They were closing the gap. Aratar had warned them that this was their moment of greatest risk. They must get close to bring lòhrengai to bear, but the elùgroth, being more powerful, would strike sooner.

Lonfar raked his gaze over the wood but saw no sign of the other lòhrens, and the elùgroth's deadly attention remained fixed on them. The wych-wood staff came to bear once more. The sorcerer paused momentarily then flung a bolt of elùgai to Lonfar's right. Too late did Carangar dodge, and a blast of crimson fire against his chest knocked him down. He staggered to his feet but was hammered down again. He screamed as fire ripped through his cloak like a knife and drove into his flesh, which smoked and withered. He went still, and Lonfar and Aratar ran on.

The tall figure now sensed the danger behind him and spun around as the lòhrens closed on him from the wood. They were dim figures moving between the fog-shrouded tree trunks. Long tendrils of mist curled out ahead of them, and on touching the elùgroth they firmed like rope and tightened around him.

He struggled against the bindings and forced the staff up. He cast a sheet of red flame in their direction, and they dived and scattered, then came to their feet and flung lòhren-fire back. The cords about him gripped harder, and he was driven to the ground, kneeling on one knee as lòhrengai struck him repeatedly. The wych-wood staff dropped from his hands.

He bowed his head and remained still for a moment, and then bunched his shoulders and drove himself up on his long legs. Red flame flickered around him. While he struggled with the bindings, the lòhrens behind worked in unison to send a sheet of fire at him. It flashed and fluttered in the air before landing on him like a blanket.

He turned and twisted. For just an instant Lonfar thought they could win, but with a surge of elùgai that sparked in all directions, he burst the bonds. Cords of fog burnt away in wisps of steam, and the lòhren-fire faltered.

The elùgroth stood still for a moment. He was tall, dark and angry. His robes, tattered and burnt at the edges, smoldered. Aratar closed on him, and Lonfar was only a few paces behind. The sorcerer raised his hand, and fire streamed from his fingers knocking them sprawling.

He picked up his staff and spun back to the lòhrens. He sent a succession of shattering bolts at them until the white trunks of the birches were scorched, and smoke roiled upward through their branches. The lòhrens dodged behind cover, but he probed them out with bolts of flame.

While they fought, Lonfar crept past the unconscious figure of Aratar. He dared not stand and draw attention to himself. The mist around him had turned to vapor and rose with the smoke from the burnt grass. It offered little cover, but with the Raithlin cloak it could just be enough to get him closer.

The elùgroth sent jagged fire at one of the lòhrens. It knocked his legs from beneath him and pinned him to the ground relentlessly. His robes smoked and burned, and he shouted in agony as he died. The other lòhrens desperately flung fire at the elùgroth, but their strength was fading, and he shrugged their weakened attacks aside. He swept a wall of flame at them, and they reeled back and fell. They crawled for cover, but the red elùgai ate away at their bodies while they screamed.

Their cries tortured Lonfar. These were the weakest lòhrens, ill-suited to opposing such an enemy, and though they could have turned and fled they were fighting with all they had to try to save Lòrenta. He could do no less, and moved by white-hot anger, he surged to his feet only a dozen paces from the elùgroth.

The sorcerer sensed him and spun, red fire flickered at the tip of the wych-wood staff. Lonfar had kept his vow and left his sword behind, but he could not make himself face an elùgroth empty handed. He drew one of his Raithlin knives, doubt tugging at him that he had still broken the spirit of his promise, and hurled it with the skill of long years of practice. It wheeled and cut through the smoke and steam-laden air.

The knife struck the sorcerer in the upper arm instead of the neck. Nevertheless, bright blood spurted from an artery. He reached for a second knife and felt its weight in his hand, but the enemy was too swift. Red fire burst toward him and beat into his chest. It sent him flying to the ground and pinned him. He felt the stab of burning flesh and smelled it in his nostrils. Consciousness flickered and he prepared to die, but as quick as it came the flame ceased, and he felt the sudden release of its pressure.

He looked up through nauseating pain and streaming tears.

The elùgroth had thrown down his staff and clamped a hand to his wound. Red fire erupted from his palm, and he loosed a high-pitched scream from his throat. It was more animal than human and was filled with rage and pain.

Lonfar realized the sorcerer was cauterizing the wound to stop the bleeding that might otherwise kill him. In moments he would be done and would pick up the staff and continue the attack. Lonfar tried to rise but fell back to the ground. Suddenly bright fire burst from behind him. Aratar was up again, and the lòhren-fire hit the

230

elùgroth, but the dark figure merely shrugged it aside as he concentrated on his task.

The lòhren-fire faltered and went out. Aratar was spent, but Lonfar felt his strong hands on him as the lòhren picked him up and lurched back toward the fortress. It was hard to believe that an old man could have such strength in his bony arms, but lòhrens were always surprising.

They passed by the broken body of Carangar and then neared the portcullis, which was opened. It was dark inside, and with a loud clang the great gate closed behind and they were safe. Of the six who had made the venture, only they had survived.

Aratar laid him down and staggered back as lòhrens came to help.

"I'm sorry," Lonfar said. "My plan failed."

Aratar's face was gray with fatigue. He rubbed it and shrugged.

"Do you think so? We were never likely to kill him. But we've wounded him, and we'll see if it makes a difference in the end."

****

The next day Lonfar stood on the battlements. He was tired and weak. His burns throbbed, and he felt like he was being stabbed each time he moved, but the lòhrens had given him a drink infused with elendhrot that eased the pain. They had also applied honey from the moors to his skin, which soothed and healed. His chest would carry scars for the rest of his life, however long that may be, but at least he was alive.

Aratar stood beside him. He must have been in just as much pain but showed none of it.

"It begins," he said ominously.

And it was true. Lonfar felt cold as he watched. One after another, elùgroths emerged from the birch wood and slowly gathered about their leader. That dark figure moved gingerly, and Lonfar watched in grim satisfaction. His wounds troubled him, perhaps even badly.

Lonfar counted them as they came. There were eleven. With their leader, they totaled twelve, and there was power at their command to unnerve an army.

It was hushed on the battlements. The lòhrens watched silently and gave no indication of their feelings except by their very quietude. Aratar looked on stoically, and Lonfar felt a surge of unexpected affection. This man had risked his own life to save him. He had also done everything he could to protect Lòrenta, and it was not his fault that he was outmatched.

Pain washed over Lonfar, and he felt despair for the first time in his life. It was crushing. It made him think that all he had ever done had been for nothing and that he might as well have never lived. He regretted using the Raithlin knives even though he knew he was justified in doing so.

The elùgroths discoursed solemnly for some time. They were alike, black-robed and tall, their wych-wood staffs ominous with the threat of elùgai.

After a while their discussion broke up. They sat cross-legged and formed a wedge that pointed at the fortress. Their pallid hands rested easily on the dark staffs in their laps, and they soon began to chant. Their words were beyond hearing at first but grew louder and clearer until they soared over the battlements. Lonfar had never heard the language before. It was harsh and guttural, but it swelled with slow and sure power.

"They're already connected to the Morleth Stone," Aratar explained, "but wherever it is, and whatever energy they're transforming, they're making the binding deeper before they call on the stone's powers."

Lonfar looked at them with mounting desperation. He searched for some way to fight, but nothing came to mind. To just wait and watch went against all his instincts, but to attack again was folly. He swept his eyes over them once more and noticed something that intrigued him. He made sure of it before he spoke, uncertain of its consequences, but hope fluttered in his heart.

"Aratar . . ." he said.

The lòhren turned to him.

"I counted eleven as they arrived. And their master makes twelve."

"Yes," the lòhren said. "It's their number of power."

"But there are only eleven in the wedge."

Aratar's eyed widened, and he spun back and looked over the battlements. After a moment his hands went white and trembled where they gripped the stonework forcefully.

"Yes!" he shouted.

Lonfar was heartened by the lòhren's excitement. "There," he said, pointing over the battlements. "The master sits in the shadow of the trees with his back against a fire-blackened trunk. He's not chanting and isn't part of the wedge. What does it mean?"

Aratar gave him a fierce smile. "It means that your plan was successful, and my brothers didn't give their lives for nothing. The elùgroth leader isn't linked to the Morleth Stone. His power and skill, the highest of them all, won't be added to their sorcery."

"But what effect will that have?"

Aratar shrugged. "It's hard to say. This much is certain though – it'll take them longer to achieve their purpose."

Lonfar took heart at the lòhren's words. They had defied those who would destroy them and struck a blow of their own. There was yet hope, however little, and he would not despair. It was not the Raithlin way, and sword

233

or no sword, he was a Raithlin and would remain one all the days of his life.

He sensed a change in the air over the next few hours. It grew cooler. The colors of the moors and the woods became muted, and he felt something pressing at him and enveloping the fortress. The horizon blurred and dimmed with a grayness that was not fog.

Aratar looked at him. "Do you feel it? It's the spirit world cutting us off from life."

Lonfar gave no reply. Nothing could be added.

20. Nightmare

Lanrik rolled over on the hard ground. He wanted to sleep, but his Raithlin cloak was uncomfortably damp, and his boots, which he dared not take off in case Mecklar and Gwalchmur found the camp and attacked, were cold and clammy.

The travelers had stopped by the edge of a willow-rimmed tarn. It had been drizzling for days, and everything from the misty tops of the trees to the root-bound soil was saturated.

He curled his knees up to his chest but still shivered under the cloak. There was no fire. Aranloth might have been able to start one but had remained true to the lòhren principle of using lòhrengai only at need.

For over a week, they had ridden hard and kept the northern bank of the Carist Nien in view. The lands they journeyed through were lush and green. Aranloth said the sea was only some fifty miles away, and its influence caused heavy rainfall between the coast and the river.

They were further away from the sea now, in the hills of Lòrenta, but the rain had followed. Of the enemies that pursued them there was no sign. This only served to worry Lanrik more. He knew Mecklar and Gwalchmur would not give up and would be somewhere in the surrounding wilderness. Ebona was also on his mind. He had rebuffed her, and she was obviously a dangerous enemy.

They had lost sight of the river when they reached the hill country and started toward the interior of Lòrenta. Aranloth led them unfailingly, for this was the land of the lòhrens. They had lived here since long before the founding of Esgallien or any of the eastern cities, and while they wandered all over Alithoras they always returned. Aranloth rode with lingering glances at the misty

235

hills and wild moors, yet his love of the land had not slowed his pace.

The area around the tarn was uneven, and the dank soil was strewn with rocks and moss-covered boulders. Some places were crowded with green bracken while others were darkened by stands of gloomy willow trees. Their long branches drooped over the stagnant pond and dripped slow beads of water onto its scum-crusted surface.

Lanrik had woken Erlissa when it was her turn to keep watch and had tried without success to sleep. He pulled part of the Raithlin cloak over his head so that he could no longer see the low clouds scud across the dark sky or feel the fine drops of rain on his face.

Eventually he went to sleep with one hand on the hilt of the shazrahad sword. Though he was asleep, his mind remained strangely alert, and he could think rationally. Everything was vivid and clear. His dreams were dark though, and when he felt himself plunge from a great height, he desperately tried to wake himself up.

He fell with a crash that should have broken his body, but instead his dream-self surged upright. He was in the deep bottom of the tarn, but it was now empty of all water. Far above the willow trees still dripped, yet the beads of moisture had turned to blood. They dropped onto the parched soil near his feet and also ran in long rivulets down the woven roots in the walls of the pit.

Stepping back, his boots crunched on the ground. He turned to look and saw that the bottom of the tarn was littered with ancient bones. Scores of carrion crows perched atop skulls, their plumage velvety-black against the bleached surface. Fat-bodied adders lay coiled in the shadows and tested the air with long tongues. Far away on the fells, he heard wolves howl and then the answering echo from rocky crags within the lonely hills.

He looked up at the rim of the pit and searched for a way of escape. Crows had replaced the leaves of the willows. There were thousands of them, and they hung upside down from the branches and made them lurch and sway. Instead of the rustle of leaves, he heard only their croaking, and when they opened their beaks drops of blood dribbled from the sharp tips.

A disembodied voice cried his name. The crows with him in the pit flapped their wings and hopped from skull to skull while the adders uncoiled and hissed.

It was Lathmai, and her words stabbed into his heart.

When will you fulfil your oath?

He fell to his knees.

Why have you betrayed me?

He clamped his hands to his ears.

I want blood. Blood! Blood! Blood!

The hair on his head prickled. The willows leaned over the tarn as though sealing the entrance of a tomb, and the wolves howled again. They were closer than before, and he knew they had his scent and hunted him. His heart thudded wildly in his chest, and he drove himself upright and ran along the base of the pit. He stumbled over rocks and bones while the crows swarmed up and battered his face with their black wings.

The roots of the trees writhed, and their tips broke through the dry ground beneath his feet. They snatched at his ankles. He suddenly sensed his body in the camp and felt it thrash beneath the Raithlin cloak. There were hands on him too, but in the tarn he was on his feet and leapt and dodged. He attempted to climb the side of the pit, but everything he gripped turned to dust in his hands. He fell back and ran once more.

This time he heard the pound of hooves behind him. He turned and was frozen by the horror of a white mare that towered over him. She was fleshless: a creature of bone, sinew and tattered hide.

The mare reared, and her bones creaked and rattled. She snorted silently, and the stench of rotted flesh filled the air. The bones in her long neck lengthened, and she lunged and nipped at him with the sharp incisors at the front of her skull. He found the will to move and leapt back, thinking the mare would chase, but her teeth merely clicked together, and she stayed where she was. Her head turned though, and she eyed him with one of the empty sockets of her long skull.

She drummed the hoof of a foreleg against the brittle bone and rock of the dry tarn bed, and he heard Ebona's voice in the sound.

"Die! Die! Die!"

The words grew clearer with each beat, and even as he listened in terror the dark walls of the tarn began to cave in and fill the pit. Dirt and bone-dust clogged his nose, and he could not breathe. He was being buried alive.

Hands gripped his arm and shook him urgently. He screamed and his eyes flicked open. The misty stars were above, and Erlissa was leaning over him.

"Wake up!" she yelled.

Her fingers dug into his flesh, and she continued to shake him. He gasped and shuddered as he drew in ragged breaths of clean air. He was drenched with icy sweat, and his tunic and hair were dank. Slowly his breathing returned to normal, and Erlissa loosened her grip but did not let go. There was something in her look that he had never seen before. It was worry. Deep worry. She had appeared less disturbed in the shazrahad's tent or during any of the moments of danger since then. She felt for him, and her care blazed unguarded in her eyes.

"Are you all right?" she asked.

He shivered. "It was a nightmare."

Drawing calmer breaths, he spoke again. "I dreamed of . . . Lathmai. Then things got worse. It all seemed so real."

238

Erlissa rubbed his arm soothingly.

"It was so *real*," he repeated.

Aranloth stood behind her, the oaken staff held tightly in his hand, and he also looked concerned. Lanrik realized that he must have made a lot of noise in his sleep, maybe even screamed before Erlissa had managed to wake him. He felt ashamed.

He closed his eyes for a moment and tried to relax. The hilt of the sword in his hand was burning to the touch, but he did not let it go. Somewhere in the nearby hills the wolves howled excitedly. He had heard them in his sleep, and the nightmare still felt real. He tried to shake off the feeling, but with inexplicable clarity he knew the wolves hunted them in truth.

He staggered to his feet and drew the sword.

Erlissa stepped back. "What is it?"

"The wolves!" he said." They're hunting us!"

"It was just a dream, Lan."

She stepped slowly toward him again, but he shook his head adamantly. "No. I feel it. They're coming for us. That part of my dream was real."

"Wolves aren't likely to attack a group of people," she said reasonably.

Lanrik gritted his teeth in frustration. He could not make her understand; he did not understand himself, but he knew it was true. Aranloth peered at him closely then wheeled around to face the night.

"It may be as he says," the lòhren stated with his back to them. "I feel Ebona's touch in this. Get the horses and tether them near the edge of the tarn."

They did as Aranloth asked, and then waited. The horses were secure, and no harm could come to them from behind. Standing in front of them they looked outward into the darkness. The howling increased until it seemed the hills were alive with wolves.

"The spirit of Ebona cannot come into the camp," Aranloth said. "Yet even so, she might have found a way into Lanrik's dreams. Sending nightmares is one of her skills."

Erlissa looked concerned. "Can she hurt him that way?"

"Not really. For all her power and wisdom she can be spiteful though, and distressing him would have been her main purpose. Yet if so, it was foolish. Her mind would have been linked to his in order to do it. And just as some of his thoughts would be open to her, some of hers would be open to him, and he might have discerned her plan. Especially now that he wields the shazrahad sword and the lòhrengai in it."

Lanrik did not know how he knew. It might have been the sword or something else, but he *knew* the wolves were coming. By the time he spotted the first one the last remnants of his nightmare had slipped away, and he was ready to fight.

"There!" he pointed.

They all saw it. A great white wolf padded toward them from the darkness and surveyed them before retreating into the night. There were scuffling noises, and soon dim eyes appeared all about them.

Several wolves ventured into view. They were smaller but just as white as the first. Deep ruffs of fur encircled their necks, and compared to the wolves Lanrik had seen in Esgallien they were heavy and of a more rounded body shape. Their muzzles were short, and their ears were thick tufts of fur rather than long and pointed.

"They're strange wolves," he said.

Aranloth did not look at him and kept his gaze on the shapes moving about the perimeter of their camp.

"They're not the wolves of Lòrenta," he replied. "Around here they're lean and gray like most in Alithoras. And as Erlissa suggested, they avoid people. These come from the cold mountains of Anast Dennath, a haunt for evil creatures, some of them otherworldly."

"They're a long way from home, then."

"Yes," agreed the lòhren. "Which means they've been called here."

"Ebona?" Lanrik said.

The lòhren did not have a chance to answer. One of the wolves raced sleekly toward them over the rock-strewn ground.

Aranloth lifted his staff and stabbed lòhren-fire at it. The animal dodged and turned back swiftly into the darkness.

Lanrik took a tight grip of his sword. He knew Ebona was behind the attack. The blade had given him sensitivities, and he had felt her presence in the nightmare. He thought of Lathmai. Was her apparition also Ebona's doing? Had she seen into his mind and found what most troubled him? His hands trembled with anger, and when the wolves rushed he strode forward to meet them.

Lòhren-fire seared the night, and the shazrahad blade flickered with its own killing light. The wolves howled and yelped but seemed driven beyond reason and continued to attack until there was a pile of white bodies. Only the great white wolf that must have been the leader of the pack was left.

Lanrik charged toward it as it leapt at him. His blade sang through the air and cut through the thick rough of fur about its neck. He could feel ùhrengai in the creature's blood, and it flowed up through the sword and into his body. He felt dizzy with power.

The corpse thumped to the ground, its snow-white coat red with blood. He looked at the dead animal and laughed. The urge left as suddenly as it came, and he turned his face to the sky, graying with the coming dawn.

"Ebona!" he screamed.

All the frustration and anger he felt flooded his voice, and his arms and legs trembled. When he turned back to the others, he saw that Aranloth leaned on his staff and surveyed him watchfully. Erlissa, wide-eyed and white-faced, dragged her gaze away from his eyes and refused to meet his glance anymore.

He realized that the sword was changing him. He would do anything to have Erlissa look at him as she used to, even cast the blade aside and go back to being his true self. But the hilt was warm and comforting in his grip, and he felt its strength infuse him. He would need it when he finally fought Mecklar and Gwalchmur. That he would do so was beyond doubt. He must fulfil his promise to Lathmai, whatever the cost. Without a word, he wiped the blade clean and sheathed it.

They did not speak as they broke camp in the growing light. Quickly and efficiently, they packed up and left the willow-rimmed tarn behind. Lanrik tried repeatedly to catch Erlissa's glance, but she looked steadfastly ahead. After a while, he gave up and used the silence to think.

He noticed that Erlissa, however unwilling she was to look at him, had no such reluctance when it came to Aranloth. She stared at him often, and her eyes bored into him angrily. The lòhren pretended not to notice. He rode calmly, finding the easiest paths through thickets, dells and meadows. He took them up onto the high moors and always knew exactly where he was going and the quickest way to get there.

It was a lonely and wild land. The drizzle soon ceased, but gray clouds hung low and oppressive in the sky. Occasionally the horses disturbed quail, and the drab-colored birds burst into flight like arrows thrumming from a score of bows. Hares, crouching and hidden, stayed still until they were nearly trodden, then zigzagged away at speed while agile-winged kestrels hovered and banked in the air, studying all below with eyes that saw everything.

Aranloth turned aside. He avoided a hollow that was spongy with water that seeped into it from higher ground, and Erlissa caught his eye and spoke.

"The sooner we're finished, the better," she said.

"We're getting close," the lòhren replied casually. "See how the ground is turning boggy? We're nearing the source of the Carist Nien, and beyond that is the fortress of Lòrenta."

"I didn't just mean the fortress," she said. "I'm done with the whole venture. I've had enough of being hunted and attacked."

Aranloth gave no answer, but his silence did not stop Erlissa from speaking her mind.

"And the lòhrengai is the worst of it."

Lanrik felt her glance slide over him and quickly shift away.

"Nothing with lòhrengai is as simple as it seems," she continued. "I'll find the Morleth Stone, but that will be an end to it. I'll do no more."

Aranloth stiffened as she spoke, but he eased back into his saddle and rode on.

Lanrik had not seen the lòhren react like that before. Erlissa looked away and went silent without noticing the effect of her words. But there *was* an effect, and Lanrik had the sudden feeling that there was more going on than what the lòhren had told them. Her words were about the sword, but he felt that Aranloth's reaction had something to do with Erlissa herself. He knew the lòhren would never hurt her, but he also knew that he did what was necessary. Would he lie though? Lanrik did not think so, but that did not mean he had told all of the truth. The more he thought about it the more he knew he was right. He fondled the sword hilt absently as he searched for answers.

The day drew on. The headwaters of the Carist Nien came into view, and then late in the afternoon Lòrenta itself appeared against the horizon. It was a mighty fortress, white walled and many towered. Legends described it as shinning with an inner light, and while he could see why that was so, with his hand on the sword, he realized there was also a grayness about it that was neither mist nor fog. He felt the otherworld; he sensed elùgai, and at the same time Aranloth let out a long sigh.

"We're nearly too late," he said quietly. "The fortress is assailed, and all that is in her, the artefacts of the lòhrens, the wisdom of the ages and the people dwelling there, are imperiled."

He spoke with a catch in his throat. The fortress and the danger it was in meant something more to him than just a battle against enemies, however important that was. This was his home. It was a place that he loved, but one that he may never see again.

Lanrik understood how he felt.

21. On the Brink

The afternoon light faded swiftly, and darkness veiled the remote hills. Night shadows swallowed Lòrenta, but Aranloth, deep in thought, stood unmoving and stared in the direction of his fortress home. Lanrik and Erlissa set up the camp and did not disturb him.

They lit no fire. The lonely wilderness pressed in, and Lanrik could scarcely remember his last hot meal. He did not complain though. Food was the least of his troubles, for somewhere nearby were elùgroths. Nor could he forget Mecklar and Gwalchmur. They troubled his thoughts constantly, and he would have no peace until he fulfilled his promise to Lathmai.

They eventually ate a meagre meal. Aranloth, the oaken staff resting in his lap, spoke when they were finished.

"The Morleth Stone has nearly done its work," he said. "We must hurry, yet we can't be sure where our enemies are. The elùgroths are likely to be at the front of the fortress, but Mecklar and Gwalchmur could be anywhere."

"Could they have beaten us here?" asked Erlissa doubtfully.

Aranloth shrugged. "We traveled fast, but they're driven by Ebona. If they're not here already, they'll arrive soon. They won't spare their horses."

Lanrik had no doubts. Their own alar mounts and the lòhren's roan had been pushed hard, harder than most in Esgallien could have endured, but Mecklar and Gwalchmur had quality horses and would squeeze every drop of life out of them. He knew they were close by somewhere. And there was Ebona too. She would arrange more trouble if she could.

If Aranloth was concerned, he did not show it. "We can't afford a confrontation with any of our enemies, but there are many entrances into the fortress, and not all of them can be watched. We'll go through a hidden way at the back and use the cover of night to conceal our presence."

For a little while longer, they sat together without speaking. The end of their quest was in sight, but all that they had suffered and risked would be in vain if they did not save Lòrenta.

Lanrik thought of what had brought them to this point. It had started with the plume of smoke on Galenthern, and he had known at the time that his life was going to change. He had not known to what extent though. Who could have predicted the things that had happened to him since that morning?

The best of it all was Erlissa. But he was losing her and could see no way to prevent it. He would not betray Lathmai by failing in his promise to find and kill Gwalchmur. Yet Erlissa would condemn him for it.

He needed the sword to accomplish his goals, even if she thought otherwise. He now recognized the truth of her advice that its lòhrengai was changing him, but it was a sacrifice he must make. He turned toward her. She rested her chin in the cup of her long-fingered hands and stirred when he looked. She refused to meet his glance though. She was still angry with him . . . or maybe disappointed. It was a new thought, and it shook him.

He sensed that she still had some feelings for him. Irrespective of her easygoing attitude, he knew that her emotions ran deep. That she had lost both her parents when she was young made it hard for her. She was forced too early in life to learn that love inevitably led to loss, yet he thought that she was strong enough to overcome that.

Aranloth stood up and broke the silence.

"We'll rest for a few hours. Get what sleep you can – I'll keep watch."

The lòhren moved to the edge of the camp. The rain had stopped and the sky was clear, but toward the fortress it was dark. Lanrik felt sorcery at work. It throbbed at his senses like a distant storm. He intended to doze lightly because he was fearful of Ebona's influence on his dreams, yet he was near exhaustion and drifted into a deep sleep. It only seemed moments though before Aranloth gently shook his shoulder.

"It's time."

The lòhren showed no signs of tiredness, even though Lanrik was sure he had not slept. It was another reminder that he was something more than just a kindly old man. He could not match a dozen elùgroths, but he was still a power in the world.

The hills were hushed. The evening was old, and the stars bright as on a winter's night. Silvery dew lay thick on the grass, and the horses left tracks as they walked toward the fortress. A fox crossed the slope ahead, its fur slick with moisture. It hastened to its destination with less caution than it would usually have used and paused in mid-stride when it saw them. It observed things intently for several seconds but sensed no danger and paid them no further heed as it trotted away purposefully.

They continued on their own journey until the fortress was only a few hundred paces away; a dark shape in the night that seemed little more substantial than a midnight shadow. The air grew cold, and the warm breath of the horses turned to vapor. Even as they drew close, it remained little more than a vague outline. Aranloth was right; the elùgroths had nearly accomplished their task.

The lòhren turned and signed for total quiet before going forward cautiously. The ground angled upward as the rear of the fortress was built on a stony outcrop. Tufts of stunted grass studded the uneven surface, and the rock was pale in the dim light.

The slope steepened, and they dismounted and led the horses by hand.

"Be careful," Aranloth whispered. "Noise travels far at night."

Erlissa nodded her understanding, and Lanrik studied the fortress wall higher up on the outcrop. He could not see any entrance but noticed that it appeared more like a weak reflection in murky water than something solid. The closer they got the more he sensed that something was wrong.

The fortress was still over a hundred feet away, but insubstantial or not, it towered above them. Soon they reached a cliff-like face on the outcrop, and Aranloth led them to a cave, its opening wide and obvious.

Lanrik leaned in close to the lòhren and spoke softly. "This is a *secret* entrance?"

Aranloth appeared amused. "Yes. Why don't you go first, and see if you can find the way?"

Lanrik hesitated then took the lead. He paused in the cave mouth to allow his eyes to adjust to the dark interior and to listen for any noise. He studied the ground in front of him as well, but there was no sign that anyone was inside.

He led them into the cave. It was not large but would shelter several people and their horses. The floor, of sand and scattered rocks, contained in its center a fire-pit surrounded by large stones. A pile of fine kindling and wood was stacked nearby. Aranloth took some of the kindling and ignited it with his flint. When it came to life he set alight a branch, which he held aloft to illuminate the cave.

They studied the walls about them. The chamber was round, though not man made, and the dome-like roof was darkened by smoke.

248

Aranloth handed him the improvised torch. "Do you see the way into the fortress?"

Lanrik looked about him intently then walked around the walls and checked them closely. They were all solid and without any crack or crevice that might indicate a secret door.

He returned from his inspection. "I can't find anything."

Aranloth gave him the roan's reins. "The best way to hide something is to put it in the open."

He walked to the fire pit and knelt to the side of one of the larger stones that circled it. He placed both hands on it and used force to pull it in the direction of the cave entrance. It did not budge, but there was a loud click. The lòhren stood and used his foot to push once more against the rock, this time in the opposite direction.

The floor of the chamber thrummed, and there was a grinding noise. To Lanrik's surprise, a large portion of the sand covered ground slid forward smoothly until an opening revealed a wooden ramp. It had a steep downward slope but was wide enough for a horse to use. The flickering light of the torch did not reach the bottom.

Lanrik shook his head and pursed his lips. "I'd never have found it."

Aranloth shrugged. "It's not meant to be found. But once used the sand is disturbed and shows the false floor. That's not a problem coming out because it can be brushed back to look natural again. Going in, as we are, is another matter."

Aranloth took his horse's reins back. "We have to hurry now. There's still much to do before we enter the fortress."

He led his horse down the ramp. It did not like the narrow confines or the steep slope, but with coaxing it went forward, and the others, seeing it going that way, followed without trouble.

The lòhren held the branch up when they were all through, and the mechanism for the opening flickered into view. It was a device of oiled iron wheels and a slab of stone. He closed it, and when the outside world vanished from sight, went to the front again and led them on.

The narrow tunnel soon went forward at an upward angle. They followed, the hooves of the horses muffled by sand-covered stone. The passageway did not last long however. After a little while it opened up into a cavern. They could not see much but could tell from the hollow sounds that the area was large.

Aranloth touched his burning branch to several torches on the wall. Soon the chamber was lit with dancing light, but the tunnel remained a dark mouth behind them.

Ahead, a set of stairs was carved into the stone and led to a raised platform. Beyond that was a massive iron gate set in the wall of the fortress. The bars were pale with rime and contrasted sharply with the darkness beyond them. That darkness, Lanrik knew, was the inside of Lòrenta. They were on the brink now.

"I don't see any sentries," he said.

Aranloth followed his glance toward the gate. "No," he replied. "Lòrenta is built as a fortress and has ramparts and towers. But that's symbolic rather than practical. What it guards, what it's a sanctuary for, is protected instead by ùhrengai. Nothing can enter that the lòhrens don't allow. I'll mark you each with a special kind of lòhrengai before we go in. Otherwise, you would be repelled."

"Repelled, or killed?" asked Erlissa, distaste of lòhrengai in her voice.

"A good question," Aranloth said. "In your cases, repelled. Others, such as an elùgroth, would be killed. But they would retreat when they felt the power stir against them."

The lòhren was done with explanations. "There's little time left," he said briskly. "Lòrenta is deep in the spirit world, and I must prepare the mistletoe before we cross the threshold."

He retrieved the three berries from his cloak. They were still fresh, unchanged since they were picked, and they glimmered in his hand with a hint of pale light. Lanrik was reminded of the half moon rising over the dark forests of Enorìen.

"To invoke their power," Aranloth explained, "I have to use complex and tightly controlled lòhrengai. Whatever happens I mustn't be disturbed. Otherwise, the properties of the berries will be lost, and we won't be able to enter Lòrenta."

The lòhren walked up the stairs to the raised platform in front of the gate. Lanrik and Erlissa left him to his work and waited in awkward silence. He wanted to talk but could not find the right words.

He sensed her discomfort and thought the sword was on her mind. She had warned him against it when Aranloth first infused it with lòhrengai. She had warned him again when he used it to fight off Mecklar in the gorge that led up from the Angle. He had rebuffed her, the last person in the word that he wanted to, and had created the distance between them. She had ceased trying to warn him, but he sensed something else of her mood; she had not ceased to care. That was why she was upset.

Aranloth's voice drifted from the platform. He sat near the rime-coated gate and chanted softly in a foreign language. It might, or might not have been, Halathrin. Lanrik could not hear it properly, but the lòhren's words flowed sonorously and filled the cavern. There was power in them too, and he felt lòhrengai grow and strengthen as the chanting deepened and became more urgent.

He suddenly stiffened. He had heard something out of place. Something from beyond the light of the torches, back toward the beginning of the tunnel. He strained his ears and listened intently. He no longer heeded Aranloth's chant or Erlissa's soft breathing. He concentrated only on the passageway.

He was right. He heard it again, closer now, and he stood up and motioned Erlissa to stay back. He stepped toward the opening of the tunnel and drew the shazrahad sword. Its warmth pulsed through him, and something else too; eagerness.

He soon knew why. What he had long feared, or long hoped for, he was no longer sure which, had occurred. Mecklar and Gwalchmur walked from the dark mouth of the tunnel into the flickering light. They led their mounts, pitifully spent and gaunt creatures with dull coats caked by dirt and sweat. The horses stepped slowly and their heads hung low. Their lackluster eyes looked at the ground, and they showed no interest in their surroundings. They had been cruelly used, and anger rose in Lanrik. In response, the pulse of lòhrengai in his sword quickened.

He observed his countrymen, and they looked back at him. There was no surprise or hurry among any of them, merely a sense of the inevitable coming to pass. Events that had begun on the wide expanse of Galenthern would find fruition in the hemmed in land of the lòhrens, at the very gate of their fabled fortress.

"We've caught up with you, at last," Mecklar said conversationally.

Lanrik looked at him coolly. "The day of reckoning has come."

The King's Counselor let go his horse's reins. It stood exactly where it was, a miserable and exhausted creature.

Mecklar had lost weight and been hardened by the long journey, but he was still a large man. Lanrik remembered how fast he could move, as well as the strength and skill of his blows. None of these things would have diminished. If anything, he would be more dangerous. Nor had he lost the heavy-lidded gaze that weighed, judged and planned to minute detail in a single glance

Mecklar slowly drew his sword. "I'll finish things now – as I should have done on Galenthern."

Lanrik stepped forward. His eyes flicked to Gwalchmur, but the Raithlin remained still and silent.

Mecklar noted his look. "Gwalchmur will stay out of it. The pleasure of killing you will be mine."

Lanrik felt a sense of rightness settle over him. "We'll finish the fight we began at the Spring Games."

Mecklar cocked his head. "The Spring Games? A strange thing to say. I'd almost forgotten our match, but I've not forgotten that it was finished. And I won." He raised the tip of his sword. "As I will again."

"You didn't win. The king merely awarded you the prize."

Mecklar shrugged and stepped closer. His sword wove slowly through the air, and his eyes burned feverishly. The fight was about to begin, and he did not answer.

Erlissa spoke from behind, and Lanrik heard concern in her voice. "Be careful, Lan."

The combatants drew close and he saw Mecklar grimace. Was he injured? That would make the fight easier, but then he sensed the presence of Ebona and saw the likeness of her haughty expression creep over his opponent's face. The witch wanted to kill him and make certain of things herself. Gwalchmur also watched, a sick look on his face.

Lanrik's sword throbbed, but the lòhrengai subsided when Mecklar groaned and thrust Ebona away. He sensed it would be for the last time. Her influence was growing stronger, but at least this battle would be man against man, steel against cold steel.

Mecklar looked at him viciously. Hatred, frustration and the lust to kill blazed in his eyes. Ebona was not in control, but he had long since succumbed to her ùhrengai. It fed on the darkness within him, and its power magnified it.

He had passed beyond the threshold of sanity.

22. Death is Become Life, and Life Death

Mecklar, nimble on his feet, moved in quickly and attacked with a flurry of swift blows. Confident in his skill and sure of success, he struck with effortless grace and ease.

His strokes were not light though. Lanrik felt their force jar his bones and run down to his feet. He tried to deflect rather than block, but his opponent had an uncanny ability to anticipate his defense and catch him in unfavorable positions.

He felt the first trickle of panic and strove for a sense of calm. The fear that Lathmai might not be avenged prevented him from attaining it.

He retreated, but Mecklar shadowed him seamlessly and continued his attack. Lanrik gritted his teeth. He had not defied an army of elugs and rescued a prisoner from the shazrahad's tent only to be killed by a single man. It was time to retaliate. He swayed away from a brutal stroke and surged forward. He thrust, struck and sliced at killing points and forced his opponent back.

Mecklar gave ground adroitly. His blade turned and shifted in harmony with his footwork and deflected all blows. He absorbed the attack, and when Lanrik's momentum slowed, he launched his own blistering offensive.

Lanrik retreated once more, but he felt better now. Mecklar was not holding back. His eyes burned feverishly, and though he attacked with all his skill and strength, none of the blows landed. Lanrik started to relax his muscles and allow the tenseness of his body to flow away. It felt as

255

if there were no past or any future, only the here and now, the fight his entire existence.

His opponent continued to shift smoothly between attack and defense, advance and retreat. He showed no fault or weakness to exploit. His iron-hard muscles, hidden beneath layers of fat, were infused with skill from years of practice. His expertise, strength and bodyweight were unified so that he struck with power, and the harsh clang of metal against metal crashed about the chamber.

The fight ebbed and flowed. Mecklar's eyes flared with ever-greater fury, and he struck with increasing viciousness. Lanrik became calmer though, and his body more supple. He was surefooted, and retreated again and again to absorb his opponent's attacks, but advanced when there was opportunity.

Their contrasting styles were evenly matched, yet no fight conducted with sharp-edged blades could continue for long. The slightest error by one would give a killing chance to the other, and Lanrik made the first.

He slashed at his opponent's neck, and the shazrahad blade sang through the air only inches away, but he committed himself a little too far and was vulnerable to Mecklar's counterattack. His blade was high while his enemy's was low. Mecklar, his eyes wide in triumph, surged forward in a classic thrust. He drove up from his feet, added the power of his waist, and stabbed with the point of the weapon.

Lanrik could not bring his sword to bear or retreat quickly enough. He reacted by instinct and performed a technique his uncle had made him practice for desperate situations. Instead of trying to move back as expected, he twisted sideways at the last moment. The blade scraped along his stomach and burned like a lash of fire, but he avoided the lethal blow.

The king's counselor was surprised and started to withdraw, but Lanrik stepped in and ruthlessly smashed the hilt of the sword into his face. There was a loud crack of bone, and his enemy reeled away. Lanrik followed him and ran him through with the same classic thrust that he had just avoided himself. The blade slid underneath Mecklar's ribcage, and the point stabbed up toward his heart.

Bloody foam frothed at his mouth. His eyes had been bright with madness but now showed disbelief. They closed as Lanrik withdrew the sword, and he slumped to the ground and coughed wetly. He tried to rise, then went suddenly still, and a dark pool of blood seeped onto the stone floor.

Mecklar was dead, and all was silent except for the chanting of the lòhren. Lanrik felt a rush of triumph. He had killed his enemy with the shazrahad sword, though not by any advantage of lòhrengai. He could feel power in the blade. It raged from the metal into his body like a wild animal seeking to destroy those who had caged it.

He stood where he was and trembled, drawing in ragged breaths. He felt something within him grow and expand. His sense of sight sharpened; his hearing became acute; he had greater insight into the world and the intent of the people around him.

He understood that everything was in a state of flux and that this was a pivotal moment in his life. It would set the direction of his future just as seeing the plume of smoke on Galenthern had led him to Lòrenta.

He observed with detachment as Ebona struggled to control Gwalchmur and make another attack. The Raithlin had never been as deeply under her influence as Mecklar though, and was divided in his loyalties. He would not succumb, at least not yet.

The bloodstain slowly expanded about Mecklar's corpse, and Lanrik perceived how he had been dominated by ùhrengai. Ebona had planted the seed of his destruction in the fertile soil of his lust for power and

257

wealth. He realized that something similar was happening to him but felt powerless to contest it. The lòhrengai was feeding on the darker side of his mind, drawing strength from him, and its roots felt too deep to pluck away. And why would he want to? With the lòhrengai, he would be a power in the world. He did not need Ebona. He saw the path that he could take to become king of Esgallien and set right Murhain's wrongs.

He looked back at Erlissa and saw that her eyes were intense with fear. He knew instinctively that it was not for herself, but for him. Doubt clouded his mind, and for just a moment he closed his eyes.

When he opened them again, he saw Lathmai, and she seemed so real that he involuntarily groaned. Her legs were broken, and shards of bone gleamed white through patches of bruised flesh, but she stood upright. Her tattered cloak was soaked with blood.

Slowly, she raised her arms in supplication. "Must I beg you to keep your promise?"

He tried to speak, but his throat was dry as ash.

She shambled forward, and the bones in her leg grated against each other. The wound in her side opened and glistened with fresh blood.

"Why haven't you killed him yet?"

She stopped and swayed before steadying herself. One eye gazed at him, clear and pleading; the other was a ruined socket.

He tried to look elsewhere but could not. Her features sharpened; the burnt and blistered skin of her scalp, where her hair had burned away, flushed purple.

She raised a fist. "Traitor! Look at me. *Look at me!* Do you see what I endured? Will you betray me?"

Tears sprang to his eyes and ran down his cheeks. The moment of final choice had come, and the future would follow as it must.

He remembered Lathmai as she lay dying on the Tor. Once more, he heard her ask for revenge, and he perceived the dark source of pain and suffering that was its wellspring. If she had lived she might have conquered it, but she never had that chance. He sensed something similar in Mecklar, who had the time to change but succumbed instead.

His promise to her had been wrong. It was better to break it than let the darkness within overwhelm his life. He turned toward Gwalchmur and cast the shazrahad sword to the ground. Lathmai's image faded. As though from a great distance, he heard Aranloth's chanting reach a crescendo.

He was about to speak when Lathmai appeared again. This time she was beautiful and looked just as she had at the Spring Games.

He gazed at her through stinging eyes, and she smiled sadly. "Thank you," she said. "I wouldn't have asked you to make such a promise had I known its cost."

Her smile brightened. "I couldn't take my words back. But you've given me your last gift – you did it for me."

He shook his head and found his voice. "Not the last. The last is that I'll never forget you."

Her eyes gleamed and she vanished.

He looked at Gwalchmur. The Raithlin had, at least for the moment, suppressed Ebona and his expression was one of surprise. The visions of Lathmai must have troubled him, and the last thing he would have expected was that his enemy would face him without a weapon. Lanrik acted swiftly to take advantage of the moment.

"Your betrayal of the Raithlin was shameful," he said. "Yet all who live make mistakes. Yours was worse than most – but I forgive you."

He looked at his enemy with steady eyes. "There's been enough killing. Will you leave us free to try and accomplish our task?"

Gwalchmur stared at him. A long time he remained motionless, his hand hovering near the hilt of his sword. Lanrik realized that the lòhren had ceased chanting.

Like a man who had just woken Gwalchmur blinked repeatedly, and his hand relaxed.

"Much has happened that I don't understand," he said. "But I too am tired of killing. I'll leave you in peace, though I fear that Ebona will usurp my mind."

Lanrik heard dread in the other man's voice. The power of the witch was strong, just as the lure of the sword had been.

"You've rebuffed her," he said, "and her influence over you will diminish as you walk away. Her power is like a flame – it needs kindling to start. If you leave with hope and goodwill in your heart, she'll have no further hold on you."

Aranloth spoke from behind. "Already her power is lessened," he said. "Look inside yourself, and you will know."

Gwalchmur nodded slowly. "You're right." He ran a hand through his hair. "But after what I've done, how can I dare to hope?"

Lanrik looked at him with pity. He was a tortured man, and his deeds would haunt him all the days of his life. And yet, his senses still acute, Lanrik had a sudden feeling that Gwalchmur's regrets would drive him to great accomplishments. He would play a pivotal role in the future of Alithoras.

"You have rare skills," he said. "While you can never return to Esgallien, they could be used to benefit people all over the land. Perhaps, in helping others, you'll help yourself."

Gwalchmur bowed his head. "You don't seek to punish me." A moment later, he looked up, his expression fierce and determined. "But I'll punish myself. I pledge my life to the service of Alithoras, even though it costs me dearly."

He retrieved Mecklar's sword and scabbard. Removing his own he strapped the new one on, and then, carefully, he stepped forward and offered Lanrik the hilt of his old one. "I'm unworthy," he said. "You would wear it for the greater Renown of the Raithlin."

Gwalchmur gathered the reins of Mecklar's horse and his own, then led them from the chamber without looking back.

The sword felt heavy in Lanrik's hand after the shazrahad blade. He withdrew it part way from the sheath and revealed the motif of the trotting fox looking back over its shoulder. It was identical to the one he had lost in Esgallien Ford.

He had a Raithlin sword again, and it felt good. But he realized that while he still treasured their teachings he no longer defined himself by being part of them. The world was wider and deeper, more perilous and infinitely more mysterious than any single worldview encompassed.

He heard footsteps behind him and turned around. It was Erlissa. Without hesitation, she took him in her arms and hugged him tightly. He felt the barrier between them drop away, and when she released him, Aranloth approached.

"That was well done," the lòhren said.

He glanced at the shazrahad blade on the ground. "You needn't fear it anymore. You know what's inside us all. If you allow the lòhrengai to draw only on the good, you'll achieve much."

Lanrik picked up the sword, and it felt weightier than he remembered. He had two now, and did not know which to use, but that was a problem for another day. There were more pressing matters.

He looked at the lòhren. "Was it really Lathmai?"

Aranloth sighed. "I cannot be sure." He swept a hand all around them. "Several forces are at work in this chamber. The power of the mistletoe berries has been invoked, and the Morleth Stone has brought Lòrenta to the brink. There's the lòhrengai of the sword, not to mention the ùhrengai of Ebona. Also, there were *two* images of Lathmai. They needn't have had the same source. We're caught between worlds, and the laws of nature are distorted, even reversed. The normal and spirit spheres are conjoined, and it's as though night and day existed at the same time. Death is become life, and life death."

"I hope it was her . . . she seemed happy at the end."

Aranloth gazed at him with compassion but did not answer.

"What do we do now?" asked Erlissa.

Aranloth gripped his staff tightly and looked determined. "What we came for. We must use the mistletoe and pass into Lòrenta."

He opened his hand, and the three berries lay on his palm. "Take one and eat it," he instructed.

Lanrik noticed that they had changed. They gleamed brilliantly and had swelled. His was heavy in his hand when he picked it up, and when he placed it on his tongue it was cold. He bit down, and its juices filled his mouth. He could not describe if it was sweet or bitter, but it tasted like nothing he had ever eaten before. He felt its power, the ùhrengai that it contained, creep through his body. It was cold and slow to act whereas the lòhrengai of the sword was hot and fast.

Erlissa ate hers slowly. The lòhren ate last, but he consumed the berry quickly and waited for the others to finish.

"We must leave the horses," he said.

Lanrik was loath to do so, and Erlissa seemed upset. "Must we?"

"We have no choice," the lòhren said. "They cannot enter the spirit world with us."

He went over to his roan and ran a hand along its neck. "We'll return for them soon. They'll be safe until then."

He turned away from the horse. "Come!" he said. "It's time."

He went to each of them in turn and placed a hand on their forehead. He muttered a brief phrase, and lòhrengai warmed his palm.

"We can enter Lòrenta now."

He took a torch from the wall and walked up the stairs to the rime-coated gate. Three times he tapped the metal with the end of his staff, and three times lòhrengai flickered. On the third, the gate creaked and opened. Ice shattered and fell from its bars like snow, and a momentary blast of cold air struck them. When they had passed through Aranloth swung the gate, and it closed with a loud clang.

Lanrik felt an immediate change. They had been on the threshold in the previous chamber, but now they were inside Lòrenta, within the spirit world. The air was still and cool. Everything about him seemed tinged with gray and void of color and life.

He wondered if they would be able to save the fortress. Most of all he wanted to know what Aranloth had hidden from them on the journey.

Erlissa's hand was in his as they walked forward. They would soon find out.

23. Erlissa's Choice

They walked as ghosts through the halls of Lòrenta. Aranloth's torch was the only spark of life in the shadow-cluttered passages. Dust lay undisturbed in the long corridors, and closed doors, hinged with bands of rusted iron, flanked their sides. Outside, there were bright walls and flag-flying towers, but deep inside the buttress of rock that formed the base of the fortress, it felt like a tomb.

Lòrenta dominated the history of Alithoras, and Lanrik felt strange walking through it. Lòhrens journeyed far and long, their exploits the stock-in-trade of bards across many lands, but this was where they all started from.

The bare stone was gray, and he grew tired of the changeless walls and floor. The very air seemed dreary, all color and life washed away by sorcery. The fortress would remain that way, trapped in a nowhere world, until they broke the power of the Morleth Stone.

The drudgery was only relieved by ornate stairwells that led to higher levels. Stone rails spiraled upward, carved with a decorative finish, but the steps showed the wear of passing feet: smooth hollows in their middle. How many years had that taken? He could not guess, but Lòrenta was old, even ancient.

He glanced at Erlissa. She had been silent and withdrawn for some time.

"What's wrong?"

She frowned and searched for an answer. "Something troubles me . . . I don't know what."

He touched her elbow reassuringly, and they turned another corner. Her instincts had proven correct since Galenthern, and he would not doubt them now. If she was worried, there was a reason for it.

They climbed yet another stairwell and at last reached the aboveground chambers. The passages widened and glass windows, framed by peaked arches of carved stone, looked to the outside world. Little was visible though except a gray dawn, dull and muted.

Mosaics decorated the floors, and the doors on either side were now open. Some rooms were bare, but many contained apparatus that he had never seen before and for which he could not even guess a purpose.

One room however, larger than most, contained things he understood. It was an armory. Near the entrance were swords carefully mounted on individual stands, and behind them was an array of others collected on racks. There were rapiers, scimitars, long and broad swords: he knew all their various types, but the artisanship was different from anything in Esgallien. Some were finely worked pieces of art, others plain and brutal killing weapons. It looked like they had come from many lands, possibly even different eras.

Behind the swords were more weapons: hammers, clubs, long-handled axes, halberds and spears. There were darts, slings, recurve and long bows, javelins, hauberks, helms and all manner of war accoutrement. There was even a battering ram, a massive construction of oak and rusted iron. The timber was blackened by fire and oil, the iron warped and dented. It had seen use in war, and a quick glance at the other artefacts showed many were damaged too. The room was not just an armory; it was a remnant of the history of Alithoras. A shiver ran through him. What battles had these weapons been used in? What long dead heroes once held them in their living hands?

Aranloth strode by without slowing, and soon they came to another room. This one contained musical instruments. There was a wide variety of pipes, harps, cymbals, zithers and gongs. There were also elug war drums and against the far wall the man-high carnyx horns of Esgallien. At least Lanrik thought so; it would not surprise him if they came from other Camar tribes or even from before Conhain had led his people into Esgallien.

"Why do the lòhrens collect all these things?"

Aranloth barely slowed his stride. "To preserve history. Much is lost – it always is from age to age, but a glimpse is kept alive here. And it's studied too. How could lòhrens teach if they didn't know the land's past?"

They turned a corner into a great hallway. A series of vast chambers ran off from it, each containing innumerable shelves packed with books and scrolls. Aranloth halted and swept his arm in a wide arc.

"The Halls of Lore," he said. There was a hint of pride in his voice.

Lanrik was amazed. The books seemed numberless, and he got an inkling of how much knowledge the lòhrens collected and their role in Alithoras. Small wonder the enemy wanted them destroyed.

They walked on but paused when they came to the doorway of yet another massive room. It too was part of the library, its walls cased with bookshelves and desks, though its center was clear. Children played in the open space and did not notice the weary figures grouped at the dark entrance. Many laughed loud and free, showing no fear for the fate of the fortress, but worry marked the somber faces of the eldest.

After several moments Aranloth strode away. Renewed determination stiffened his back, and he led them into a great courtyard. Morning had come, but the day remained gray. The lawn felt soft and lush but looked dull to the eye. Neat and well-tended flowerbeds were everywhere, but they too were drained of color, and the leaves of the trees were lackluster. Lanrik glanced up at the sky, and it was heavy with scudding cloud.

In the middle of the courtyard was a fountain, and Aranloth walked swiftly past. Lanrik paused and studied it carefully though. It was built of white granite, and the centerpiece was a statue of a lòhren. It seemed just as old as the rest of Lòrenta, yet the likeness to Aranloth was striking. It even caught the expression of compassion that so often filled his eyes. Could there be truth to the legends? Had he lived through the centuries? It seemed impossible, but the world was stranger than Lanrik had ever imagined, and he was no longer so quick to dismiss things.

It was not the only change. His instincts were now heightened by lòhrengai, and he sensed that the fountain was the heart of the fortress. It welled with tranquility, though it also had something of the feel of Ebona or Carnona. And just as the Guardian had searched his thoughts in the hills of Enorìen, his mind was even now being assessed by ùhrengai. He got an impression of the true defense of Lòrenta, but there was no time to consider it.

Aranloth hurried him on with a quick gesture. "We're nearly there. The elùgroths must be at the front gate, and the lòhrens on the battlements above."

He led them to the far side of the courtyard and back inside the fortress. Contrary to his words, they walked through many corridors and climbed a lot of staircases before they finally reached the ramparts, and Lanrik wondered if he had been purposefully distracted.

They reached the battlements, and a small group of lòhrens turned around. They were dressed in flowing robes and leaned on tall staffs. Their faces, gray with worry, lit up like children whose father had come home when they saw Aranloth. They seemed to revere him, and his presence invigorated them.

They bowed and shook his hand. Some called him *Careth Tar,* which Lanrik understood to mean "Great Father". It was a term of respect as well as the title of the head of their order, the fabled leader of the Lòhrenin.

Lanrik realized that his uncle Conrik was there too. It was the first time he had seen him in years, but he had not changed except for the absence of his Raithlin sword. It was strange to see him without it.

Conrik made his way through the lòhrens and embraced him warmly. When he was done, he stood back and looked him over slowly. "You've grown, Lan."

"It's been a long time, Uncle Con."

"True enough. How did you get mixed up in this business?"

Lanrik shrugged. "I've had a bit of trouble – it's a long story though."

Aranloth was watching them, and Conrik glanced in his direction. "The lòhren has a habit of showing up when there's trouble. But he usually knows how to fix it."

Lanrik noticed that his uncle wore bandages and realized that he moved gingerly.

"It looks like you've had your own problems," he said. "Where's your sword?"

Conrik hesitated. He glanced at Aranloth again, and then looked Lanrik in the eye.

"I no longer carry it. I've killed too often, and I'm always tempted to fight when I can feel the hilt in my hand. I've got a new name and job these days. I'm Lonfar . . . the librarian."

Lanrik understood. Violence now repulsed his uncle, and he nodded slowly.

"It's strange to see you without a blade, but I don't blame you."

Lonfar stared at him, at a loss for words at such easy acceptance when he had obviously expected a different reaction. Aranloth merely smiled.

"The journey has changed your nephew," he said.

The lòhren shifted his gaze to Erlissa, as though assessing how she might also have changed, and Lanrik wondered what he hoped to see.

Aranloth was diverted again by the other lòhrens, and he took his scrutinizing gaze off her.

"How did you get inside Lòrenta?"

The speaker was a bony wisp of a man, old and wiry, but if he was anything like Aranloth he was much less frail than he looked.

"Sorcery has removed Lòrenta from the ordinary world, Aratar. Yet there are powers more ancient than lòhrengai and elùgai."

The lòhrens looked highly interested, and Lanrik realized they could discuss such matters all day long. His uncle typically got straight to the point though.

"I don't give a damn how you got here," he said. "I want to know if you can help."

Aranloth must have been used to his bluntness, for he showed no offence at all.

"That remains to be seen," he said. "Our first task must be to destroy the Morleth Stone."

The lòhrens looked confused. "But how?" asked Aratar. "We don't even know where it is."

Aranloth turned to Erlissa. "I've brought a Seeker," he said softly.

Aratar looked hard at her for a moment. "That's a rare talent." He nodded slowly. "Yes, I begin to see how it could be done. But—"

"There's little time left," Aranloth interrupted him. "We have to find the stone quickly."

Lanrik noticed the two lòhrens exchange a glance. There was something more to finding the stone than had been spoken aloud, but Aranloth was already guiding Erlissa to the edge of the battlements.

They all looked over the crenellations. The elùgroths sat in a wedge, and their malice thrust toward the fortress. Dark clouds seethed in the airs above, and the birch wood bent to an unnatural wind. It stripped leaves from the trees and swirled them wildly about the sorcerers, but they remained as still as carved statues, their concentration unwavering.

Lanrik felt the cold blast envelop the fortress and sensed elùgai in the air. Erlissa shivered, and he guessed why. Somewhere among the sorcerous brethren was the elùgroth who had captured her, and she would be reliving that memory.

Aranloth stepped to the very brink. He stood to his full height, the staff crooked through the inside of his right elbow, and lifted his arms skyward. He addressed the elùgroth leader, his voice couched in a ceremonious mode suitable to enemies who had opposed each other for centuries, and aided by some art of lòhrengai, his words rolled loud and clear from the ramparts right down to the wood.

"Elù-Randùr!" he said, allowing disdain to drip off the name like the dregs of a drink from an overturned cup.

"Hear me, thou creature of the shadow! Hear me, thou craven who hidest from the light of the sun! Hear me, and cease the spell-making of thy servants!"

Aranloth waited, and a hush fell over the world. Those on the battlements watched him in amazement, fearful of the reaction his insult would provoke.

A stir passed through the elùgroths in the wedge, and they cast their gaze to the ground. Their master was challenged, and the potential for death and destruction charged the air.

The elùgroth leader emerged from the shadows of the wood, and a slow reply came. It welled up as though from deep beneath the earth and rumbled over the wedge to Lòrenta's battlements. Like the cold wind it buffeted them.

"I hear thee, old man. I hear thee, and thine hollow words. Dost thou challenge me? Thou hast not the strength! Mine is the power, and it will prevail over all that is and all that shall be. Thou hast naught but trickeries, for thou dost not embrace the Master."

Aranloth, immutable, answered in a calm and certain voice. "Thy power is not thine own. I sense he that upholdeth thee, he that is thy master, and he for whom thou hast entered thralldom. Thou art but a tool."

The voice of the lòhren rang with authority, and the silver circlet on his brow gleamed in the dim light.

"I know thee, Elù-Randùr, lòhren that was. I know thy past, and surely, even as we speak, I see thy future. Get thee gone! Leavest while thou may, or thou and thy servants shalt be overthrown. Trickster thou callest me, but my words are true. Have I not the sight?"

The elùgroth stepped forward, and the wych-wood staff in his grip shivered with suppressed power. His answer, cold and final, resounded as a pronouncement of doom in the chill air.

"I will think of thee, old man," he said, "when thou art imprisoned in thine own fortress and I lead an army over the spent bodies of those who would defend the cities of the north."

Aranloth lowered his arms and abruptly turned away from the Elùgroth. The discussion had ended as swiftly as it began.

He looked to Erlissa. "The time has come."

Lanrik watched closely as Erlissa nodded and closed her eyes. He could almost see her opening her senses, searching out the sorcery that emanated from the wedge below and tracing it to the faraway Morleth Stone. She toyed absently with the gold bracelet about her wrist while the cold wind tugged at her hair. The lòhrens were silent and motionless, waiting for the outcome. Conrik observed the enemy below with a stony mask of detachment.

Erlissa shuddered, and her eyes flicked open.

"I have it!"

She turned to Aranloth. "You can destroy it now."

Aranloth leaned on his staff and looked at her with pity.

"I cannot."

Her eyes narrowed and bored into him. "What?"

"The lòhrengai that found the stone is yours. I cannot use it."

"Then *why* bring me here?"

Aranloth held her gaze and searched for the right words. Lanrik realized that Erlissa was the only one who could break the stone. She would not have come if she had known though. To destroy the stone was to kill the elùgroths, and that went against everything she believed in.

Erlissa shouted. "I won't do it!"

"I cannot make you break the stone," Aranloth said. "You must choose to do so, or opt to walk away. I brought you so that you could see Lòrenta's need."

"I can't do it!"

"Then how will Lòrenta be saved?"

Erlissa trembled all over. "I *won't* do it, even if I have to stay and suffer the same fate as the fortress."

Aranloth shook his head. "You needn't do that. You've eaten a mistletoe berry and can leave. If you choose not to break the stone I'll have someone guide you back to your horse."

Erlissa studied him for a moment. "And then?"

Aranloth took a firm grip on his staff. "Then I'll attack the elùgroths by myself."

Lanrik did not think he could succeed. There were too many of them, but he would not have to make the attempt alone. He too could leave the fortress. And the lòhrengai in the shazrahad sword would give him a weapon. That way there may be at least some chance of defeating them.

Elù-Randùr glared up at them from far below and spoke again.

"I perceive what thou hast done, old man. Thou wouldst turn the Seeker into a lòhren, but if she accomplishes thy design, she will instead be an elùgroth."

The sorcerer slowly lifted his wych-wood staff and pointed it straight at her.

"I told thee on Galenthern that thou wouldst join our order. I welcome thee, sister."

The elùgroth moved back to the edge of the wood, and Erlissa reeled away. Her eyes were bright with tears, and Lanrik put an arm about her shoulder.

"I wish they'd killed me in the shazrahad tent! Why did you save me?"

He cast his mind back to that time. "Because the need of the one can outweigh the good of the many."

She closed her eyes, and her breath shuddered through her chest. When she opened them again she was more composed.

"I trust you, Lan. What should I do?"

His heart broke for her, and he realized that she might destroy the stone and kill the elùgroths if he asked her to. But he could not do it. He knew her beliefs and understood them. They were reasonable in their own right, but the sacrifice of her parents had made them sacred. They gave meaning and purpose to her life. Should she betray them the emotional damage might be intolerable. It would be better for him and Aranloth to fight the elùgroths, though he would not tell her this. It would only push her toward breaking the stone.

He took her hands in his. "The old me, the one you first met in the dark of the shazrahad tent, would be sure of the answer. Now, I won't pretend to know what you should do. I'll tell you this, though. Follow your heart and do what you think is right. One thing is certain. I'll support you – whatever you choose."

Erlissa stared at him. She took deep and slow breaths. "What will happen if I don't break the stone?"

273

"Aranloth, the other lòhrens, and the children could be lost."

"And if I do?"

"You'll go against your beliefs and kill. The elùgroths, though killers themselves, are people that might yet be redeemed."

Erlissa bowed her head. All along Lanrik had expected that the end of their quest would be a simple physical act, the breaking of the stone, but it had turned out to be more complex than he could have guessed. It hinged on a choice. Some would call it a moral choice, others spiritual. He knew that in her case it was an impossible one.

Erlissa straightened. "I was right to trust you, Lan. You've told me the truth. *Both* of them."

She looked away over the battlements and ordered her thoughts. The wind stilled, the elùgroths watched from afar, and the lòhrens gazed on her in silence.

She squeezed his hands firmly and let go. "You said the need of the one can outweigh the good of the many. But the reverse is just as true."

She turned to Aranloth. "I should hate you, but you did what was necessary to help Alithoras, and I think it's hurt you as much as me."

Her glance went back to Lanrik. "All along you've used violence to protect me, and I accepted it. Just as all over the land there are those who fight so that others may enjoy peace. Who living in Esgallien could sleep at night except for the vigilance of the Raithlin and the readiness of our army? Yet those who value peace must be prepared to fight for it . . . if the fight comes to them."

Her face was white as snow, and her eyes red-rimmed.

"I'll break the stone," she said, "but I've only sensed things before and never done anything with lòhrengai. I don't know how."

Aranloth looked at her solemnly. "You must imagine it," he said simply. "Wherever the mind goes the lòhrengai

274

follows. Sense the stone and shatter it in your thought. The lòhrengai will do the rest."

She gazed far out over the battlements. Lanrik knew she was not seeing the wood or even the faraway fells but concentrating on some inner vision. Suddenly her hands clenched into fists and she sagged.

He caught her before she fell. Wind rose up like an angry snake that hissed and spat venom. It howled around Lòrenta and gripped the birch wood, bending trunks toward the ground and thrashing branches. The wedge of elùgroths moaned. They staggered to their feet, but then screamed and toppled like hewn trees. The morning sun flashed through jagged rents in the cloud, and fresh air washed over the ramparts.

The wind stilled. Nothing moved now except Elù-Randùr. He picked his way carefully through his dead comrades, and his voice was cold as death when he spoke.

"Thou art become an elùgroth, *sister*. Do not forget it. And thou, old man, art not the only one with the sight. I know Esgallien shall fall. I have seen Cardoroth run red with blood and Kûn Dennath burn to firebrands and ashes. Lòrenta will surely follow."

Aranloth gave no answer, but his face was stern and his posture stiff with defiance. Elù-Randùr turned away and walked slowly into the woods.

The lòhren glanced at Erlissa. There was great compassion in his eyes, but it gave way to surprise. She was made of sterner stuff than even he had guessed, and she stood straight and tall, unmoved by the elùgroth's taunt.

"I'm not one of them. And never shall be," she said. "I've now killed, as have they, but I took no joy in it. That separates us."

Aranloth nodded, and Lanrik held her hand tightly. Her grip was firm and strong as she rested her head lightly on his shoulder.

275

He was exhausted but felt at peace for the first time in a long while. It would not last though. Even as he relaxed he sensed change in the air. He knew that his future was different than it had ever been before. Erlissa's was too, but for the moment he would enjoy their feeling of closeness. There was something special about her. She could endure the worst that fate offered, and neither the changing fortunes of life nor an elùgroth could break her.

Epilogue

High summer swept northward over Lòrenta and the balmy days held a mood of celebration and relief. The sky was clear, the sun hot, and the air that drifted over waterfalls, crags and deep tarns was like wine. Lanrik's long days of ease and contentment were interrupted though. Aranloth brought him to the Halls of Lore and retrieved a leather-bound tome. He sat at a table and looked soberly over the top of the unopened book.

"Do you remember the inscriptions on the shazrahad sword?"

Lanrik doubted this conversation would bring good news. "It was made for the Hakalakadan, some kind of over-king in Azan prophecy, which they hope will one day rule the conquered north."

"Indeed," the lòhren said. "But there were two other inscriptions that I couldn't read."

Lanrik glanced at the book. "I take it you can translate them now?"

"Yes, but I no longer need to," the lòhren said. "In studying Azan languages I learned more about the Hakalakadan and the sword. I already know what they say."

Lanrik had no idea what Aranloth was about to reveal, but it would be important. Not for nothing had the shazrahad pursued him across Galenthern and finally cursed him.

The lòhren did not even look at the book. "Assurah, the smith who crafted the sword, was an elùgroth, and he imbued it with elùgai. The second inscription confirms this. He foresaw among the many possible futures one that most appealed to him, and the sorcery reaches out to it, pulling it back to the blade. It's a physical embodiment of the prophecy, an attempt to bridge the gap between reality and possibility, and to make them one."

Lanrik frowned. "So the elùgai acts like some kind of lodestone, drawing events toward it that will lead to the future Assurah wanted?"

"That's it. Like a snowball that starts small but gains size and momentum as it rolls down a slope."

"Will it actually work?"

"A good question." Aranloth leaned back and folded his arms. "It's an ingenious idea. I can't say more at the moment."

"I see why the shazrahad wanted it so much."

The lòhren flashed him a smile. "He'd have done anything to keep it in his family. He still might too, so guard it. Always."

Lanrik nodded. "What of the third inscription?"

"It's a curse that if ever a king of the north should hold the blade his realm will be ruined."

"Do you believe that?"

"Not really." Aranloth shrugged. "But Assurah was powerful, and his elùgai remains in the sword. It has a purpose and intent of its own. If a king of the north was to hold the blade – it just might trigger the sorcery to work in some way against him."

"Perhaps it should be destroyed then," suggested Lanrik.

"Maybe," Aranloth said. "But it's a complex situation, especially now that lòhrengai infuses it. And there might even be ways to turn the blade to our advantage. I need to think on it more. Much more."

"Then it looks like I'll be staying here for a while."

"Yes." A glimmer of a smile came to the lòhren's eyes. "But you needn't be idle."

"What do you mean?"

Aranloth leaned forward. "You have skills that could be used."

Lanrik was not sure what he meant. "Only those of the Raithlin . . . and they don't even exist anymore."

"Not in Esgallien. But during our journey, I saw firsthand how useful they are. I will re-establish what Murhain foolishly disbanded. Only this time they'll be based in Lòrenta and benefit all of Alithoras instead of a single city." The lòhren looked at him intently. "What do you say?"

Lanrik was dumfounded. "That's the last thing I expected." He paused to consider things. "It's a good idea, though. But you won't find it easy to persuade the Lindrath to come here – everything he loves is in Esgallien."

Aranloth raised an eyebrow. "I wasn't thinking of him. I want *you* to be the Lindrath – to recruit, train and lead the new Raithlin."

Goose bumps stood out on Lanrik's skin. He suddenly recalled what Arawnus had said to him at Esgallien Ford after he returned from Galenthern: *You'll be the Raithlindrath one day.* He also remembered his promise to Carnona, which had seemed futile at the time, but now he felt as though everything fitted together properly at last, albeit in a way that he had never have seen coming.

****

The brief days of high summer waned, and the march toward autumn quickened. The ling flowered profusely and turned the hills purple while stags roared during the rut. The moorland was fog-ridden, and frost had browned the bracken in the rocky hollows that it favored. Word came, as expected, that the enemy's attacks along the frontier had been repelled, and the elug armies had withdrawn southward.

Erlissa spent much of her time learning the ways of lòhrengai. Now that she had used it once, that door was

279

open and could not be closed. Nor did she any longer want to. Using it had woken in her a thirst for knowledge that she had long suppressed. And she had reconciled her conflicted emotions about her parents. The confrontation with the elùgroth had taught her that there were many ways to serve.

When she was not occupied by her studies, she explored the hills with Lanrik, roaming long and far. He told her of his plans for the new Raithlin, and she spoke of lòhrengai and her growing desire to learn more.

On a cold day when incessant rain kept them indoors, Lanrik showed her the new Raithlin motif. It was the same trotting fox as always, looking back over its shoulder, but a half moon had been added above. He told her that it signified the hidden powers that existed in Alithoras beyond the usual recognition of men. It brought back memories of their journey to the fortress and she grinned.

****

Lòhrens started to return to Lòrenta, and the lengthening nights were spent talking before warm fires. One traveler gave Lanrik and Erlissa word of an emerging legend. There was a man, silent and grim, whose dark past drove him to risk his life fighting for the innocent weak against the evil strong.

"What's the man's name?" asked Lanrik.

"He's called Gwalchmur."

Appendix A. The Red Cloth of Victory

Halls of Lore. Chamber 7. Aisle 23. Item 346
General subject: Migration of Camar tribes
Topic: The founding of Esgallien
Author: Careth Tar

People can say what they want. I know the truth.

It is told that Conhain grew restless under the sway of the Halathrin and was eager to lead his tribe toward the fertile lands of the east. Certainly, report of other clan-chiefs who had established free and prosperous realms in those wide regions sparked such a desire in many.

Other stories suggest that a lòhren foretold him a difficult journey but long life, lasting fame, and wealth for his nation if he led the migration.

The truth is that the less people know the more they invent.

Conhain had great love for the Halathrin. All he wanted was to dwell among them, to roam their great forest domain and learn of their lore. The immortals had enriched his life, as they had his entire clan. Their influence had ennobled generations of migrating tribes, often primitive and barbaric races fleeing turmoil in the west of Alithoras. They taught them the higher arts of civilization and formed a federation that resisted the northward incursion of elugs.

Nevertheless, Conhain knew his people wished to migrate and that they would march eventually. He had decided that when the time came he would relinquish his chieftainship and remain in the lands that he loved: until I spoke with him.

I did not predict long life and fame. Indeed, I warned him that if he led his people eastward he would not survive to establish a kingdom.

Yet I asked him to go anyway. I foretold that if he participated in a battle when they reached their destination, his people would be victorious. If he did not, they would be destroyed. No more had I seen, no more did he ask of me. In a quiet moment, away from witnesses, friends or family, he resolved to sacrifice everything for his people.

Necessity often drives me against my will, though seldom has it filled me with such anguish, for Conhain's like is rarely seen. He was a vigorous leader, always willing to listen to his people, quick with a smile and slow to anger. Slights he swiftly forgave and was generous to friend and stranger alike. When I told him of the danger to his clan, even the death that awaited him, he did not rail against circumstances or show anger at the lòhren who asked so much of him. Instead, he thanked me for helping his people.

This much is true of what the stories say. There were great eastward migrations, and the lands toward the coast were lush and fertile. The free cities had begun to flourish. However, word of their prosperity was ever exaggerated, and the hardships of the earlier resettlements glossed over.

Ebona was the chief mover of this. She held a high place in the counsels of some clan-chiefs, though most had ceased to listen to her and turned their ears toward the wisdom of the Halathrin and the teachings of lòhrens. Consequently, her power and authority was much diminished and her time passing. This, she could not endure, for being a creature of ùhrengai that had left her birthing lands when the ancient Camar moved toward Halathar, she had been sustained instead by their worship and blood sacrifice. But they had emerged from those dark days and put the primitive ceremonies of their ancestors behind them.

Yet once, she was a goddess, and she craved that again. She wanted kings to rule beneath her, to guide the destiny of the multitude at her direction and to increase her strength by their veneration and sacrifice. I know this to be true, for I sought to dissuade her from that path. However, my attempt was futile. She despised me, for I held the trust of many chiefs and the more they heeded me the hotter her hatred grew.

On a time, when fresh rumors of the east were stirred up, Balmur, a young clan-chief, came to prominence. He was a favorite of Ebona, and he heeded me not, nor any other lòhren, and seduced by the prospect of kingship and rule by the side of a goddess he gathered many to him. He promised them a realm free of Halathrin influence, governed according to ancient Camar custom.

Whether by accident, or as I think more likely, the design of Ebona, there was at that time a great attack by the enemy who sought to force a crossing of the ford in the Careth Nien just east of Halathar. A joint regiment of warriors from several Camar tribes guarded the ford, and Conhain was their leader. The ford was defended, with great loss of life, and the enemy repelled. However, during the battle messengers were sent to the Halathrin for aid, but it never eventuated. I discovered afterward that the messengers never reached their destination, nor were they ever seen again.

Balmur proclaimed that the Halathrin had left them to fight and die in their stead and urged that the time was right to migrate. There was great anguish, and his words caught like fire in dry grass. Swiftly he acted, Ebona always nearby, and a host nearing ten thousand was readied, though ill prepared to march.

At the dawn of a bleak day, the people commenced their journey. Conhain, against his true desire, led a great mass. Balmur another, though not so large, and he was irked that although he had goaded the people into this action most still followed Conhain.

They marched side by side, the bulk of the warriors at the front, and then the women and children. Behind each column was a ragged band of wagons that carried their hastily gathered supplies. Last of all was a rearguard of warriors that drove cattle and other stock. It was a great mass of humanity; some on horseback but most on foot, and it flowed and ebbed like a second river along the north bank of the Careth Nien.

During the long march, Ebona was ever at the side of Balmur, and they headed their column on matching milk-white steeds. They were surrounded by her hounds, great black beasts that snarled at all who neared them. Conhain, though he had a great roan warhorse, chose to lead it by hand instead of ride. He spent most of each day walking up and down the line, sharing a quick joke with the people and offering encouragement.

Neither Balmur nor Ebona had specified a destination. However, Conhain knew that they could only travel so far before building shelters. Summer was swiftly passing, and the cold and wet would soon set in. It would be foolish to continue the journey into winter, for the frail would be at risk of sickness and exposure, yet Balmur refused to discuss the issue, saying only that they must travel as far as possible from Halathar. Contention grew between the leaders as the weeks passed.

Conhain, like all his people, had been born near Halathar and had never left the region. But I had. Of all the host, including Ebona, I was the only one who had traveled the lands we now traversed. Each day I discussed the upcoming terrain with him and his retinue, and a time came when I told them we approached Esgallien Ford. I knew it was a good place to settle. The land was fertile, and the climate conducive to raising crops and stock. Also, the ford could be defended against enemy attack; a benefit to the Camar and the rest of Alithoras. Conhain considered my advice for several days then announced that he would winter at the ford and establish a city there.

Balmur was incensed and stormed into the camp. He insisted, to no avail, that Conhain reconsider as the ford was too close to the influence of the Halathrin. Then, in an unseemly rage, he drew his sword. Conhain signaled for his retinue to eject him. Disarmed and ashamed at his treatment, he returned to Ebona, and together they conceived a great evil. Balmur would suffer no denial of his will, and Ebona coveted blood sacrifice.

Within the week, the host reached the region of the ford. Balmur might have led a portion on, but many repented their earlier haste and saw the necessity of establishing winter shelters. He knew he could not muster a sufficient number to face the perils of travel or to found his own realm. Discontented, he undertook the guard of the ford.

Conhain camped a few miles upstream, and more of the people now looked to him for leadership, and he ordered things to his will. Most importantly, he sent forth scouts to survey the country. These had been specially trained in Halathar and were named *Raithlin*.

When the Raithlin started to return they brought tidings of good lands, fertile soils, expansive forests and game. Most influential were reports of a gold-rich creek only a day's march to the north. Conhain, unusually silent and withdrawn, rode there and inspected it. After some time, with a strange expression on his face, he proclaimed that he would establish his city there, with all the high knowledge and skill the Halathrin had given his people, and that it would act as a bulwark against the enemy.

On a hill above the site, he ordered his banner planted in the ground and left. When he rode away he did not look back. I knew he would never return, and I think he felt it too. It is said that when the shadow of death is heavy upon some men they see a vision of the future. I do not know if that happened to him. He did not say so, and I did not ask, but his manner suggested it.

During the journey back to the camp, we learned from Raithlin who had crossed into Galenthern that an elug army swiftly approached. Further on we heard that Balmur's guard had ceded the ford after a short battle and fallen back to Conhain's encampment. The enemy now faced the Camar on the north bank of the Careth Nien.

When we returned I sensed treachery, and ùhrengai too. It was spread out in an invisible net over all our people; men, women and children alike. Instantly, but still too late, I deduced Ebona's plan. She had sent word to the enemy and brought them here. Thus, a battle would be fought and the spilled blood committed to her as a sacrifice.

I had no doubt that she arranged it. The enemy was perhaps larger than she had anticipated, for their force was a third greater than our own. But that is the way of perfidy – the betrayer is often betrayed. Yet though she had miscalculated, I did not sense any worry. The total destruction of our host would only increase her power all the more, and greatly enhanced, she would return to Halathar and attempt to dominate other Camar tribes.

There was fear and despair in the camp, for the warriors doubted they could defeat the elug army, especially with divided leadership, yet they could not retreat swiftly enough with women, children and the elderly to avoid battle.

Balmur came once more to Conhain, and this time Ebona was with him. She demanded a sacrifice, and promised that fortified by blood, she could ensure a Camar victory. Conhain did not consider it. He refused, and it was the only time that I saw him lose his temper. In great fury he scorned Ebona and ordered his retinue to cast the two of them from his presence.

Ebona must have thought he would be forced to agree. At first she shrank away from his wrath, then her eyes flashed with hatred. Had I been quick enough I might have prevented what happened next, but Balmur drew his sword and slashed at me while Ebona cast flame from her fingers among Conhain's retinue. They were forced away from their lord, and she turned her power upon him. Her fire struck the sword from his grip and drove him to the ground where she set her hounds upon him.

Swiftly I killed Balmur, but not soon enough. I glanced at Conhain, and the mad din of the barking hounds pierced my ears, and their bloodthirsty snarls caused my hair to stand on end. Never will I forget the sound.

Conhain was in trouble. He was viciously mauled, some of his flesh hanging in ribbons, his fine clothes shredded, and his face smeared with blood. He kicked with his legs and with his arms struggled to keep the dogs from his throat. Yet I saw that already he was mortally wounded.

I flung lòhren-fire at the hounds and scattered them, but a blast of ùhrengai smashed me to the ground. Ebona strode toward me, and the hatred of all the long years where her power had been eroded by lòhrens and Halathrin blazed in her eyes.

"Die!" she screamed.

She stabbed at me with fingers that spurted ùhrengai, and a battle ensued. Word of what happened afterward spread far and wide. Great was her strength even though she was diminished from what she once was, but necessity drove me, as it ever does, and at length I found a way to prevail.

Men saw that she, who was once a goddess, was now humbled and stripped of the remnant of her power, and the hounds whimpered and yelped as they fled with her into the wilderness. What they did not see was the dispersing of the net of ùhrengai that she had cast over the people. So ended Ebona's influence over the Camar, but she will hate me so long as the world endures.

I staggered toward Conhain, thinking to find him dead, but somehow he held the breath of life to his broken body. We tended his many wounds and staunched the flow of blood with linen. I fixed a square of the white cloth to a gash in his scalp, but it, like the rest, was soon stained red by his lifeblood.

He turned weakly toward me. "It's as you foretold."

I nodded, unable to speak. Only a man of great heart could cling to life with such injuries.

"I'm nearly done," he said. "But help me one last time, old friend. I have a final duty to perform."

With disbelief I helped him. He should already have died, but we assisted him to his warhorse, and he commanded that his feet be tied to the stirrups and his waist lashed to the saddle. It was done, but I do not know what kept him upright except the iron-like power of his will that for a time was stronger than fate.

Slowly we proceeded to the battle lines. Word went ahead that Ebona was banished and Balmur slain. Men saw Conhain on his warhorse. They realized that their leader, whom they loved, was coming to fight with them and their hearts swelled. The despair that was in them transformed into sudden hope, and they chanted his name. But even as they did so, the enemy attacked and swept toward us as a dark wave.

Conhain made a sign, and men with carnyx horns stood forth. They who bore them were tall, and the bronze horns matched them foot for foot. The warriors held them high, the mouths of the horns twelve feet above ground, and voiced their unearthly moan that sounded like an otherworldly beast.

The Camar believe the horns invoke supernatural aid, and having heard them rend the air before a battle, I know why. Whether Conhain believed it himself, or merely used them for effect on the superstitious elugs, I do not know. Nevertheless, the elug host faltered until their own war drums quickened, and then there was a sudden tumult.

As the enemy approached, Conhain undid the square cloth from his head. It was soaked red with his blood but he held it high.

For a moment he glanced at me, and above the din of horn and drum he spoke.

"Nothing lasts forever, Aranloth. Not men, nor chiefs . . . nor even cities."

He turned to the elugs again and suddenly jerked his arm down. Even now I can see the droplets of his lifeblood splash to the ground.

"Charge!" he yelled.

The Camar warriors moved forward, and the two forces met with a horrendous clash. It was a great battle, but this is a testimony of the founding of Esgallien and the man who made it happen, not a record of the fight. It is enough to say that the Camar prevailed.

I do not know when Conhain died, for I did not see it. There are stories that he slew twenty men. Others say that his warhorse killed many by hoof and tooth. For myself, I doubt he lived more than moments after he signaled the charge with what was afterwards called the Red Cloth of Victory.

Thus was Esgallien founded. In the end it was a good thing, for long will the city help to protect the north, yet even as I write on my return to Lòrenta, after some ten years of advising his son, I still feel Conhain's blood on my hands.

Thus ends *Renown of the Raithlin*. The Raithlindrath series continues in book two, *Lore of the Letharn*. Once again, Lanrik and Erlissa are caught up in events destined to shape the future of the land.

Sign up below and be the first to hear about new book releases, see previews and learn of upcoming discounts.
http://eepurl.com/Rswv1

Visit my website at www.homeofhighfantasy.com

Appendix B. Encyclopedic Glossary

Many races dwell in Alithoras. All have their own language, and though sometimes related to one another, the changes sparked by migration, isolation and various influences often render these tongues unintelligible to each other.

The ascendancy of Halathrin culture, combined with their widespread efforts to secure and maintain allies against elug incursions, has made their language the primary means of communication between diverse peoples.

For instance, a soldier of Esgallien addressing a ship's captain from Camarelon would speak Halathrin, or a simplified version of it, even though their native speeches stem from the same ancestral language.

This glossary contains a range of names and terms. Many are of Halathrin origin, and their meaning is provided. The remainder derive from native tongues and are obscure, so meanings are only given intermittently.

Some variation exists within the Halathrin language, chiefly between the regions of Halathar and Alonin. The most obvious example is the latter's preference for a "dh" spelling instead of "th".

Often, Camar names and Halathrin elements are combined. This is especially so for the aristocracy. No other tribes had such long-term friendship with the Halathrin, and though in this relationship they lost some of their natural culture, they gained nobility and knowledge in return.

List of abbreviations:

Azn. Azan

Cam. Camar

Chg. Cheng

Comb. Combined

Cor. Corrupted form

Duth. Duthenor

Esg. Esgallien

Hal. Halathrin

Prn. Pronounced

Alar: *Azn.* A strain of horses raised in the southern deserts of Alithoras. Bred for endurance, but capable of bursts of speed. Most valued possession of the Azan people, who measure wealth and status by their number. In their culture, where a person on foot is likely to die between water sources, horse-theft is punished by torture and death.

Alithoras: *Hal.* "Silver land." The Halathrin name for the continent they settled after the exodus. Refers to the extensive river and lake systems they found and their appreciation of the beauty of the land.

Alonin: *Hal.* "White gathering." Large forest in eastern Alithoras. Once contained a fortress city of the Halathrin, now destroyed by war. The name refers to an abundant variety of deciduous tree that bears white flowers.

Alonùradth: *Hal.* "White lady." A Halathrin noble killed during the elug sacking of Alonin.

Anast Dennath: *Hal.* "Stone mountains." Mountain range in northern Alithoras. Contiguous with Auren Dennath and location of the Dweorhrealm.

Angle: The land hemmed in by the Carist Nien and Erenian rivers, especially the area in proximity to their divergence.

Aranloth: *Hal.* "Noble might." A lòhren.

Aratar: *Cor. Hal.* "Ara(n)tar(an) – noble father." A lòhren.

Arawdan: *Esg.* A Raithlin. Brother to Arawnus.

Arawnus: *Esg.* A Raithlin. Brother to Arawdan.

Arn: See Letharn.

Assurah: *Azn.* A renowned sword-smith of ancient Azanbulzibar, capital city of the Azan people. He was also adept at elùgai, and his work was sought by the rich and powerful of many nations.

Auren Dennath: *Comb. Duth.* and *Hal. Prn.* Our-ren dennath. "Blue mountains." Mountain range in northern Alithoras. Contiguous with Anast Dennath. Home of the Duthenor, a tribe of people related to the Camar.

Aurochs: The wild forebear of domesticated cattle. They are larger and more aggressive than their tamed descendants and prefer to graze and forage in swamps and wet forests. The "s" at the end of their name is both singular and plural.

Azan: *Azn.* Desert dwelling people. Their nobility often serve as leaders of elug armies. They are a prideful race, often haughty and domineering, but they also adhere to a strict code of honor.

Balmur: *Cam.* A clan-chief of the Camar during the migration from Halathar to Esgallien.

Bakert: *Esg.* A hound of the otherworld.

Balert: *Esg.* A hound of the otherworld.

Bikar: *Esg.* A hound of the otherworld.

Bilar: *Esg.* A hound of the otherworld.

Caladhrist: *Hal. Prn.* Kal-ath-rist. "Gold gorge." A valley north of Esgallien. Rich in gold and the source of much of the city's wealth subsequent to the depletion of closer alluvial deposits. Many others mined the valley through the history of Alithoras. A dangerous place and believed by many to be haunted.

Camar: *Cam. Prn.* Kay-mar. A race of interrelated tribes that migrated in two main stages. The first brought them to the vicinity of Halathar; in the second, they separated and established cities along a broad sweep of eastern Alithoras.

Camarelon: *Cam. Prn.* Kam-arelon. A port city and capital of a Camar tribe. It was founded after Esgallien as the waves of migrating people settled the more southerly lands first. Each new migration tended northward. It is perhaps the most representative of a traditional Camar realm, while Esgallien is the most influenced by Halathrin culture.

Carandùr: *Hal.* "Red blade." A Halathrin noble famous for victorious battles against the elugs. Wounded near to death in the attempt to save his wife, Alonùradth, during the sacking of Alonin.

Carangar: *Hal.* "Red Star." A lòhren.

Cardoroth: *Cor. Hal. Comb. Cam.* A Camar city, often called Red Cardoroth. Some say this alludes to the red granite commonly used in the construction of its buildings, others that it refers to a prophecy of destruction.

Carèthlath: *Hal. Prn.* Kareth-lath. "Great joy." A student in Lòrenta.

Careth Nien: *Hal. Prn.* Kareth nyen. "Great River." Largest river in Alithoras. Has its source in the mountains of Anast Dennath and runs southeast across the land before emptying into the sea. It was over this river (which sometimes freezes along its northern length) that the Camar, Duthenor and other tribes migrated into the eastern lands.

Careth Tar: *Cor. Hal.* "Careth Tar(an) – Great Father." Title of respect for the leader of the lòhrens.

Carist Nien: *Hal.* "Ice River." A river of northern Alithoras that has its source in the hills of Lòrenta.

Carnyx: The sacred horn of Conhain's people and related tribes. An instrument of brass, man high with a mouth fashioned in the likeness of a fierce animal, often a boar or bear. Winded in battle and designed to intimidate the foe with its otherworldly sound. Some believe it invokes supernatural aid.

Carnona: *Cam.* The Guardian of Enorìen. A creature of ùhrengai who has remained in her birthing lands.

Cheng: *Chg.* "Warrior." The overall name of the various related tribes united by Chen Fei. It was a word for warrior in his dialect, later adopted for his growing army and last of all for the people of his nation. His empire disintegrated after his death, but much of the culture he fostered endured.

Clear like water, cold like ice: A mnemonic saying of the Raithlin. The perfect state of mind during a crisis. Emotions, pain or discomfort are momentarily ignored in order to facilitate rapid and logical thought processes.

Condred: *Esg.* A king of Esgallien.

Conhain: *Comb. Esg & Hal.* First element unknown, second "hero." Accounted the first king of Esgallien.

Conmur: *Esg.* A king of Esgallien.

Conrik: *Esg.* A former Raithlin and uncle of Lanrik.

Danhain: *Comb. Esg. & Hal.* First element unknown, second "hero." A grandson of Conhain.

Drùgluck: A pattern of three slanted lines, going from right to left and each one longer than the previous. Used by elugs as a warning to stay away from a place because it is a sacred area that serves as a gateway between the spirit and normal worlds. Such areas are used in ceremonies and invocations for help or retribution against enemies. It is believed that at certain cycles of the moon and seasons the barriers that separate the worlds are weakened and the gateway opens. Also marks a place where the effects of elùgai linger or where there is some unspecified but lethal danger. Often it signifies all three at once.

Dweorh: A race of people who establish underground homes within mountain ranges. They possess tremendous strength and are the finest workers of stone in Alithoras. They have a reputation of being fierce to foes and true to friends. They are fond of cider, feasting and humor. A complex people of which few in Alithoras have learnt much because of their tendency toward secrecy. However, their ancient feud with the Lethrin is famous.

Ebona: *Cam.* A witch. A being of ùhrengai who has long since left her birthing lands.

Elendhrot: *Hal. Prn.* Elen-throt. "Treasure tuber." A bush type plant with a tuber that contains pain-reducing substances, though too much will kill. The tuber has a purplish skin and slightly bitter pith. Its use was discovered by the Halathrin, but it was deliberately planted by Raithlin near areas they frequent. They similarly spread other medicinal plants.

Elùgai: *Hal. Prn.* Eloo-guy. "Shadowed force." The sorcery of an elùgroth.

Elùgroth: *Hal. Prn.* Eloo-groth. "Shadowed horror." A sorcerer.

Elugs: *Hal.* "That which creeps in shadows." A cruel and superstitious race that inhabits the southern lands, especially the Graèglin Dennath.

Elù-Randùr: *Hal.* "Blade of the Shadow." An elùgroth leader. Formerly a lòhren.

Enorìen: *Cam.* The Eastern Hills. A land where ùhrengai runs strong. Protected by the Guardian Carnona.

Erenian River: A river in northern Alithoras. Some say its name derives from a corruption of the Halathrin word "nien," meaning river. Others dispute this and postulate the word derives from a pre-exodus name adopted by the Camar tribes after they settled the east of Alithoras.

Erlissa: *Esg.* A young woman of Esgallien. Also known as the Seeker.

Esgallien: *Hal. Prn.* Ez-gally-en. A city established by King Conhain. Named after the nearby ford.

Esgallien Ford: *Hal.* "Es – rushing water, gal(en) – green, lien – to cross: place of the crossing onto the green plains." A ford of the Careth Nien.

Exodus: The arrival of the Halathrin into Alithoras from an outside land. They came by ship and beached north of Anast Dennath.

Faladir: A city founded by a Camar tribe.

Foresight: Premonition of the future. Can occur at random as a single image or as a longer sequence of events. Can also be deliberately sought by entering the realm between life and death where the spirit is released from the body to travel through space and time. To

298

achieve this, the body must be brought to the very threshold of death. The first method is uncontrollable and rare. The second exceedingly rare but controllable for those with the skill and willingness to endure the danger.

Founding: The arrival of Conhain and his people near Esgallien Fŏrd. This was nine hundred and fifty three years ago at the time of Lanrik's meeting with Erlissa and Aranloth.

Free cities: A group of cooperative city states that pool military resources to defend themselves against attack. Founded prior to Esgallien. Initially ruled by kings and queens, now by a senate.

Galathar: *Hal.* "Green dwelling place – a forest." Hero of the immortal Halathrin whose deeds have been studied by the Raithlin and whose actions have passed into legend.

Galenthern: *Hal.* "Green flat." Southern plains bounded by the Careth Nien and the Graèglin Dennath mountain range.

Ghash: An elug term for a mischievous (and sometimes malicious) spirit intent on causing harm (or death).

Gilhain: *Comb. Esg & Hal.* First element unknown, second "hero." A Raithlin.

Graèglin Dennath: *Hal. Prn.* Greg-lin dennath. "Mountains of ash." Chain of mountains in southern Alithoras. The landscape is one of jagged stone and boulder, relieved only by gaping fissures from which plumes of ashen smoke ascend, thus leading to its name. Believed to be impassable because of the danger of poisonous air flowing from cracks, and the ground unexpectedly giving way, swallowing any who dare to tread its forbidden paths. In other places swathes of molten stone run in rivers down its slopes.

Guardian: A creature of sentient ùhrengai that preserves its birthing land.

Gwalchmur: *Esg.* A Raithlin.

Hainer Lon: *Hal. Prn.* Hiner lon. "Heroes way." The main thoroughfare of Esgallien.

Hakalakadan: *Azn.* A revered title among the Azan peoples.

Haladhon: *Hal.* "Bright tower." A tower in the Halathrin fortress city of Alonin.

Halathar: *Hal.* "Dwelling place of the people of Halath." The forest realm of the Halathrin.

Halathgar: *Hal.* "Bright Star." Actually a constellation. Also known as the Lost Huntress.

Halathrin: *Hal.* "People of Halath." A race named after a mighty lord who led an exodus of his people to the continent of Alithoras in pursuit of justice, having sworn to redress a great evil. They are human, though of fairer form, greater skill and higher culture. They possess an inherent unity of body, mind and spirit enabling insight and endurance beyond other races of Alithoras. Reported to be immortal, but killed in great numbers during their conflicts with the evil they seek to destroy.

Halls of Lore: Library of records maintained by lòhrens of the history, knowledge and wisdom of the nations of

Alithoras. Accumulated over millennia and one of the treasures of Lòrenta.

Hamalath: *Hal.* "Sorrow joy". An open-air theatre where dramas of history, tragedy and humor are conducted. Derived from the Halathrin who built many. In Esgallien called simply "The Hamalath," as there is only one of significant size.

Haranast: *Hal.* "Horse race." A racetrack. Its form was derived from the Halathrin but the love of horseracing by the Camar predates the exodus of the immortals. A successful rider, or horse, could be more famous and better loved than tribal chiefs or kings. The stealing of a racehorse is punishable by death.

Headdress: A turban. Worn by the Azan people as protection from desert heat. Can be lowered in a sandstorm to protect the eyes and breath. Its color, and the manner in which it's worn signify military rank or social status.

Karlenthern: *Hal.* "Games field." The location of many events during the Spring Games and other athletic competitions during the year.

Kûn Dennath: *Hal. Prn.* Kuun Dennath. "Defended mountain." A man made hill fort. Now the town center of the oldest of the free cities.

Lake Alithorin: *Hal.* "Silver lake." A lake of northern Alithoras.

Lanrik: *Esg.* A Raithlin.

Lathmai: *Comb. Hal. & Esg.* "Joy and unknown element." A Raithlin.

Letharn: *Hal.* "Stone Raisers. Builders." A race of people that in antiquity ruled much of Alithoras. Only traces of their civilization remain.

Lethrin: *Hal.* "Stone People." Creatures of the Graèglin Dennath. Renowned for their size and strength. Tunnelers and miners.

Lindrath: *Hal.* "People lord." A shortening of Raithlindrath. Commander of the Raithlin organization.

Ling: Heather. Predominant plant growth of moorland. Purple flowered in late summer and provider of food for deer, and food and cover, for grouse. Prevalent in Lòrenta.

Lòhren: *Hal. Prn.* Ler-ren. "Knowledge giver – a counselor." Other terms used by various nations include wizard, druid and sage.

Lòhren-fire: A defensive manifestation of lòhrengai. The color of the flame varies according to the skill and temperament of the lòhren.

Lòhrengai: *Hal. Prn.* Ler-ren-guy. "Lòhren force." Enchantment, spell or use of arcane power. A manipulation and transformation ùhrengai, the natural energy inherent in all things. Each use takes something from the user. Likewise, some part of the transformed energy infuses them. Lòhrens use it sparingly.

Lòhrenin: *Hal. Prn.* Ler-ren-in. "Council of lòhrens."

Lonfar: *Hal.* "Way of peace." The librarian of the Halls of Lore.

Lòrenta: *Hal. Prn.* Ler-rent-a. "Hills of knowledge." Uplands in northern Alithoras in which the stronghold of the lòhrens is established.

Mecklar: *Esg.* A senior member of King Murhain's retinue.

Menetuin: *Cam.* A city founded by a Camar tribe.

Merenloth: *Hal. Prn.* Mair-en-loth. "Words of power." A place for philosophical debate, reciting poetry and the chanting of bards. Derived from Halathrin practice. Often full to capacity during times of change. King Danhain, disguised as a bard, often frequented the Merenloth and chanted pre-founding lays passed down from his grandfather. After the performance he discoursed with the crowd to determine what the people thought of the king's rule. He sometimes changed his decisions after such debates.

Morleth Stone: *Hal.* "Round Stone." The name signifies that such a stone is not natural. It is formed by elùgai for sorcerous purposes. The stone is strengthened by arcane power to act as a receptacle of enormous force. Little is known of their making and use except that they are rare and that elùgroths perish during their construction.

Murhain: *Esg.* The current king of Esgallien. He was a younger son of the previous king and assumed the throne unexpectedly. Earlier in his life, he had attempted to train as a Raithlin but failed their vigorous standards.

Musraka: *Azn.* A shazrahad.

Nudaluk: *Cam.* A bird of the woodpecker family.

Otherworld: Esgallien term for a mingling of half-remembered history, myth and the spirit world.

Pattern-welded: A blade forged and reforged from bundles of iron rods that are twisted and beaten. This creates a flexible core to which a hard edge is added. The process produces superior, distinctive and sought-after weapons.

Raithlin: *Hal.* "Range and report people." A scouting and saboteur organization. They derive from ancient contact with, and the teachings of, the Halathrin. Their number is always 100.

Raithlin motif: A trotting fox looking back over its shoulder. Symbolizes cunning, stealth and boldness.

Raithlin crawl: A famous technique of stealth. It requires that the palms rest on the earth and the elbows remain tucked in to the body for support and silhouette reduction. The bodyweight is borne on the forearms and only one leg. The other is carefully brought forward in order to avoid making noise while moving.

Raithlin creed: "Our duty is to serve and protect. Our honor is to fight but not hate. Our love is for all that is good in the world."

Raithlin principles of concealment: The Raithlin believe the eye recognizes movement first, silhouette second and color last. Using this principle enables them to best determine how to remain unseen in varying circumstances.

Raithlindrath: *Hal.* "Lord of range and report people."

Rapier: A lightweight sword, still deadly in skilled hands, but advantageous for Raithlin mobility which is their prime concern.

Red Cloth of Victory: The highest symbol of courage and determination in Esgallien society.

Rhodlin: *Esg.* A Raithlin. Brother to Rhodmur.

Rhodmai: *Esg.* An inn servant who married King Danhain and ruled as queen after his death. Her reign was noted for civic constructions and marked for its peace. So much so that a prosperous period for the city has ever since been known as "Rhodmai's Peace."

Rhodmur: *Esg.* A Raithlin. Brother to Rhodlin.

Seeker: A person with a rare talent of finding lost things. It stems from a latent use of lòhrengai.

Shazrahad: *Azn.* The Azan who commands an elug army.

Sign of death: See drùgluck.

Sorcerer: See elùgroth.

Spring Games: A series of athletic and skill-based competitions in Esgallien deriving from antiquity. Other Camar peoples also conduct the games, sometimes under a different name. Before the tribes diverged, they met at various sacred sites marked by standing stones. There, amid sporting games, feasting and trade, chiefs were chosen, disputes settled and ceremonies conducted.

Talnak: *Azn.* A large goat-like animal that survives and even flourishes in the most remote and inhospitable regions of the Graèglin Dennath. Its preferred habitat makes it perilous to hunt, but its horn is highly valued by the Azan people and used in ceremonial roles.

Ùhrengai: *Hal. Prn.* Er-ren-guy. "Original force." The primordial force that existed before substance or time, light or dark, life or death, good or evil.

War drums: Drums of the elug tribes. Used especially in times of war or ceremony. Rumored to carry hidden messages in their beat and also to invoke sorcery.

Wych-wood: A general description for a range of supple and springy timbers. Some hardy varieties are prevalent on the poisonous slopes of the Graèglin Dennath mountain range and are favored by elùgroths as instruments of sorcery.

From the author

I'm a man born in the wrong era. My heart yearns for faraway places and even further afield times. Tolkien had me at the beginning of *The Hobbit* when he said, ". . . one morning long ago in the quiet of the world . . ."

Sometimes I imagine myself in a Viking mead-hall. The long winter night presses in, but the shimmering embers of a log in the hearth hold back both cold and dark. The chieftain calls for a story, and I take a sip from my drinking horn and stand up . . .

Or maybe the desert stars shine bright and clear, obscured occasionally by wisps of smoke from burning camel dung. A dry gust of wind marches sand grains across our lonely campsite, and the wayfarers about me stir restlessly. I sip cool water and begin to speak.

I'm a storyteller. A man to paint a picture by the slow music of words. I like to bring faraway places and times to life, to make hearts yearn for something they can never have, unless for a passing moment.